The Deaf Heart

The Deaf Heart

A Novel

WILLY CONLEY

Gallaudet University Press
Washington, DC

Gallaudet University Press
Washington, DC 20002
http://gupress.gallaudet.edu

Second printing 2017

Library of Congress Cataloging-in-Publication Data
Conley, Willy.
The deaf heart : a novel / Willy Conley.
pages ; cm
ISBN 978-1-56368-603-0 (softcover) — ISBN 978-1-56368-604-7 (ebook)
1. Deaf culture—Fiction. 2. People with disabilities—Fiction.
3. Interpersonal relations—Fiction. I. Title.
PS3603.O536D43 2015
813'.6—dc23
2015029841

♾ This paper meets the requirements of ANSI/NISO Z39.48-1992
(Permanence of Paper).

For my son,
Clayton Lee

Well I remember how you smiled
To see me write your name upon
The soft sea-sand – 'O! what a child!
You think you're writing upon stone!'

—from "Well I Remember,"
WALTER SAVAGE LANDOR

Contents

List of Illustrations

Acknowledgments

I WOULD LIKE to thank the following medical photographers, who graciously hosted me, treated me to delicious meals, and allowed themselves to be interviewed as part of my research visit to Galveston: John Glowczwski (biomedical photographer extraordinaire, who went above and beyond by giving tours of the photo and medical facilities and sharing the use of his clinical photography manual), Roger Stone (in memoriam), Steve and Cynthia Nussenblatt, and Tom Bednarek. And to the medical photographers who moved out of Galveston to other parts of the country: Dave Zagorski, Steve Murbach, Dave Joern, and Margaret Latta: I am so grateful for all of your wonderful comments, memories, and answers to my research questions via e-mail.

I wish to thank Dr. Robert Panara (in memoriam), who first taught me what it means to write from "the Deaf experience." A ton of thanks to my eagle-eyed readers Perry and Kitty Conley, Jim Conley, Ingrid Weidner, Dr. Carol Robinson, and especially to Dr. Edna Sayers, who so promptly and tirelessly gave me crucial feedback every time I asked for it. Special thanks to the Gallaudet University Schaefer Committee, which granted a professorship that allowed me to do further research for the book; to David Hays, who encouraged me to send my big, fat "literary scrapbook" of essays, photos, poems, and short fiction to Robert Rubin, who kindly took the time to write and tell me point-blank to whittle it all down to a series of linked short stories. Hence this novel.

I am indebted to Ivey Wallace, my editor, who saw the potential in my early manuscript years ago, encouraged me to continue writing, and helped shape this book along the way.

To Mark Mueller, my childhood buddy who turned me on to photography, and to Tom Coughlan, the first Deaf biomedical photography major at RIT and the nation's, if not the world's, first Deaf medical photographer, who had an illustrious career at Yale University's School of Medicine—if it weren't for you guys, this book would not have been conceived.

Credits

Portions of this work first appeared in the following publications:

Fiction

"Characters in El Paso." *Deaf American Prose:1980–2010*, ed. Kristen Harmon and Jennifer Nelson, 62–67. Washington, DC: Gallaudet University Press, 2012.

"The Deaf Heart," originally titled "It Could've Happened to Anyone! (anyone that is deaf)." *Symposium Magazine.* 2 (Spring 1981).

"Every Man Must Fall." *The Deaf Way II Anthology: A Literary Collection by Deaf and Hard of Hearing Writers*, ed. Tonya M. Stremlau, 171–83. Washington, DC: Gallaudet University Press, 2002.

"A Photographic Memory," the next incarnation of "It Could've Happened to Anyone! (anyone that is deaf)." *Kaleidoscope* 18 (Winter/Spring 1989), 16–18.

"The Seawall." *No Walls of Stone: An Anthology of Literature by Deaf and Hard of Hearing Writers*, ed. Jill Jepson, 39–45. Washington, DC: Gallaudet University Press, 1992.

Excerpt from "The Face of Grace." *Urbanite* (December 2006), 25.

Excerpts from "Kindergarten to College—A Personal Narrative" in "A Tale of a Hangnail and a Horn." *Post-Secondary Education and the Hearing Impaired Student.* London: Routledge, 1991.

"The Horn." *Hearing Health* 12 (5, September–October 1996), 9–10. ["A Tale of a Hangnail and a Horn" is adapted from this story.]

Photographs

"Girl in Truck Bed." *Off the Coast* 38 (Summer 2012), 64.

"Infant Skeletal Development." *34ʰ Parallel* 5 (2009), 4–5.

"Tropical Storm Aftermath." *American Photographer* (May 1985), 34.

"Used Car Shack." *Arkansas Review* 43(2012), 84.

"Human Heart Tricuspid Valve and Trabeculae." *Kaleidoscope* 18 (Winter/Spring 1989), 18.

The cover and interior photographs are all by Willy Conley except for "LeRoy Colombo Memorial, near 53ʳᵈ Street on the Seawall" on p. 143. That photo is by John Glowczwski.

The Deaf Heart

Mar. 7, 1981

R.I.T., Wallace Memorial Library

Dear Mom & Dad, am in a study room with my trusty Smith-Corona typewriter you gave me for Christmas. I "heard" you -- can't read my chicken scratches, so will type from now on. Just got your letter today. Decided to write back right away and include a copy of the Student Preparation Manual of that residency program in Galveston, Texas that I was telling you about. Last week, Dr. Nelson Robb, the director of the program, was on campus to give a ~~lecter~~ lecture to all of the students in the biomed photo program about the residency. Luckily, I had an ASL interpreter there. The program's really impressive! It'll be like getting a Masters in Biomedical Photography. What they do is help prepare you -- in one year -- for certification as a Registered Biological Photographer. Normally it requires five years of on the job experience before anyone can apply for certification. If one gets accepted into the program in Galveston, the board of registry ~~wavesxxx~~ waives those five years because of their recognition of this intensive residency. Accepted applicants will be working for the Department of Pathology full time while preparing for certification after hours and on weekends. One caveat -- only two students are accepted every year.

After the lecture, I went up to Dr. Robb with my interpreter, to ask some questions about accommodations for potential deaf applicants, and whether the program would be open to them.

He said absolutely, and that they would look
into it if the applicant showed promise.

It's a lonnnnnng shot for me. We've got over
35 biomed majors and I'm the only deaf one.
Chances are they'll go for the top hearing
majors -- why would they want to get involved
with the complications of working with a deaf
person? But, I figured what the hell? At least,
it gives me a push to get my photo portfolio
ready for the job market.

Oh -- almost forgot to tell ya -- we got
this biomed photo assignment that requires us
to photograph specimens, i.e. -- human heart,
brain, animal organs, or chicken embryos. I made
arrangements to get to a slaughterhouse and
bought a pig's lung and heart ($2.50) and eyes
($1.50). Photographed the tracheal tubes from
the lungs, did a section of the heart, and some
close-ups of the eyes. Also bought a couple of
fertilized chicken eggs (75 cts. apiece). Was

basically doing an "autopsy" in the bathroom sink. Messy work. But, in spite of it all, I think I got some really cool Lennart Nilsson-inspired shots. Ever see his photos? They look like they were shot <u>inside</u> the human body and you wonder how he ever squeezed a Nikon in there. I'm gonna use some of the specimen shots to go with the residency application (which requires a mini-portfolio of five black-and-white prints). Spring break is coming up and I plan on sticking around on campus to work in the photo labs to put together the portfolio and application packet for Texas.

Dad -- I found another leak in my anti-freeze system after I replaced the heater hose in the LTD. A deaf guy on my floor who used to work as an auto mechanic took a look at the problem. He fingerspelled slowly in my face: F-O-R-D. Asked me if I knew what those letters stood for. I said no. He signed, "<u>F</u>ix <u>O</u>r <u>R</u>epair <u>D</u>aily." Smartass!! Turns out I need a new water pump. He's going to show me how to install the whole shebang.

Let me know your plans about coming up for graduation. Can't believe four years here have slipped by already. Your little baby that you thought was deaf and dumb is finally gonna make it. Ain't we gonna have a party!
All my luv,
Max
P.S. Don't forget to let me know what you think of the manual and the residency program. This is only a copy of the first four pages from the manual. The rest of the pages are photo instructions on how to shoot stuff in a variety of medical situations -- too many pages to copy and didn't want to bore you with them.

STUDENT PREPARATION MANUAL
FOR EXAMINATION
AS REGISTERED BIOLOGICAL PHOTOGRAPHERS

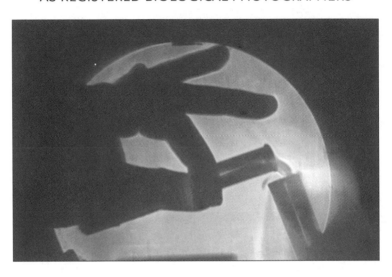

INTRODUCTION

This manual is for new, incoming pathology photography residents. As part of your 12-month training toward certification as a Registered Biological Photographer (RBP), you will serve a number of one- to two-week rotations to other departments on campus as well as to other off-campus departments within the University of Texas system (when applicable). This is in addition to your responsibilities in handling the lab's day-to-day pathology photography services in the Department of Pathology at the University of Texas Medical Branch in Galveston, Texas. Familiarize yourself with the main aspects of biomedical photography as seen in the following pages. Chances are you will most likely encounter them at some point during your one-year residency.

The RBP certification program was established to raise standards in the biomedical photography industry and to provide scientists, physicians, veterinarians, biologists, and medical personnel a criterion to go by when hiring biomedical photographers who have been certified by the Board of Registry of the Biological Photographic Association. Having the initials "RBP" next to one's name indicates that one has completed the three-phase written, practical (portfolio), and oral examination. The Registered Biological Photographer has been thoroughly evaluated in a diverse range of theoretical and practical applications in biomedical photographic communications. Doctors, research scientists, and clinical staff will know that a photographer with this prestigious credential is best qualified to take photographs for: a) a patient's medical condition for permanent record-keeping, assessment, and diagnosis; b) educating future medical personnel; and c) publication in medical textbooks and journals.

Each resident will be paid a monthly stipend in exchange for 40 hours/week in the photo lab. A two-week paid vacation is provided, including a standard university benefits package.

Arrangements have been made for you to take the written examination portion on campus. The pathology photography lab provides all necessary materials toward completion of the portfolio portion; however, you are responsible for arranging the shipment of your portfolio to the examiners. For the oral examination portion, you must arrange your own transportation and lodging for your oral defense before the Board of Registry in the city in which the national Biological Photographic Association convention takes place.

All necessary textbooks are available either in the photo lab or in the Moody Medical Library. An extensive bibliography of biomedical photographic communication resources is available upon request.

We are a "white glove publication laboratory." Each resident will be provided with a white lab coat, a pair of white lintless gloves, a hospital photo identification tag, and a set of protective clothing. Bring an extra pair of shoes to be used only in the autopsy suite.

Galveston is an island city, with a mild climate, located sixty miles south of Houston, Texas, in the Gulf of Mexico. The city dates from the early 1800s and is a port of entry. The University of Texas Medical Branch (UTMB) was founded in Galveston in 1881. Presently, the University and Medical complex houses a Medical School, the School of Allied Health Sciences and Nursing, and seven hospitals. Around 6,500 people are employed here, making UTMB one of the major employers on this island of 62,000 people.

Nelson Millard Robb, LL.D., R.B.P., F.B.P.A., F.R.M.S.
Teaching Associate, Department of Pathology
Director, Pathology Photography Residency Program
University of Texas Medical Branch
Galveston, Texas 77550

The First Heart

Reflective Objects   Occasionally, you will be required to photograph medical specimens that are in glass containers. Most of the time, you will not be able to remove the specimen from its container. The best way to photograph such a situation is to ask to have the specimen brought to the lab, where we have various-sized light boxes. Set up a light box vertically on top of a black velvet–covered table, and use that as your photographic background. All of our light boxes are balanced at 5500K. Be sure to use daylight film, not tungsten; otherwise, your results will come out with a bluish tint.

At thirteen years of age, Dempsey Maxwell McCall, otherwise known as Max, saw his first human heart—a large, grayish-yellow clump of bulging veins at the bottom of a jar of formaldehyde. Mr. Orendorf, the biology teacher, kept prodding his students to keep the jar moving up and down the rows of lab tables. "People, stop lollygagging!" he said. "If you're shocked, think of it as a piece of raw chicken."

Max looked at Orendorf, who had a tendency to quiver his lips after speaking, and then over to Flathead, his lab partner, who had the jar in front of him. Flathead was pale and looked ready to make a dash for the lab sink to upchuck. He sat there heaving, his eyes fixed straight ahead at the Periodic Table of Elements, as if the atomic numbers and symbols provided a calming effect. Max did Flathead a favor and took the heart. It bobbed around the bottom of the jar, waving its cut veins with endings flared in perpetual screams. Max took a long look at the heart, noticing through the murky fluid in the jar that on the seat in front of him, Carolyn McCormick's slip was showing its frilly lace. His eyes began to water. When Orendorf gestured for him to pass the jar along, Max lifted it over to the next student—who seemed as eager to see the heart as Flathead was. Max's eyes stopped watering. He realized they'd been affected by the jar's fumes, not by the excitement of seeing some creamy skin and lingerie.

Even though the jar hadn't yet made it halfway across the classroom, Orendorf opened class discussion by scribbling on the blackboard: "syphilitic aortitis."

"Would any of you ladies and gentlemen like to take a stab at the meaning of these two words?"

Max looked over at Flathead, silently trying out the words on his lips. His color was back.

"Hello? What's the matter, folks, are you deaf?" Orendorf rapped his knuckles on the board.

A redheaded kid with bad teeth leaned over to Carolyn, cupped his hand to her ear, and whispered, "No, but Max is." Both of them snickered. The kid had cupped his hand from Orendorf's view, not from Max's. Max was able to lipread in plain view. He thought about what the consequences might be of removing the jar lid and upending the contents over the kid's pimply face. The kid caught Max looking at him.

"Why don't you take a picture, it'll last longer," said Redhead. Max kept his eyes on him, daring Redhead to maintain eye contact.

"Peeee-ple!" Orendorf knocked on the board again. "Definition, please?"

Flathead hesitantly put his hand up.

"Looks like VD to me," said Flathead. The class had been studying venereal diseases over the past week, and many of the words accompanied by medical photographs were long and scientific-looking, like the ones now on the board.

"SY-PHI-LIS!" said Orendorf, as if he were selling popcorn. "The poor gentleman whose heart is in that jar keeled over from syphilis. Ve-ne-rrrreal di-seassse!" His lips trembled. "That's right, ladies and germs . . . from that dirty, three-letter word . . ."

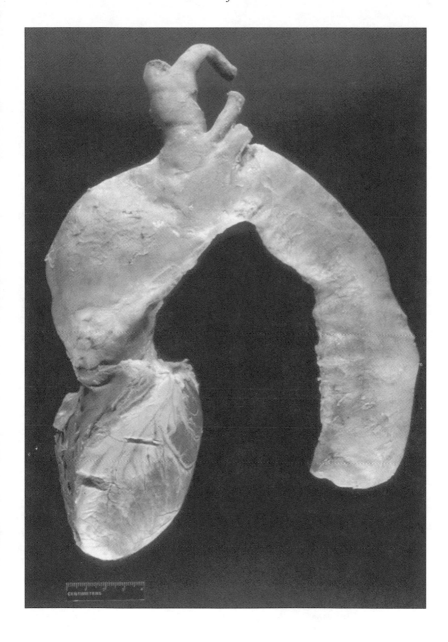

He turned his chalk sideways and wrote on the board in fat letters: "S E X."

"Let that be a lesson to the male of the species in this room who may be thinking about doing some hanky-panky in the woods with a loved one. Your heart might just blow up to twice its size, seize itself, and go blllrrrrtttth," said Orendorf with a raspberry. To underscore his point, he grabbed a sheet of paper, squeezed it into a ball, and dropped it onto his desk.

Flathead squinted skeptically and glanced over at Max. Max kicked Redhead's seat. When Redhead turned around, Max gestured with his index finger screwing in and out of his fist, then withdrew his finger and wagged a shaming "no-no."

"Now, have you lads and lasses formulated in your nimble brains any intelligent questions for me yet?" Orendorf raised his eyebrows repeatedly in an effort to bait his students. What he didn't realize was that his attempt was negated by his shivery lips.

Max raised his hand and cleared his throat. He swished saliva around in his mouth in preparation for his clearest enunciation, to minimize the sound of his deaf voice.

"If that was a normal heart," said Max, pointing at the jar, "could you tell the sex of the person it came from?"

A few smirking heads turned his way. Max could tell Mr. Orendorf either didn't know the answer or couldn't understand him. Whenever that happened, one of Orendorf's pockmarked cheeks would flutter a little, and he would rub his fingers over the deep acne scars, scars that made Max wonder just how rough his teacher's teenage years had been.

June 8, 1981
My room, Photo House, RIT

Hi Guys!

I'M IN!!!!!! Come August, I'm heading for
~~Glavx~~ Galveston. The acceptance letter for the
residency program arrived yesterday. Whew!
Can you believe it??? Dr. Robb must've seen
something in me. Went to the Red Creek last
night to celebrate with my friend Roger. He
couldn't fully celebrate 'cuz he was bartending,
but he was able to quickly quaff a few with me
when the boss wasn't looking. He also slipped
me a copy of their secret recipe for making the
chicken wing sauce.

The Creek has the best Buffalo chicken wings
and artichokes in Rochester. Really crispy and
spicy wings offset with a cool bleu cheese dip.
But don't call them Buffalo wings to anyone's
face around here -- they're <u>Rochester</u> wings. I
don't call them that, though -- too confusing
with the Rochester Red Wings, the Oriole's
AAA farm team. Speaking of the Red Wings, I've
been to a couple of their games already. Cheap
entertainment and a great place to take a date.
Been keeping my eye out on this one ballplayer
-- #5 -- who looks like an up-and-comer; hits a
lot of homers and is a great infielder. His name
is Calvin Ripken, Jr.

All is going well. The summer resident advisor
job has been a piece of cake. It's really nice
not to have to worry about paying room and board
for two months. Been doing a lot of swimming,
and playing tennis. Trying to do laps to build

up stamina. It's hard and frustrating, but I
know it's good for me.

I met up with Reuben Zagruder, the other
biomed photo student who got selected for the
residency. I only knew him superficially. We
discussed a few things about Galveston, and
agreed to share a place down there to save
money. We definitely want to live on the beach.
He seems like a super nice guy. He plays tennis
too! I have a hunch we'll get along well. He
invited me to visit him at his parents' in NYC
later in July. Will join you for Family Week
at the beach in Ocean City in mid-August, and
then plan to leave for Texas from Baltimore on
August 29th. Reuben volunteered to phone Dr.
Robb to make arrangements to stay with him till
we get on our feet. People who've been through
the program before have told Reuben that Robb is
a very hospitaɫble person. Guess we've got the
right man!

It was great having you up here for graduation
last month. Thanks for forwarding the graduation
cards, gifts, and people's mailing addresses.
I've got most of the thank-you cards all written
out. Hope to get them out soon before the post
office does something ridiculous, like go on
strike or something.

Love ya, Mmmmmmax

Every Man Must Fall

The ER   When called to the emergency room, you will most likely get one of the following cases to photograph: rape, child abuse, domestic violence, or police brutality. You MUST shoot the injured areas and the face in the same photo. When shooting, vary the flash angle to reveal the bumps, bruises, and cuts. Be sure to shoot lots of pictures—it would be disastrous to under-shoot when it comes to medical-legal situations. Each slide must be hand-labeled with your signature and date on the back in case you get called to court to testify that you were the photographer on the case. Hand-deliver the photos to the requesting physician and have him sign your log to show proof that the images were delivered. NEVER give the photos to a lawyer, a patient, or a police officer; they must ask the physician for copies.

When Max was told what the announcement over Dulaney High's public address system was all about—that his friend, Billy Hendricks, had drowned in the Loch Raven Reservoir—all he could do was sit there and stare at the wooden speaker above the door. How could such tragic news simply spill invisibly through the speaker's fabric screen? In Max's world, all information had to come to him visually. Most of his classmates and teachers had never understood that.

Minutes before Max learned of the tragedy, the sun was shining bright and cheerful rays into the classroom. Morning announcements went on dreadfully long, and to him they sounded like an alley dog barking incessantly. Since he couldn't lipread dogs and knew dogs couldn't enunciate anything better than an "arf," "yap," or "rowf," Max ignored the morning cacophony and killed time playing tic-tac-toe tournaments with Flathead.

Flathead used condoms with see-through packages for *O*s, while Max put down twisted paper clips for *X*s. The tourney winner would get a six-pack of beer. Flathead was about to drop an *O* to win a game when he suddenly stopped midway, pressing the condom between his fingers. He looked up at the doorway. Max could tell he was listening to the speaker by the way he tilted his head. Max imagined that if Flathead turned at the proper angle, a stream of words would enter cleanly into his ear, like water through a funnel. Max envied him for getting information so easily.

Flathead put the condom down and bowed his head. Max saw students behind him talking rapidly to each other. Others sat quietly, wide-eyed and slack-jawed. A few of the girls began to weep. One girl got up and rushed out of the classroom. Max looked over to Mr. Crumwell, his homeroom teacher, for some visual reference. Crumwell looked up toward the speaker, shook his head in disgust, mumbled something that looked like, "He asked for it," and went back to grading papers. Somebody in the senior class must've gotten caught in the lavatory smoking pot and wasn't going to be able to graduate—probably the star varsity pitcher or quarterback.

Max nudged Flathead's skinny arm. Flathead looked up at Max, all sad-eyed, running his hand over his crew top, soothing himself. Max gave him a questioning gesture with an upward shake of his head: "What's up?"

By now, Max knew that something more serious than a pot bust had happened. Flathead didn't get emotional unless he won at tic-tac-toe or lined up a hot date for a mixer. He flipped the tic-tac-toe sheet over, grabbed the pencil, and wrote, "Billy Hendricks died."

Max had to read it a few times. Flathead couldn't spell to save his life, and Max wondered if he'd written an incomplete sentence, like, "Billy Hendricks did . . ."

To confirm the spelling, Max whispered, "Are you saying Billy Hendricks d-i-e-d?"

Mr. Crumwell and the students in the front of the class suddenly turned their heads to look at Max. He thought he had whispered.

Flathead took a deep breath. He scrawled the words, "drowned, lock ravin."

It was then that Max took a good hard look at the loudspeaker with the coarse fabric covering, wishing that captions could come out of it during announcements. Perhaps no one else would think this was such a big deal, but Max wanted the right to get the news at the same time as everyone else, especially news concerning someone he cared about.

This was the first time an experience with death had affected Max. When one of the boys in his Cub Scout troop, a kid with asthma, had died, it had not shaken him. The kid was a snob. Only a year ahead of him in elementary school, the boy had always acted like he was more intelligent and talented than Max. Max had felt that the kid had seen him as retarded, and suspected it was because of his deafness. Max didn't know why the kid thought he was such hot shit, because whenever the troop played baseball, the kid had to take a whiff from his inhaler thing between empty swings at the plate. And here was Max whiffling balls over the stone wall in left field, rounding the bases as easily as breathing in his sleep.

One October evening at home, Max had been helping his mother carve a pumpkin in preparation for a Scout meeting. She was the troop's den mother. That night, she had received a phone call that brought tears to her eyes. He was told later that the call was about the asthmatic troop member. The kid simply couldn't get enough oxygen, and had died the previous day. How could anyone not have enough air?, Max had thought at the time. There's so much of it outside. Max asked his mother about this later, but she shrugged him off and dabbed her eyes again with a Kleenex. Now this one he really couldn't figure out. The kid wasn't *her* son.

Max approached Mr. Crumwell and asked to be excused. He was feeling all knotty inside and needed some air and water. Thankfully, there wasn't anybody in the lavatory. He didn't know what he was going to feel, but whatever it was, he wanted to feel it alone, without anyone scrutinizing his facial expressions or listening to sounds he might make. He clogged the drain with some paper towels and turned on the cold water to fill up the sink to the overflow level. He lowered his face into the water until numbness from the cold came over him. He tried to envision what Billy's face must've looked like under water. Bloated? White? Smiling? Yawning, maybe?

Max couldn't believe his buddy had been killed by a substance as weak and insubstantial as water—the very substance he worked with. Billy and Max worked side by side as dishwashers on Saturdays and Sundays at the White Coffee Pot, a family restaurant nestled between Read's Drugstore and Hardware Fair in a strip shopping center. Billy was the kind of guy who would probably have grown up to be a Klan member or the president of the local chapter of the NRA. His blazing orange hair matched a hunter's outdoor shirt, and a badly chipped front tooth gave him a smile that showed you something was missing. Although he was only seventeen years old, he had the belly of a beer drinker.

After six months of working with Max at the White Coffee Pot, Billy'd gotten fired. Max had found out why when Sylvia, the manager, called him out of the kitchen and had him sit across from her in one of the black Naugahyde booths. She stared at him a long time before saying a word. Max's heart pounded in his throat. He mentally ran through a list of all the things that he shouldn't have done in the back: dipping his fingers in the cornbread batter, taking home crab cakes, squirting the dishwasher hose at a waitress's legs, neglecting to mop the floor on the late nights when he was tired and alone.

Over-enunciating a bit for his benefit, Sylvia asked, "Have you ever looked down into the women's restroom?" When she said "down" her jaw dropped low enough for him to see that she had spent a lot of time in a dental office getting her teeth filled with gold.

"Looked down? I'm sorry, I don't know what you're talking about."

"You've never, ever looked down into the women's restroom?"

"The only time I even look in there is when I empty the trash can and mop the floor after we close. What happened?"

"You honestly don't know?" She put her index finger to her head to emphasize the word *know* in hopes that it might rouse his memory.

"No, ma'am," he said, using his best speech. "I swear." During this line of questioning, he leaned forward on the table and stroked his chin. He had read in a book about body language that this posture would show that he was seriously thinking about what the other person was saying. Max hid his other hand under the table, keeping it busy exploring hardened pieces of bubble gum, nuts and bolts, a carved-out hole . . . Then, finally, he grasped what she was asking.

Once Billy had invited him up into the rafters to take a peek into the ladies' room. Billy said he'd cut out a small hole in the corner of the ceiling—small enough that no one in the restroom would notice it, but large enough that someone in the rafters could see everything that went on inside. Virtuously, Max had told Billy that he wasn't interested. He'd tried to sound cool; he wasn't desperate to see female anatomy. Actually, he'd made a note to himself to check it out one weekend when he was the sole dishwasher. The very next time he worked alone, an opportunity presented itself. The restaurant was closed and it was just him, Esther the cook, and a couple of waitresses cleaning up. Esther was about forty, with a pockmarked face and a body pushing against an extra-large cook's uniform. She'd put down her grill scrub brush and apron, and headed for the back.

Max had quickly gone over to the walk-in refrigerator, pretending to stock up on "prep" foods for the next day. He'd timed opening the refrigerator to Esther's opening the door to the ladies' room. He'd closed the walk-in quietly, without going inside, and climbed up the ladder instead.

There were greasy handprints on the ceiling tiles where Billy had pushed them aside to gain access. Max's heart beat fast, since he wouldn't be able to hear it if one of the waitresses came by. He put his hand up to the same corner as Billy's handprints, noticing that Billy's hands were smaller than his. Amazing how ego could exaggerate one's size.

Cartons of lettuce, tomatoes, and potatoes were down below the ladder waiting to be stored in the walk-in. Max looked once more at the ceiling tile, paused, and then came back down the ladder. Being deaf was enough of a stigma. Were he caught, he would never get another job in his entire life. He predicted the rumors that would spread about the incompetencies and sexual vagaries of the deaf.

Across from him in the booth, Sylvia lit up a filterless Pall Mall. She politely bent her head to spit out some loose tobacco strands in the direction of her lap. Each *spphht* was followed by a puff of smoke.

"Well, I just fired Mr. Hendricks for lewd behavior in the back." She drew a heavy sigh and exhaled another column of smoke.

"Oh, really?" He stifled the urge to grab a napkin from the dispenser to tear apart and roll up into little balls to calm his nerves.

"I went in the back the other day to check out how many crab cakes we had left in the walk-in."

"Y-yeah," he answered, not sure if she was asking him a question.

"Well, I saw where that ladder was when I came out of the walk-in. Mr. Hendricks was standing on it, half up in the ceiling, looking down into the women's restroom."

"Oh, my God," said Max, slapping his forehead to convey disapproval.

Sylvia had ended her interrogation the same way she had opened it, with an eagle-eyed stare. He was innocent, of course, but he was afraid that his knowledge of the hole would trip this human lie detector. Finally, Sylvia put out her cigarette in the white ashtray shaped like a coffee pot and slid out of the booth. Max grabbed a napkin and quickly rolled a couple of little paper balls between his fingertips before going back to the dishes.

At school, Billy and Max happened to be in the same photography class. Billy said he'd taken photography to get out of his art requirement. He couldn't stand the idea of sitting on a stool for two hours slapping paint onto a canvas; that was for girls, and for boys who wanted to be girls.

Since there weren't enough darkrooms to go around, they shared one. Billy picked Max for a partner because of Max's premature baldness. To Billy's mind, that meant Max was the most mature student around, meaning he wouldn't give a flick about anything Billy said or did. Besides, Max was deaf and pretty much kept to himself. All Billy wanted to do was read *Playboy* magazines under the seedy illumination of a safelight.

Max had ended up doing Billy's black-and-white prints. In exchange, Billy had worked at the restaurant in Max's place any time he needed a Saturday or Sunday off to spend with his girlfriend, who lived an hour and a half away.

Having Billy fill in for him at the restaurant wasn't the only reason why Max was willing to develop Billy's prints. The fat sucker had a damn good eye for composition, and God only knew where he got it. Billy's mother ran the Laundromat at the end of the shopping center. All she did was open the place, make sure nobody walked out with a washer or dryer, lock up at closing time, and then hurry home to watch *Dialing for Dollars* by the telephone. His father worked for the highway department filling potholes and striping yellow lines on the streets of Baltimore. He also ran a plow and salt truck during the winter, when it snowed. His parents definitely didn't seem to carry any genes for a good eye in photographic composition.

In the most ordinary subjects, Billy would find something extraordinary—like, he'd shoot a rusty nail on a barn door. Big

funky deal, right? In the developer bath, that 8x10 print came
out looking like a Walker Evans or Dorothea Lange masterpiece
from the Depression. Max's pictures always ended up looking like
clichés: the proverbial sunset smack-dab in the middle of a print
with a seagull silhouetted against the sky.

Billy used his grandfather's old Leica range finder, the kind
where you looked through the viewfinder from the upper left corner of the camera. Max didn't know how Billy did it, since range
finders never recorded exactly what was seen through the glass.
Whenever he shot with that kind of camera, Max's pictures were
always off-center.

When Billy went shooting, he "burned" film. He'd shoot up a
roll of thirty-six exposures on that one rusty nail, whereas Max
hated to waste more than two frames on a subject.

"Billy, where did you learn to shoot like that?" Max would ask.

"Nowheres. I just aim and click, is all."

"But there's more to it than that. I mean, how did you come
up with stuff like taking pictures of water reflections and then
turning the photos upside down to make your images look like
the real thing?"

"Shit-if-I-know, man," Billy would say, holding his *Playboy*
centerfold up vertically for a minute.

"I've never seen anybody turn their reflections upside down.
That's ingenious! You're a regular Monet, painting with your
camera."

"What're you talking about money for?" he asked.

"Mo-nay."

"What is it? Some kind of an eel or sumthin'?" Then he would
give Max that chipped-tooth smile.

Max suspected Billy knew he was an artist, but would never let
on to anyone. Art was for faggots, and for some reason, Billy had
a backwoods, tobacco-chewing reputation to maintain.

After the day Billy was fired, Max hadn't seen him much. Billy
had stopped going to photography class. His souped-up blue '62
Valiant with the small Confederate flag on the aerial was rarely

seen about town. Max had missed Billy's brazen presence, but was so caught up in the end-of-the-year school activities that he'd almost forgotten about Billy—until the morning of the death announcement.

Several months after Billy died, Max went fishing for old times' sake at the Loch Raven Reservoir under a Fourth of July sky that was as blue as it could ever get. He stood in the water up to his knees, holding the line of his bamboo rod out by the deep pocket where he knew sunfish liked to hang out. Max kept an eye on the red-and-white bobber, waiting for it to be pulled under. When they got time off from work on some weekends, he and Billy used to troll in the area of Goetze's Cove for sunfish. Whenever a catfish snatched onto Billy's line, he'd rip the hook out of its mouth, replace it with a lit firecracker, and heave it into the air to explode like a grenade.

"What did you do that for, Bill?"

"Doin' my part for wildlife conservation."

"Man, you're a piece of wildlife. What's your part?"

"Keepin' the ugly-fish population down. It's a bottom-feeder. You ever ate one of them?"

"No."

"Tastes like a dirty dishrag from all that shit it sucks up from the lake bottom."

"Yeah, right, Bill, I guess you would know the flavor of dirty dishrags."

Up on the bank of the cove was a granite boulder big as an old refrigerator lying on its side. Max had always thought of it as Billy's rock. According to the local news, this was near where Billy's body had been pulled out of the water. It was at this rock that Max first saw Billy, after his family moved to the area. A small crowd of kids was yelling at Billy not to do whatever it was he was doing. He was a skinny little runt then. As Max snuck in for a closer view, he saw Billy pounding something against the rock over and over: it was a box turtle with its shell cracked apart and blood dripping out. Besides the prepubescent act of violence, what had also stunned Max was the cloud-colored, gelatinous remains of the tortoise. He'd never realized that turtles had a lump of jelly under their shells. And there was Billy grinning at this wondrous discovery, his eyes sparkling in the late afternoon sun. Max couldn't remember if his friend had the chip in his tooth then. In later years, Billy claimed he held his secret MPA club meetings at the rock.

"What's MPA stand for, Bill?"

"I ain't gonna tell you. You ain't a member."

Max had wondered if Billy's club had any members at all. One of the neighborhood kids told Max in confidence that MPA stood for Mashed Potatoes Association. It wasn't until the time Billy and Max worked together at the White Coffee Pot that the potato connection was made. Billy craved mashed potatoes with a crater of butter and, while washing dishes, always kept a plate of them at his side.

The bobber continued to float in place, the white half still above the water. About three feet away, an object under the water reflected the sunlight. Max tried to edge toward it, but kept slipping on smooth algae-covered rocks. He didn't want some crayfish snapping at his toes. If Billy was looking down on him at that moment and knew his thoughts, he would think he was a big sissy. In his head, he gave Billy the finger.

Max lowered the bamboo pole and tried to probe the object. Attached to it was a dark strap wavering in the water. Max caught the strap with the pole and tried to pull it toward him. The strap slid off. He dipped the pole underneath and fished for the strap again. The object felt heavy as Max was finally able to lift it up.

It was a Leica range finder. Max swung the pole over and eased the camera onto the bank. After cleaning off the mud, he could see that the film's counter was on 13. The rewind knob was taut, indicating that there was indeed film inside. He took the camera home and kept it submerged in a sink of water to preserve the film until it could be brought to school for processing.

The next morning, not many people were at the photo lab, since it was summer school. In the darkroom Max had the absurd thought that if he opened the camera back, minnows would flop out, but all that came out was musty water. He developed the film and, after fifteen minutes, turned the lights on. The moldy smell was replaced by the vinegary odor of photographic chemicals. He washed the film and held it up to the bare bulb overhead. Twelve frames had been exposed, all of somebody's face, all similar, perhaps a man's face—hard to tell since they were negative images. Max dried the film, cut it into strips, and placed it in protective sleeves. Then he took out a strip and inserted it into the enlarger.

He cranked the enlarger to blow up the image to an 8x10 size. He made an exposure and slipped the print into the developer. As he rocked the tray back and forth to agitate the chemicals, Billy's image appeared on the paper. He wasn't smiling, yawning, or giving that devil-may-care look of his. The look was more like that of a downed U.S. fighter pilot held as a POW during the Vietnam War. Billy's right eye was black and swollen shut. Across his forehead was a caterpillar-shaped gash. His nose had the unmistakable curve of a break in the middle. A thin but deep-looking cut on his chin showed that he had probably been knifed. Both cheeks were swollen. His good eye looked dead-dull.

Max's heart started pounding and his throat went dry. He leaned over the darkroom sink and drank water from the faucet. He took the print out of the developer and bathed it in the other chemicals before continuing to wash the image of Billy Hendricks. Even though Billy was dead, Max felt comforted by the thought that he was cleansing Billy's wounds. Maybe no one had been able to do this for him at the time. But what had happened? Had Billy taken these himself on a self-timer, or did some bruiser shoot the pictures to record his handiwork and forget to take out the film? Max couldn't tell from the background where the photos had been taken. It was all white—probably a wall, by the way the shadows fell behind Billy.

Max made more prints from the rest of the negatives. All turned out to be basically the same, except that the angles were slightly different in each frame. One shot was a little tilted. Another a little higher. A third, a bit to the left, and so forth. But in every one of them, Billy had that straight-ahead dead stare at the lens. It was a look Max had never seen in any of Billy's most mischievous moments.

Max cleaned up and dried everything in the darkroom. He decided not to show the prints to anyone in the lab, and walked home mulling over what to do with this newfound evidence. He didn't want to take the pictures to Billy's parents, suspicious that Billy's father might somehow be involved. Billy and his father had never got on, and often wound up having fistfights in their backyard. Billy had once said that when his old man got older, he was going to do to him what he had done to the turtle—crack the old man's skull and expose the jelly underneath that tough exterior.

If Max went to the cops, they'd start some full-blown investigation probing into everybody's lives and turning everything upside down. Max resisted the need to show the pictures to anyone because he was well aware of how human nature works, how confidential information gets blabbed away.

Fortunately, Max's parents weren't home yet. He pushed his mother's plants on the windowsill aside and opened the kitchen window. He moved the dirty dishes and glasses out of the sink and set them on the counter. He lifted the negatives and prints out of the box and set them by the sink. The soft light coming through the window made Billy look even more vulnerable. It made him think of that song, "I Shall Be Released," they always sang at the Young Life meetings he occasionally went to. Max had never really associated its meaning with anything until now, although after he'd read the lyrics his mother had written down for him, he'd assumed they were singing about Jesus Christ. "They say every man needs protection . . . they say that every man must fall." He felt all knotty again in his eyes and throat.

Max got a box of wooden matches out of the drawer and struck one. Suspending the prints and negatives over the sink, he held the match up to the corners of the photos, watching the flame grow big. The papers curled and the plastic sizzled. On the 8x10, the black around Billy's swollen eye grew bigger until it was black all over. Just when Max could no longer stand the heat, he dropped the pictures in the sink and waited until they were reduced to ashes. He brushed the soot down the drain and put in the drain plug. Turning on the hot water and squeezing in some detergent, he transferred the dirty tableware back into the sink. Then, grabbing a sponge, Max began to wash the dishes.

July 12, 1981
Lounge, Photo House, RIT

It's practically a ghost town around here --
only a smattering of summer photo students
staying on my floor in the dorms. What's great
about it is that there are very few problems
to deal with -- informing Housekeeping that
the bathrooms need more toilet paper, putting
in a work order to get a couple of burnted out
lightbulbs replaced in the hallway, letting
someone in their room because they forgot their
room key, etc. [YAWN!] It's so quiet and sparse
in the dining hall that with my hearing aids
on even I can hear the echo of pots and pans
banging in the kitchen. Almost makes me wanna
yell, "HEY, KEEP IT DOWN! I'm trying to read the
paper here." Probably useless if I yelled 'cuz
they're deaf students working back there.

What's also good about not many students
around -- I don't have to fight for getting a
darkroom in the NTID photo printing lab. I'm
catching up on printing some of my personal
work. Plus, I've made some nice, color 8x10
glossies of Grandmom and Grandpop for you guys.

I still go to my two-hour Saturday kung fu
classes on campus. I'm learning kicks now;
there's so many moves to learn. I'm still at
that awkward phase which kung fu beginners go
through during the first couple of months. In a
few more weeks I should be quick and graceful.
HI-YAHHHHH! [THWACK] Uh-oh, just kicked a hole
in the drywall in the lounge . . . just kidding!
What's Bruce Lee's favorite drink? Answer:
"WA-TAAAAH!"

Two more weeks and it's bye-bye RIT -- bound
for Merryland!

Love, Kwai Chang Max Caine

p.s. (from *Kung Fu* TV series with David Carradine)
Master Po [after easily defeating the boy in
combat]: Ha, ha, never assume because a man has
no eyes he cannot see. Close your eyes. What do
you hear?
Young Caine: I hear the water, I hear the birds.
Master Po: Do you hear your own heartbeat?
Young Caine: No.
Master Po: Do you hear the grasshopper which is
at your feet?
Young Caine [looking down and seeing the
insect]: Old man, how is it that you hear these
things?
Master Po: Young man, how is it that you do not?

[pretty deep, huh?]

Sheep Is Life

Gross Specimen Photography   If called to the morgue, most often you will be asked to photograph a gross anatomic specimen removed from an autopsy. Our gross specimen photography setup, in the far right corner of the room, is standardized for lighting and exposures (see exposure table on the wall). The very first thing to do is put on a disposable surgical gown and a pair of latex gloves. Be sure the glass tabletop has been wiped clean with Windex. There are two Plexiglas backgrounds commonly used under the specimen—blue (for color slides) and black (for black-and-white prints). In the drawer are pieces of clay to use to help prop up any dangling parts of the specimen (aortas, renal veins, lung lobes, etc.) to help minimize any depth of field problems. If the specimen is moist, pat it dry with paper towels to reduce glare and highlights. Also in the drawer is a Dymo Label Maker and metric scale. Be sure to double-check the case number when typing out the label and affixing it on the scale. Always align the scale in the lower left or right corner of the photo frame.

The second time Max saw a human heart out in the open was during a pathology photography summer internship at the Johns Hopkins Hospital in Baltimore. During his senior year in high school, he was selected to participate in a career development program. A career counselor asked him to fill out a form describing what field of study he would like to pursue and why. Max wrote down that he liked nature and landscape photography, and his reason for pursuing this was to be outdoors in the fresh air, away from offices. He felt the best way to photograph subjects was with natural, ambient light. Little did he know that the counselor would find him a job that placed him right smack in the inner landscape of the human body at one of the most famous hospitals in the world.

Down in the hospital's pathology morgue, a doctor was cutting the heart out of the body of a withered old woman. Max had never seen a dead body before. Prepared for the moment, he held on tight to his forensic camera, expecting to be shocked. He stood by the sink in case he got sick. He had prepared by not eating anything that morning. But in fact he felt detached. The body looked like a large piece of meat being butchered, which Max had seen from time to time at the grocery store. However, he had never seen a woman doing the sawing, and what he saw before him was a macabre scene of a woman cutting into another woman.

Was he destined to get a job in this morbid world? His grandfather had been a mortician, and probably a gene for an affinity with dead people had been passed along to him. Max wondered about all of the autopsies going on in the world at that moment. It was one of those things: people vaguely knew that it was happening all around them, but would just as soon not know the details.

Despite these morbid thoughts, Max was thankful to be in this special career-placement program. It got him out of the high-peer-pressure combat zone of high school. At Hopkins he was working in the real world with real people dealing with life-and-death matters. The bargain for the Pathology Photography Department was that they got an extra worker for free two days a week. They were pleased to know that he was already trained to work in a darkroom to develop film and prints. The only drawback for Max was his Swedish boss's full beard. It was impossible to lipread him. Someone always had to interpret for Max—orally or in writing—everything the boss said.

The pathologist dabbed the bloody heart and plopped it on the scale as if she were weighing fruit. She made a notation on her clipboard, and then moved the heart over to the photographic light table. Although he couldn't tell the color of her hair because of the surgical cap, Max guessed she was in her thirties. Her face was smooth, angular, and light brown, perhaps of Native American or Asian descent. For someone working in the morgue, Max expected a certain hardness, a butch look and personality that would stare down death. The doctor's gentle brown eyes looked at Max and acknowledged that the heart was ready to be photographed.

Max screwed the camera onto the telescopic stand above the table and adjusted the lights to set them at a 45-degree angle to the specimen. He slid in the blue Plexiglas background to create contrast on film with the red. With a light meter, he checked the illumination to make sure it was even around the area of the heart. Just as he was about to make his first exposure, the doctor held out her arm and said, "Whoa! You need a scale and a case number in the photograph. Haven't they taught you that?"

"No, they just told me to show up here for pictures at 10 a.m.," Max answered.

"Didn't anybody teach you how to do things around here?"

"No, ma'am, I just started working as an intern this week."

The pathologist threw up her hands and muttered something to the wall that he couldn't understand. He just stood there feeling helpless. She turned back and looked him in the eyes. Max took a step back, unsure of what to do. He felt like she was one of those people who can really look at you and see into your soul.

"Some internship you're on here, huh? I'm Dr. Dezba Yazzie." She held out a bloody, gloved hand.

"Uh—I need to put on a pair of gloves to shake your hand," said Max.

She gave him a double-dimpled smile, and gestured for him to go ahead. He nervously snapped on a pair of latex gloves and held out his hand. She gave him a firm handshake.

"Nice to meet you. I'm Max. Thanks for your patience with me."

"Where's Bob? He should be down here giving you the lay of the land."

"He got called to photograph an operation," said Max.

"Hang on a sec while I get you a little ruler," said Dr. Yazzie. "I'll show you how to type out the case number on the label maker and stick it to the scale."

Max started to breathe easier. Dr. Yazzie had a strange way of putting him at ease in this foreign environment.

"Where are you from?" she asked.

"Dulaney Senior High," said Max.

"I noticed that you have hearing aids."

"I'm profoundly deaf."

"So, I need to look directly at you when I'm talking to you, right?"

"Yes, how did you know?"

"I have a deaf sister," she said, while signing.

"Oh, cool! I don't know signs—only a little fingerspelling. I want to learn one day, though," said Max.

"I'm a bit rusty. I don't see my sister very often. If I don't use it, I lose it," she said. "It's not easy to fingerspell with these gloves on," she said with a laugh. "My sister has been away at the Arizona State School for the Deaf and Blind in Phoenix."

"Is that where you're from?"

"From Arizona, yes. You see, we are Navajo and on our reservation near Flagstaff there are no programs to help deaf children."

"I see," said Max. "Shall I go ahead and start taking photos of the heart?"

"She can wait," said Dr. Yazzie, pointing to the corpse. "She's not going anywhere."

Max could see that she wanted someone to talk to. He imagined it probably got lonely down there. Still, he felt the urgent need to take the requested photos and get back to the lab. He didn't want his boss to think it took him an entire hour to photograph one specimen.

"How did you get through school?" Dr. Yazzie asked.

"How did I what? Get through? You mean how I passed school till now?"

She nodded, showing a perfect set of even, white teeth and full lips. Her mouth formed every word seductively while she signed, though her intention was not to be sexual but to be comprehensible. Max squirmed his legs to prevent himself from getting an erection. It brought him back to his weekly sessions with his grade school speech teacher, an elderly woman. What was remarkable to him was that despite her wrinkled face, she had a mouth that perfectly shaped words that could easily be read from her lips. He felt warm fuzzies and found himself getting hard just by watching her read sentences from a speech primer. He was embarrassed. The woman was old enough to be his grandmother, and was just trying to teach him the difference between speaking words with a "ch" and a "sh" sound.

"Sh-sh-uh . . . sh-sheer stick-to-itiveness," said Max, surprised at how that came out. "That's how I got by. Just showing up and doing the work."

"Hey—my philosophy too. That's exactly how I got into medical school here!" said Dr. Yazzie. "And, let me tell you something," she said, coming closer to his face in confidence. "Don't let the bastards get you down!" Such strong, rousing words coming from a delicate-looking woman.

"Yes ma'am, I won't."

Dr. Yazzie bent down over the table and oriented the heart the way she wanted it photographed. It had been sectioned longitudinally down the middle. She opened it like two halves of an apple. She stood up and looked at Max.

"The reason I asked about your school . . . often, deaf or disabled children in the Navajo nation unfortunately don't go to school. Families are ashamed when they find out a baby was born with a defect. They blame it on some past life transgression by the mother or father. My mother took the blame because her own father once killed a white man. She thinks she's being punished for that by having a daughter who's deaf."

"You mean deaf kids are shunned by your people?" asked Max.

"Oh, yeah! The tribal elders won't let them participate in initiations, ceremonies, or powwows," said Dr. Yazzie. "The kids still get called by their baby names after they've grown up to be adults. I'm not allowed to help interpret at an initiation or ceremony. Poor deaf kids. Stay mostly uneducated all their lives, except for those families who help the kids learn by osmosis."

"Oz-what?" asked Max.

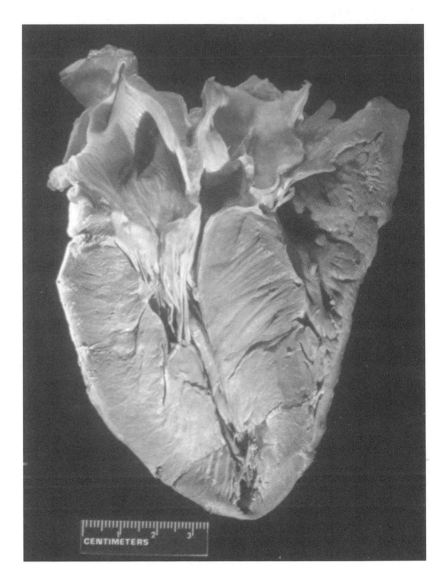

"Osmosis. You know your biology? Gradual learning from watching and doing," said Dr. Yazzie. "That's how I helped my sister. Sort of like what Annie Sullivan did with Helen Keller. I just had her hang around with me doing stuff around the house and letting her do things, too, make mistakes and learn from them."

"Did you use homemade gestures or signs with her?" asked Max.

"Some, but mostly she read my lips. In Navajo language. Then, we learned from a public school counselor that there was a school in Phoenix for deaf children. From there she learned ASL and I learned from her and some sign language books."

Dr. Yazzie showed Max the label maker and plastic ruler. She handed over her clipboard.

"Here's the chart on my case. Punch out the numbers and stick them on the corner of this ruler," said Dr. Yazzie. "I want an overall shot, and then I'd like for you to get me a close-up of the valve and trabeculae—that stringy stuff. Be sure the photo shows the abnormally thick walls there, OK?"

"Absolutely," said Max.

When he was done, Max went over to Dr. Yazzie at the autopsy table, where she was removing the old woman's digestive system. She turned her head toward him to speak while pulling out the intestines hand over hand, like rope.

"You and I are minorities, you see? You can't sit back and wait for things to happen to you. You have to actively seek out opportunities for yourself. That's how I got to be here in this world-renowned medical school. I applied for every scholarship I could find for women and minorities," she said.

"How did you get into pathology?" asked Max.

"Sheep guts!" she said, laughing, holding up a couple feet of the intestinal tract. "In our culture, 'Dibé—Diné bí' íína'—sheep is life." She laid the intestines down to fingerspell the Navajo words slowly.

Max tried hard to look beyond the bloody gloves and focus on the context of what she was spelling. The letters went right over his head.

"My father taught me how to eviscerate a sheep," she continued. "Before we killed the sheep, my mother would shear it and spin the wool to make the thread for our clothes. After my father slaughtered the sheep, he showed me how to work through the

ewe's intestines, squeezing out all of the contents. Then, we cut
the guts up for my mother, who cleaned them, and hung them up
to dry for food. My brother scraped and tanned the hides for pants
and coats. He also filed down the bones to make tools. We did not
waste any part of the sheep. So for us, sheep symbolize the good
life—living in harmony and balance on the land."

Max looked at his watch. "I would like to stay and talk more,
but I really need to get back to the photo lab," he said.

"Send the slides to me at Cardiac Pathology."

"Cardiac Pathology, got it. Dr. Yazzy—Y-a-z-z-y, right?" asked
Max.

"Not like 'jazzy'—sounds more like 'Yah-zee,' spelled Y-a-z-z-i-e."

"Thank you, Dr. Yazzie."

"Max, don't forget your word—stick-to-itiveness! My word—
stick-it-to-'em! And, remember—wear your 'freshman perfume'
proudly wherever you go."

"Excuse me, my freshman . . .?"

"P-e-r-f-u-m-e," said Dr. Yazzie, spritzing an invisible atomizer.
"It's the smell of formaldehyde that you will have on your clothes.
Out there are thousands of poor, uneducated people without jobs
who wish they were in your place."

Max wasn't sure what she really meant. He couldn't imagine
hordes of people wishing to be alone in a morgue working with
dead bodies.

Knoxville, Tennessee, Motel 6
August ~~28~~ 29, 1981

Dear Mom and Dad,

As promised I'm sending photos and letters
as I make my way to Galveston. The Blue Baby
Special is holding up pretty good, except I have
to pull off to get her gassed up every 150 miles
or so. At least it can haul all of my photo
equipment and, it has a deep trunk to keep it
well-concealed from highway robbers -- heh!

Writing to you with photos keeps me company.
You know how great the odds are of meeting
another deaf person on the road, or someone who
knows sign language. Anyhow, I'm thinking about
you guys this morning before hitting the road
again. I envision you at the kitchen table.
Dad's reading the sports page and listening
to the radio. Mom is scooping out a wedge of
grapefruit while reading the arts section.
Every now and then she accidentally squirts Dad
with bits of grapefruit juice, ticking him off.

Here's the first of the bunch . . . freshly
printed last night courtesy of Motel 6.
Surprised it's a black-and-white print and not
some One-Hour-Bang-'Em-Out color job by some
teeny-bopper in a drug store? Didn't think I'd
unpack my equipment till I got to Galveston,
right? That's why the LTD trunk comes in handy.
It's just like having an equipment closet in the
darkroom. Just ask the motel desk clerk for a
ground floor room and back the ole LTD up to the
front of the door. Instant photo lab.

One thing I learned at RIT -- the sooner you
develop your pictures, the sharper the images.
Film can only hold a latent image for so long
before it begins to fade. And you know all
things fade with time. I have this illusion that
the silver and gelatin on the film's surface
will let go of the image created by light.
Zzzzzz . . . (stop snoring, Dad!) I can see this
deterioration of the image's outline -- molecule
by molecule -- in my mind's eye. Have you ever
seen how your pictures come out a little foggy
and soft around the edges if you've sent in your
pictures a year later for development? (See, Dad
-- your $25,000 for my college education wasn't
a total waste.)

Got in the Knoxville area just off I-45 about
5 o'clock last night. Went for a walk around the
neighborhood behind the motel and shot whatever
struck my eye. Came back and mixed the chemicals
in the bathroom sink. Put a towel under the
door, turned out the lights, and loaded up the
developing reels. Once I got the film onto the
reels and into the light-tight tank, I was able
to turn on the light and do the processing.
Hung the film up to dry from the shower curtain
rack. Set up the little cheapo enlarger in the
bathtub along with some aluminum pie pans filled
with chemicals for developing the prints. Only
need to blow up the image to a 4x5 print, so
the pie pans were perfect -- thanks, Mom. Dad
-- you're probably wondering how I was able to
see in the dark while printing. I brought along
one of those 15-watt amber safelight bulbs and
unscrewed one of the bathroom bulbs. Can print
stuff in a jiffy. Piece of cake -- er, pie.

Think I oughta write this up and submit it as
a photo tip to Popular Photography magazine?
What about introducing the idea to the RBP board
as part of my certification? I don't know . . .
those Registered Biological Photographers are
very stuffy about following proper biomedical
photographic protocol. It's gonna be a long,
ass-butt-whipping year of learning strict,
"white-glove publication laboratory" techniques
for this certification. I can sense it right
from the start from Professor Robb's recruitment
lecture and the residency program manual.

Oh -- about the photo . . . these Tennesseeans
must be obsessed with hunting and fishing. On my
walk I saw this sportsman store with a vending
machine outside saying, "VEND-A-BAIT." Dad, can
you imagine getting a box of cold bloodworms
for fifty cents from a machine? Bet you wished
you had access to something like that for down
the shore, especially when stores are closed on
Sundays.

Love,
The Son
P.S. Maybe someday you'll want to put together a
scrapbook of all this. For the future grandkids
-- ha! Will send more either on the way or once
settled on Galveston Island.

A Tale of a Hangnail
and a Horn

Standardization   When shooting a series of photographs over time, the one variable that should remain constant (in order to document change) is the patient. You should always try to keep all other variables the same as much as you possibly can—camera point of view, position of the patient, background color, type and angle of lighting, focal length, exposure, type of film (preferably same film batch), and method/location of processing. Color might not always be important to an orthopedic surgeon, but to a dermatologist it might be the most critical feature when diagnosing a patient's skin ailment. Any time you take two or more photographs over time, aim for keeping everything standardized. It is a challenge to standardize all of the variables—photographs might be taken by different photographers, in different rooms, using different cameras, lenses, or films, under different lighting, and from a different distance or angle to the patient. There could be variations in the processing of film. Open a different batch of film that was mass-produced on different dates and it might show a difference in sensitivity and color. Obviously, it is important to plan well, maintain as much control over variables as possible, and be attentive to detail.

"So, Max . . . tell us why you think you're the best person to be the resident advisor for Photo House?" asked the director of the residence halls. Max took a moment to gather his thoughts. Instead of showing insecurity by fidgeting and looking away, he used the time to calmly make eye contact with the director and the other three senior RAs on the interview team. Three of them were hearing, and one was Deaf. That meant he had to suck up more to the hearing side.

In his best voice and use of sign choice, Max said, "To me, Photo House is a m-i-c-r-o-c-o-s-m," taking his time to clearly fingerspell, ". . . of what RIT is all about—the successful integration of deaf and hearing students working together in the classroom, living in the residence halls, and preparing for the work world. I understand both worlds. Photo House is where deaf and hearing residents use photography as the basis to develop communication and relationships."

The interview team immediately looked down at their forms to write. "Please give us a minute to record our notes," said the director. Max could tell the director said this for the benefit of the one Deaf RA who was not able to listen and take notes at the same time.

Beyond the large window behind the interview team, Max could see RIT's flag waving in the wind next to the American flag. It made him think of what would have happened to him if he had never come to RIT. He probably would have ended up going through life with a strained smile, a person with no Deaf identity pretending to be a hearing person teaching physical education to a bunch of public school kids he couldn't understand. When his audiologist learned that he was interested in further schooling, she advised him to look into the National Technical Institute for the Deaf at the Rochester Institute of Technology. The institute's impressive catalog convinced Max and his parents to drive to upstate New York to visit the campus. Their guide was deaf, and throughout the tour he signed, gestured, and used his voice along with facial expressions, making explanations surprisingly easy for Max to understand. Later, Max learned that the guide used total communication, a language approach employed by the faculty and staff at the time. Max was amazed to find that NTID had an enrollment of over 1,000 students, all with a hearing loss of some kind. The support services offered—tutors, note takers, and interpreters—were so luxurious compared to what he was getting in public schools—which was nothing. And to discover that he would be taught by professors who understood deafness— hallelujah! For the first time in his life he actually felt excited about going to school. Max had not known there were so many deaf people in America until he stood in the registration line for the four-week summer orientation program for incoming deaf freshmen. All around him was a representative sampling of deaf students from the four corners of the country. It was such a high that deep inside—corny as it might sound—he wanted to go up and hug each one and say, "Hi—I'm deaf, too, and I've been wait- ing all my life to meet you."

One of the hearing RAs snapped Max out of his reverie with a hand wave. "What do you mean, both worlds?"

"Umm . . . hearing and Deaf worlds. I grew up in an environ- ment where everyone was hearing—my parents, grandparents, cousins, aunts and uncles. English is my first language, so I com- municated by lipreading, speaking, and writing English. Now that I have lived with Deaf roommates for three years and been involved in various Deaf student organizations, including serving as the vice president of the student body government, I consider myself pretty fluent in ASL, and feel I could manage a floor of Deaf and hearing photo majors with my knowledge of both lan- guages and cultures."

The interview team nodded, looked down, and scribbled more notes. Max looked around the conference room. On the walls hung motivational posters: "Hang in There, Baby" (with a fright- ened baby kitten hanging from a branch); "He Who's Not Busy Being Born Is Busy Dying" (white fluffy sphere of dandelion next to a daisy); "Teamwork" (image of a rowing crew on the water at dawn); "You Are Unique in All the World" (hand-drawn illustra- tion of a star with multicolored swirls flowing from each point) . . . Max imagined that the posters were used to inspire the RAs and pump them with positivity when problems got heavy on their re- spective floors. His gaze settled on a poster of a college-aged man and woman looking at each other with the title: "Face Me When You Talk." Ah, a deafness-related one.

During his freshman and sophomore years, Max's identity as a Deaf individual had begun to surface. He discovered a part of himself that had been missing during his public school years: his roots in Deaf culture. Sign language had become his second language out of necessity, so that he could fully understand his professors, classmates, and peers, hearing and deaf. The days of spending long hours straining his eyes to try and capture bits of information, as he had in his early school years, were over. Public school teachers often turned their backs to the class while writing on the blackboard and lecturing—no matter how many times he politely asked them to face the class while talking. If Max was lucky, he could read a word or two from their lips as they occasionally turned their heads sideways. When it came to class discussions he was lost, stuck with a couple of words, trying to put together a fifty-piece puzzle that was missing forty-eight pieces. But at NTID/RIT, he was able to relax and enjoy his education. His instructors were hearing and deaf, used sign language or had an interpreter, which allowed him to comprehend everything. He was in awe of his first Deaf professor, who'd used the classroom like a stage, enacting poetic and dramatic verses in sign and voice, or sometimes in signs alone. He'd instilled in Max an appreciation for the power of language. Unlike in his primary and secondary school years, he'd finally experienced the personal reward of high marks.

Max became friends with many people, people who signed and people who didn't—their preferences made no difference to him. It was a novelty to make so many friends, because up until the summer before his freshman year, he had had very few and never so many who were understanding and unbiased about deafness. It was so overwhelming that when his second year came around, he had to slap himself to remember the main reason he was in college. He had completed a year at NTID's Applied Photography program, and then he'd cross-registered to the

School of Photographic Arts and Sciences to begin four years of study in biomedical photography. He'd had to do something that was painful—cut back on a lot of friendships and socializing, due to mounting academic pressures.

One of the hearing RAs got Max's attention and asked: "What would you do if one of the hearing students on your floor came to you to complain about their Deaf suite-mates making too much noise, interfering with their studies?" Max could tell it was probably a trick question to see which culture he favored. Under the table, he picked at an irritating hangnail that kept rubbing against his finger when he signed. Then he brought his hands above the table and told them that he would talk with the Deaf suite-mates to get them to turn down the noise.

"I would then remind those with the grievance that as hearing students in Photo House, it is a privilege to be on an integrated floor because they are granted free evening access to NTID's photo labs—the School of Photography's darkrooms are always crowded in the evenings. Secondly, the hearing students are in a total immersion environment to learn a new language and culture. Where else would they have the chance to do that? I would also tell the Deaf suite-mates basically the same thing about privilege—except to say that they are getting a real-life experience learning to work with hearing people, which will benefit them in the future when they get jobs. Whether they like it or not, it will probably be hearing people who will be hiring them, so they should learn to get along with them."

The RAs wrote more notes, then looked at each other, as if trying to figure out who should ask the next question. They excused themselves for a minute to confer with one another. Max looked away to give them privacy.

Max wondered where his amazing bullshit answers were coming from. He had days when he absolutely detested hearing people and their condescending ways. He put his finger to his mouth and chewed on the hangnail, trying to get rid of it. He thought about a derogatory term that was going around campus among

the hearing students. They were calling Deaf students "nids," a derivative of the deaf college's name NTID. This slur was the equivalent of calling black people "niggers." Max became so infuriated any time he saw a hearing guy say "nid" that he wanted to just sucker punch him in the face.

He had only hit someone once in his entire life. It had happened during lunch recess in junior high school. Students were sneaking smokes and experimenting with marijuana. Some were doing strange stunts like hyperventilating and then squeezing each other around the abdomen to pass out. Max was standing around by himself, fiddling with the volume on his hearing aid, when an eighth grader came up to make fun of him by showing off in front of the other kids. The kid told them that Max was an alien from another planet communicating with UFOs using a space radio in his ears. He went up to Max's chest and yelled into the hearing aid, "Warning! Warning! This does not compute!" This drew snickers from the other kids. "Danger, Will Robinson!" More laughter when the kid started moving like a robot.

Max instinctively pushed him away. The kid, not expecting this reaction, immediately put up his fists and started swinging them at Max's hearing aid. Max knew his parents had spent a lot of their hard-earned money to buy him the most powerful body aid on the market at the time. He'd been told to do everything he could to protect it—whether from rain, bumping into things, or, in this case, wild punches. The teen was one of the cool and popular ones—a "Prepster"—because he was good-looking and a smooth talker, and always dressed preppy.

Max's eyes zeroed in on the kid's stupid, smirking, superior expression. He moved in close and delivered a hard, cobra-fast strike on the nose, and strode away. He didn't bother to look back and see the blood spilling all over the kid's pastel yellow Izod alligator shirt with the turned-up collar.

Later, in the principal's office, Max was absolved of any wrongdoing by explaining he had merely been protecting himself and the costly "medical assistive device" he wore daily. The preppy kid ended up getting suspended from school for a week. From then on, the Prepster gave Max a wide berth when passing him in the hallways.

"Do you have any questions for us?" asked the residence halls director.

"Yes. Is it true that I would get free room and board for a year if you were to hire me as an RA?"

"That's correct. You would have to take 24-hour call for one weekend per semester and attend our weekly RA meetings," he replied.

Another RA added, "You also need to be on campus one week before students arrive in the fall, and one week after they leave for the summer. There will be a lot of administrative paperwork . . ."

Max went into his autopilot listening mode, nodding attentively but letting his mind drift back to his anger at hearing people—until the Deaf RA leaned toward him and tapped the table to get him to look up.

"Anything else you would like to add before we close?" the Deaf RA asked.

"I just want to say that—"

"Hold on—your finger is bleeding," said the Deaf RA. "Anyone have a Band-Aid?"

"I do," said the director. She pulled out a drawer from one of the filing cabinets and took out a box of assorted bandages. The Deaf RA took the box and retrieved a strip of bandage. She offered to put it on Max's finger. Max held out his finger sheepishly.

"How did that happen?" asked the director.

With only his left hand free, Max signed without speaking: "hang," as if he were hanging himself. Then "nail," hammering an imaginary nail.

The director copied Max and said, "Hanging hammer? I don't understand."

Max pointed to his bandaged finger and—since he was right-handed—he awkwardly fingerspelled: "H-a-n-g-n-a-i-l." The

hearing RAs all nodded in understanding. The Deaf RA already
knew, for she'd seen the finger wound and understood Max's lit-
eral sign translation.

"Go ahead, what were you planning to say?" she prompted.

"Oh, no! I've got the equivalent of a sore throat now," Max
said with a wink. That drew an immediate laugh from the Deaf
RA. The others looked on with blank expressions. "Well, as I was
saying . . . I think the time is ripe for Photo House to have a Deaf
RA. Since it was formed three years ago, there have been three
successive hearing RAs. I believe I would be just as good as a
hearing RA, if not better, because of my bilingual and bicultural
background." The Deaf RA smiled, while the hearing RAs main-
tained their poker faces.

That evening, Max drove over to his girlfriend's off-campus
apartment. He filled her in about his interview, feeling good that
he'd aced it, but also having sensed a weird vibe from the hearing members of the interview team. He also told her about his
bloody finger, which she softly kissed. They chatted for a little
bit about the nagging condescension they had felt at times from
hearing people, and then, to quickly forget about the topic, they
wasted no time in necking on the sofa by the window overlooking
the parking lot. Both being deaf—though they'd had arguments
over whether to call themselves deaf or hard of hearing—they left
their hearing aids on, since they enjoyed hearing the sounds of
their own lovemaking.

It was an unusually warm Rochester evening for late April. The
windows were open, and the interior lights were out. Suddenly,
in the middle of a smooch, they heard a loud, continuous sound.
They stopped and looked at each other. "Was that you?" they
asked each other. Somebody yelling? Nobody can hold a yell that
long. A train? But there was no train nearby. A foghorn? Ha! In
the middle of suburbia?

Both slowly got up and went to the window, and poked their
heads between the curtains, their naked butts hidden from the

outside world. Lights came on in the apartments adjacent to them. A guy ran out wielding a bowie knife. The landlady came out in her pink polka dot bathrobe. People spilled out in their pajamas. Max and his girlfriend laughed at the seriousness of everyone's body language and expressions. Both buried their faces in the sofa cushions, stifling giggles. The loud, continuous sound droned on.

The neighbors closed in on a row of cars on the lot. One of the neighbors went up to each car and put his ear up close to the grille. Max signed: "Some jerk's car alarm probably got tripped." Then they all gathered around the blue Ford LTD with the bumper sticker that said: "I'm NOT deaf. ^ & I'm just ignoring you." The cross-out, insert, and ampersand symbols were handwritten. Everyone looked up to their window.

Max got dressed and went out, headed straight to his car, ignoring the neighbors all talking to him at once. He put his hand on the dashboard, which confirmed that the sound was coming from his car. He jiggled the steering wheel spokes. The horn continued to blare on.

Finally, Max opened the hood and yanked out the horn's wires. He remembered how he'd acquired this horn problem. A few weeks previously, he'd been looking for subjects to photograph while driving along Main Street in Pittsford, a snooty little town about seven miles east of the campus. An old man in a Cadillac cut in front of him, and he'd pressed on his horn for a long time. The man had practically jumped out of his seat from the sudden horn blast. When he let go, the honking continued for the next five blocks. Passersby stopped and watched Max drive by. He'd waved and smiled while discreetly joggling the horn spokes on the steering wheel with his other hand, finally managing to get the horn unstuck by manipulating one of the spokes.

After the horn-awakening night with his girlfriend, Max took his car to a shop. He wanted it fixed, because he loved the control the horn gave him over hearing people. It shocked them. Made them get out of his way. It caused them to curse and gesture—all because he was lightly pressing a little lever.

When Max found out repairs would be too expensive, he went home and figured out a system. There were three places on the steering wheel designed to activate the horn—the spoke at three o'clock, a spoke at six o'clock, and one at nine o'clock. The three o'clock spoke wouldn't produce a sound. The one at six o'clock would give him something but only when it felt like it, and when it did, it would get stuck. The one at nine o'clock worked fine. He would just have to remember the nine o'clock spoke if he needed it in a moment of quick decision . . . or to provoke hearing people.

A week after his interview, Max received an envelope from the campus housing department. He fumbled opening it with his left hand; the finger on his right hand was infected and throbbing. Despite repeated rinses with Bactine, the finger was getting worse. He needed to find the time to force himself to walk the half mile across campus to student health services to get it checked out. His biggest fear was an infection so bad it would require his being admitted to the emergency room at a hospital in downtown Rochester. He envisioned losing a full day just when end-of-semester finals and projects were coming up. Beneath the RIT letterhead, he read these words over and over: "We are pleased to offer you the position of Resident Advisor for Photo House commencing on 1 August 1980." He felt a huge sense of relief and validation.

In the examination room, the student health nurse looked over his finger and told him it was indeed infected, but that he would not need to go to the emergency room. She cleaned and dressed the wound, and gave him a tetanus booster shot since it had been over ten years since his last one. Max, feeling giddy at not having to go to the ER, asked the nurse, "Will this shot provide me with immunity from hearing people?"

The nurse stopped and looked at him with a questioning expression.

"Never mind," he said. She finished bandaging his middle finger. It looked noble, wearing a tall, white turban. He held it up and found that he had a visual weapon, albeit temporary, for combating any future inane actions or remarks from hearing people.

August 29, 1981
Motel 6, Baton Rouge, Louisiana

Evenin', y'all!

Well, as luck would have it, I found another
Motel 6 right off of I-10. Decided to pull over
in Baton Rouge after being on the road for 10
hours. Tomorrow I should have an easy 5-hour
drive to Galveston. Found a local restaurant
that served crawfish. Never had them before but
they were real spicy and tasty. Hard to believe
they're the same creatures as the crayfish we
used to catch in our backyard stream. If I had
known you could cook them, I would've caught
you a bucketful for a good crawfish boil. If
you love steamed crabs, you will like these
crawdaddies.

I'm keeping this brief. Am all tuckered out
from the drive. No makeshift motel darkroom
tonight -- ha! I want to be fresh, alert, and
ready for Galveston and whomever I may meet at
the hospital there.

G'nite,
The Weary Wayward Man

Destination: Galveston

Films   The following are films designated for specific types of shooting situations. Kodak Ektachrome 64 Slide Film Daylight: use for all clinical and OR photographs; Kodak Ektachrome 200 Slide Film Daylight: use for special shots such as photos through the fiber-optic scope; Kodak VPS 125 Color Print Film: use for Employee of the Month shots; Kodak Plus-X Black-and-White Print Film: use for applications, passports, and portraits.

The road to the Port Bolivar–Galveston ferry took Max along the marshy coastline of Louisiana and Texas. Once the Gulf of Mexico became visible, the scenery of bayous, cypresses, and airboats dissolved to palm trees, bait shacks, and deep-sea yachts. The sulfuric swamp smell was swept away by the briny Gulf breeze. He passed signs that read, "Texas's First Shorebird Sanctuary" and "Galveston: 30 Miles." Getting across the bay to Galveston Island would be a test: he would be severing the emotional and financial lifeline to his family. No more weekly college allowance checks in the mail. No more collect phone calls home. No more impromptu family dinner visits. Yet he was excited to begin his new life doing a medical photography residency on an island 1,245 miles from home—the farthest he had ever been away from his family.

The old self-confidence issues kept resurfacing—would he be skilled enough for the job, would people respect him, could he survive totally on his own, would hearing women date him, and so on. It was strange that he was feeling all of this now, after four years of college, when he'd hardly had any self-doubts or feelings of inferiority. Maybe it was because he'd been cocooned with good

Deaf friends, supportive professors, and the self-contained community of college life. Now he felt like he was suddenly back in high school, where he'd been the only deaf student, fending for himself in a swarm of competitive hearing people. He'd discovered how tough it was to win respect from others if you're different from the norm—like having a huge purple birthmark on your face, or needing to get around in a wheelchair, or walking with a cane. Max had gone through high school with a gigantic mother of a hearing aid. He kept thinking, "How am I going to keep down the stares and snickers?" Then it hit him. Sports! Be an athlete. The guys would be impressed that he could actually hit or kick a ball. The girls would be in awe. "Look at those legs. And his arms . . . he even has muscles!" he imagined them saying.

One of the team sports he'd joined was wrestling. Max guessed it was because everybody involved seemed friendlier than in the other sports. After pinning a few hearing guys during tryouts, he made the varsity wrestling team. Suddenly, people started to take an interest in him. He enjoyed the fact that most of the wrestling managers were girls. The old try-to-impress-'em male routine had kicked right in.

Max had found out that most of the wrestlers were part of a Christian youth group called Young Life. They went to weekly meetings during which they read Bible passages, sang songs, and afterward had cookies and Hawaiian Punch. He was not very religious, but what he liked about the organization were the nice, wholesome-looking girls. He *was* religious about girl-watching. Besides, he wanted friends—any friends.

As Max drove past the small Texas seaside town of Gilchrist, he recollected a weekend during his junior year when Young Life had gone away on a retreat to a barrier island resort called Harvey Cedars in New Jersey.

It was a Friday night, and there must have been two hundred people milling about. Max stood around confused, nodding his head like a puppet to strange people who introduced themselves to him. So many people were talking at once. Finally, everyone settled down in groups and listened to someone behind a podium speak about what he assumed were Bible passages from a very thick black book with bookmarks. The speaker was so far away that lipreading was impossible. Max sat there killing time by counting how many girls in the room had blonde hair, how many were brunettes, redheads, etc.

His roommate for the weekend was the star wrestler of his team. Max was very impressed by him. He was an all-state champ and a devout Christian, and went out with the best-looking girl in their high school. Now, he thought, if he could become a devout Christian like his roommate, he could find himself a good-looking girlfriend. On Friday night, after reading Bible passages and counting heads, Max was back in his room by curfew. Wide awake, he didn't know what to do. So he sat on his bunk bed and watched his roommate on the floor doing push-ups for the longest time. He wrote in his little journal, "Aha, read Bible passages, do push-ups." Then he hopped off his bunk and did some push-ups along with his roommate.

On Saturday, Max thought he would never get through the Bible workshops and lectures till Sunday, when they were supposed to leave. Sunday morning he walked over to the gymnasium to shoot some baskets to work off his pent-up frustrations. The buses weren't leaving until a few hours later. A few people were bouncing balls around, each alone with a basket. One girl wore a white T-shirt, straight-legged blue jeans, and blue Converse high-tops. She had a cute dribble that was coordinated with her tongue sticking out of the side of her mouth. Swish. She was throwing foul shots. Swish. The girl was good. The scene was the epitome of the 501 Jeans commercial, before the ad ever came out. He decided that if there was anyone to share a basket with, she was the one.

Before he walked over, he tugged at the front of his reversible gym shirt to make his hearing aid unnoticeable. Whenever hearing people looked at the wires going up to Max's ears or at the front of his shirt, where the hearing aid was supposed to be hidden, he felt his self-esteem fall a few notches.

Max let out a hearty laugh and hit his horn. A couple of white herons fluttered away from the passing wetlands along the Gilchrist seashore. What good was stretching his shirt to hide the box? He still had these hideous wires coming out of his neck, connected to ear-molds that were plugged into his ears.

As Max and the 501 girl shot baskets, they learned each other's names and where they were from. He could not believe a girl so friendly, pretty, and curious was actually talking to him. Her name was Renee. Before the buses left, they exchanged phone numbers and addresses. She lived in Frostburg, in western Maryland, two hours from his home in Baltimore. He wrote his first love letter in bumpy handwriting on the way home. Very soon, he was receiving letters from Renee, and they fell in love . . . through Christ, as she would say. He was not so sure about that, but he went along with it. Every letter from her ended with this phrase adorned with little red hearts: ". . . but these three remain: faith, hope, and love, and the greatest of these is love. 1 Corinthians 13."

For a year they developed a loving long-distance relationship, held together by weekly letters, occasional phone calls, and sporadic dates when his father would let him borrow the car for the drive to Frostburg, or when her father drove her to Baltimore during one of his errands to the city. Two months before graduation, he got a call from Renee. Sometimes his mother was in the kitchen and helped him out over the phone. He couldn't hide anything from her. They had an amplifier on the phone receiver, which practically broadcast his personal calls. It didn't matter if Max stretched the cord to his bedroom and closed the door. The sound projected that loud. Max and Renee talked for a little bit. Then she asked him something out of the blue. When people spoke with Max on the phone, they had to slowly warm him up to their conversation topic.

"Hi, how are you?" Renee asked.

He'd expected that question, so he said, "Fine, and how are you, Renee?"

"Fine. Fine."

He expected that answer.

"Good. You know," he said, "I really enjoyed dancing with you at your school's mixer last Friday."

"Yeah, me too. I had fun."

He expected that answer too.

He said, "Well, today I'm helping my parents clean out the attic. What a drag, huh?"

Renee said something that he wasn't expecting and couldn't decipher. He covered the mouthpiece and looked over at his mother, who was chopping celery for a tuna-fish salad.

"Mom, what did she say?"

His mother mouthed Renee's words: "Do you want to open a bank account together?"

Max covered the mouthpiece. "Mom, what does that mean?"

The last he heard of Renee was a couple years after graduation. He was a sophomore in college. Someone told him of a rumor that Renee had married a fireman and had three children. And, he was pretty sure they had a joint bank account.

In the car, Max rewound a cassette tape until he got to the song "Shooting Star." He passed a sign that indicated Galveston was ten miles away. "Mama came to the door with a teardrop in her eye / Johnny said, 'Don't cry Mama, smile and wave good-bye.'" Max knew the song not from listening to the radio but from memorizing the words that his high school buddy, Flathead, had written down for him. Flathead helped him follow the song by mouthing the words and moving his index finger over the lyrics like a bouncing ball. It took some serious convincing that Flathead wasn't wasting time writing song lyrics for someone who had a 95-decibel hearing loss in both ears.

Sitting on the front porch steps of Flathead's house, Max had said, "Flat, I'll give you two fancy-tail guppies if you write down those words for me." Max had saved up his lawn-mowing and snow-shoveling money to buy himself a tropical fish aquarium with the works, including a little breeding tank from which he was able to get a spawn of guppy fry.

Flathead tooled with his Nikon F, taking the meter housing apart from the camera body and meticulously cleaning the glass surfaces with lens cleaner. His father had found a great deal on a box of used camera and darkroom equipment and bought them for him as a birthday gift. Flathead loved separating camera parts and putting them back together—more so than actually taking pictures.

"What the hell for?" Flathead finally said. "I don't believe you can hear that song."

"You're the one who turned me on to music, Flat. Remember the 45s you gave me of 'Hey Jude' and 'Let It Be'?"

"You didn't understand any of the words. I lip-synched them for you," said Flathead. He opened the camera back and blew out whatever piece of dust might have snuck inside. As with sports, Flathead was better with the preparation aspects of things: the primping, the preening, the posturing. When it came to actually hitting baseballs, shooting baskets, or taking photographs, he was terrible.

"Flat-dick, for your info, I couldn't follow the words to your beloved Beat-off songs because of two reasons. One—"

"I hate it when you call me that," he said, holding up a box of Kodak film which he was ready to wing at Max.

"Two reasons," Max continued. "One, the music to your beloved Beatles songs drowns out the vocals. How can I hear the words? And two, your big lips make it awfully hard for me to lipread."

Max ducked, just missing getting hit in the eye by Kodak.

"One more wise asshole remark like that and I'll pull your ear-plugs out, and then I'll whack the springs out of that hearing aid box. You'll be stone deaf and never enjoy music again. You reading my lips, Robot Boy?"

Max grimaced.

"OK, Flat, my apologies. I saw Bad Company perform 'Shooting Star' on TV during *Midnight Special*. The lead singer Paul Rodgers' vocals really stood out above the music—beautiful enough that I was moved by it."

"But you didn't get the words," Flathead said.

"That's right. If I could get my hands on the lyrics, I'd be able to memorize them and follow along with the music."

After graduating from college, Max had looked into getting himself a set of brand-new behind-the-ear hearing aids for his medical photography residency in Galveston. The hearing aids of the strength that he needed had just come out on the market and were reputed to be as powerful as the body-type hearing aids he'd worn throughout his public school years. He assisted a photo professor on a wedding shoot, and helped out another professor with some tabletop studio photography. This netted him five hundred dollars, which bought him a pair of flesh-colored hearing aids that became almost invisible behind his ears. He grew his hair a little longer in case people could see them from the back of his head.

When Max arrived at the ferry landing, he had heard the song nine or ten times already. He was sick of it and turned off his tape deck. But his mind, beyond control, took over by playing a music loop of the same song. It kept taking him home, to the neighborhood, to the little yard in front of Flathead's house where the "Shooting Star" lyrics had been written on the cover of a Kodak box. What had convinced Flathead was a deal on a swap for male and female fancy-tail guppies. A red female swordtail was thrown in for words to a couple more songs that Max wanted to know.

The world of tropical fish that Max introduced to Flathead seemed to pale in comparison to the ships full of marlins and tunas moored in the docks by the ferry landing. Piles of fish lay in the boats, waiting to be sold. Flathead had gone on to work as the manager of a store that sold tropical fish. Max had taken a high school photography course and become fascinated with the endless world of image-making.

He'd grown interested in the fancy camera equipment that Flathead carried around in his bag. The two of them eventually made an even bigger deal on their fishes-for-photography hobby swap. Ten-gallon aquariums, pumps, filters, gravel, plants, lights, aerators, and an array of tropical fish species in exchange for a Nikon F 35mm camera, a tripod, a darkroom enlarger, chemicals, timers, a light box, film, and photo paper.

Max pulled his car up to the gate of the ferry landing. The outgoing ferry had just left five minutes ago and was crossing the Houston Ship Channel. The next one wouldn't arrive for a half hour. Max turned off the engine and got out, taking Flathead's camera bag with him, and walked up a one-lane road to the point where the Port Bolivar Lighthouse warned oceangoing vessels of the shoals around Bolivar Peninsula. Through the camera's viewfinder, he could see a cloud of gulls following the outgoing ferry's wake a half mile out on the water. Beyond that he saw the Galveston shoreline and the blue-gray outline of the city, with its freighters, cranes, and port authority buildings. A water tower stood sentry over them all. Off to the left was a cluster of tall buildings of steel and glass, the University of Texas Medical Branch—where he would be employed beginning at eight o'clock the next morning. Max took some basic shots of the lighthouse and the Galveston skyline, just to have them on film. Then he

walked back to the landing area to a little shanty on a dock with two picnic tables and a blue tarp overhead. He placed an order for a shrimp po'boy and a Dr. Pepper.

While waiting for his food, Max strolled over to a historical marker overlooking the water:

> Galveston—The Oleander City'—founded in 1836. Population: 61,902. Literally a sandbar resting between Galveston Bay and the Gulf of Mexico. The Spanish explorer Cabeza de Vaca and his crew were shipwrecked on the island in November 1528, calling it *Isla de Malhado* (Isle of Doom). Site of the University of Texas Medical Branch, Galveston College, the U.S. Coast Guard, and the Texas Maritime Academy. Over 5,000 lives lost and much of the city destroyed by a hurricane on September 8, 1900. A massive seawall was then built to protect the city.

Ignoring the small text, Max framed the bold letters of the city's name and its population in the lower left corner of his viewfinder. He liked this potential shot and proceeded to load up his camera with Kodak Tri-X film, as he wanted to make a black-and-white print for a postcard to send home. Since the metering system in his Nikon F was broken, he took out a handheld meter and took a reflected light reading of the panorama before him.

After setting the shutter speed and depth of field, Max positioned the Galveston skyline in the background and the historical marker in the foreground. He raised the camera higher to see what the frame looked like with more sky in the picture, then lowered it to get a sense of it with more water. He had trouble finding the right perspective, a point of view that would capture this new era in his life for the folks back home. He didn't know if any single image could do that. He hadn't gotten there yet, but still here he was, holding in the palm of his hand the entire island of over 61,000 people in the viewfinder.

Seeing that his po'boy was ready and the incoming ferry several hundred yards away, he quickly settled for a grab shot of the Galveston skyline with a seagull perched on a shit-splattered pylon in the foreground.

8/31/81
Galveston, Isla del Sol (west end), in a double-
wide trailer
Hi Guys!
   All is going pretty well in spite of a few
minor adjustments down here:
1) just tonight, 4 tornadoes were spawned in the
community next to the one where I'm staying.
2) spent some time apartment hunting and found a
nice, clean, medium-sized beach house on stilts
in a fghtrxywqw-
         -- the power just went off here -- had to
light a candle . . .
   I was telling you about the tornadoes . . .
it's been thundering and lightning with a heavy
downpour all day. Anyway, about the house
. . . it's up for $325 a month plus utilities.
It's about 14 miles from work, but it's at a
nice location and only a couple hundred yards
from the Gulf. The place has central A.C. and
heating (it gets down to the low 30s, sometimes
20s even, during Jan. & Feb.) It won't get
cold until about the end of December and it
only stays that way for two months. The house
is just down the road from the other medical
photographers. Can't move in till after the
Labor Day rush, and we have to be out before the
Memorial Day onslaught. If we stay within those
parameters, then the rent stays cheap.
   Reuben (a.k.a. Zag) and I have been getting
along really well. Remember my mentioning
him? He's the hearing RIT photo grad that got
accepted into the residency program. I think
we'll be good housemates as soon as we get out
of our temporary quarters. I'm staying with
a photographer named Howard Bolarsky (a.k.a.

Bimbo, sometimes HoBo). He lives in a mobile home on stilts. He's been nice enough to let me crash at his place, but he's kinda strannnge. Doesn't have many social skills.

Swam in the Gulf a few times. Refreshing, and "body-surfable."

It's really humid down here. I thought Maryland was humid but this place is worse. It's hell on my hearing aids. I'm constantly putting them in a silicone gel pack to suck out the moisture.

Today was my first day. Did mostly paperwork for personnel, running around getting an I.D. made, picking up a parking tag, and helping out with cleaning the photo storage room and did an inventory. Dr. Robb wants us to be familiar with what they have already. We're to think of what supplies we'll need for making our portfolios. It's getting late and I want to get up early for a run on the beach. I want to get this letter out asap so you have an address to send $tuff (hint hint!) to. Write to the hospital's address, attention Pathology Photography Residency Program. We can't get mail delivery out on the west end of the island. I'm getting sleepy.

love y'all!
Max
P.S. One more thing . . . can you buy me a bunch of hearing aid batteries and send them down? They're hard to find on the island, and when I do find them, they charge me way up the wazoo. Get the Gould's High Performance Zinc Air brand, #675.

The Hierarchy of Hearing People

Perspective   Most medical photographs are taken from a cus-
tomary perspective. It is this perspective that determines how
depth is perceived to your subject matter. It is crucial that you
are mindful of how you alter the photographic viewpoint on
your subject matter (objects, people). Changes in perspective
affect how your subject will appear to the scientific viewer. For
example, when photographing teeth, if you use a 28mm wide-
angle lens up close, the perception of a patient's teeth will be
skewed because the optics of a 28mm lens will stretch the
image of teeth. Whereas if you use a 105mm lens, you will be
photographing teeth in a 1:1 life-size ratio which will portray
the teeth more accurately and free of distortion. The 105mm
lens is good for most clinical situations; however, when distance is needed, or when in close quarters, go with the 55mm
lens.

On his first day, Max arrived at the campus of the University
of Texas a half hour early to be sure to give himself time to
locate his new place of work. He immediately liked the campus
for its many tall palm trees. Just looking at them gave him a sense
of warmth and serenity. The sun was out in an azure sky with the
temperature in the eighties, a total reversal from the gray cold of
Rochester, New York. He eventually found the pathology photography lab, which turned out to be in the cavernous basement of
the Pathology Building.

When Max knocked on the door, a woman answered. After he
introduced himself, she welcomed him in. She was the lab secretary, and her name was Audrey. Max's vision of a massive, clean,
well-staffed, white-glove-publication laboratory went out the

window. The place was much smaller, older, and run-down than he'd imagined. Exposed pipes ran along the walls. Paint was peeling. Various pieces of photo equipment looked to be vintage 1960. The lab smelled of photo chemicals and mildew. A huge cockroach scampered across the floor unseen by Audrey, who seemed dwarfed by tall piles of papers, magazines, books, and coffee mugs on her desk.

Off the main photo finishing room, Max saw Dr. Robb in a little room working with a photomicroscope. He waved to Max and gave him a "just a minute" gesture. A pathologist was seated next to him with a tray of microscope slides. Max later learned that Robb was not a medical doctor, but had several honorary degrees; he was, for example, an honorary fellow of the Royal Microscopical Society. Max was sure that Robb was milking his titles for all they were worth to elicit special perquisites. The lab was an example of such a perk—Robb had convinced the Pathology Department that they should donate space and money to invest in a photo lab that exclusively served pathologists. When he was at RIT for the recruitment lecture, his introduction as "Dr. Robb" had endowed him with the distinguished air of a medical doctor.

As soon as the pathologist left, Max could see Dr. Robb's false MD veneer peel away. In the days and weeks to come, Robb's true character would emerge. He was highly verbal, mercurial, and opinionated, yet also oddly charismatic. Reuben Zagruder, Zag as he preferred to be called, had despised Robb early on during the residency and continued to despise him till the end. But Max saw something in Robb that he found endearing. This was the man who'd selected him over thirty other biomed photo majors. Sometimes it paid to be Deaf—it made one stand out in a crowd and receive special attention because of one's so-called disability. Whenever Max was around, Dr. Robb made a conscious effort to clearly articulate his words. He included Max in discussions, and truly listened to what Max had to say, something most hearing people didn't do.

Every morning, Professor Robb greeted Max with "How ya feel?" He liked to make little jokes or puns, and to laugh at himself in short, staccato bursts of horse laughter, which made his face look old and maniacal.

One day Dr. Robb treated Max to lunch at a hot dog stand across the street from the photo lab. A sign next to the hot dog cart proclaimed: "A UTMB study stated that hot dogs are good for the mind, body, and soul."

Max and Dr. Robb sat at an outdoor table shaded by an umbrella. Clipped to the umbrella was a rack of potato chips hanging and swaying in the breeze. At one point, it almost fell off and hit Robb in the head. He said to the hot dog vendor, "If I get hit in the head and get brain damage from those chips, I'm gonna hafta sue ya—hahahahahahaha! My brain may just need a new chip, hahahahahahaha! Well, I need a new chip in my head anyway, hahahahahahaha!"

Robb's bright, even teeth and large mouth made it easy to lip-read him. The downside was that Max had to tolerate Robb's bad breath and the white spittle that would form in the corners of his mouth. To make matters worse, boogers were often to be seen lodged in his nostrils—right in the line of sight of reading lips. The tradeoff was that Max sensed he was getting a real street education by being around Professor Robb.

"Max, this is Big Red. He's a retired fireman from Texas City. Cooks the meanest hot dogs on the island," said Dr. Robb.

Big Red was wearing a pin-striped gangster outfit and a black fedora. He held out his beefy hand and said something incomprehensible to Max.

"He's deaf," said Dr. Robb. "You gotta be sure you're facing him. Speak your words clearly; don't give him none of that Texas City mumbo-jumbo."

"With this guy around, I'm always putting out fires," said Big Red with a wink.

Max nodded and grinned.

"Not only does he sell hot dogs, he plays Halloween. Every day he has on a different costume," said Dr. Robb.

"Hey! It's good for the business," said Big Red. "People like it."

As they munched on their hot dogs, Dr. Robb and Max watched doctors, medical students, and nurses walk by. Once in a while, they spotted groups of tourists in gaudy outfits walking toward Galveston's historic district, which was a few blocks away. At the table next to them was a heavyset, middle-aged couple wearing Reagan–Bush T-shirts. Max noticed out of the corner of his eye that the wife had been watching him. Finally, she leaned over to Max and asked, "Do those things really help you lose weight?"

Max looked at Dr. Robb for translation help.

Robb looked at the woman and asked, "What things are you talkin' about, ma'am?"

"Those things on his ears. Do they help with weight loss?" asked the wife. The husband was busy wiping ketchup off his shirt.

"She wants to know if your hearing aids help you lose weight," said Dr. Robb. He turned his back to her and stuck his index finger into the closed orifice of his other hand, indicating to Max: "Fucking asshole!"

"Umm . . ." Max searched for a tactful reply. "Well—."

Dr. Robb took a deep breath and turned back around toward her. "Ma'am—those things are his hearing aids." He gritted his teeth while smiling. "They help him hear, not lose weight. Have a nice day."

Robb looked at Max and clearly enunciated, without using his voice: "Tourons! They come to the island with a shirt on their back and a five-dollar bill in their pocket, but never change either one." He took one last bite of his hot dog and opened a bag of potato chips.

With food still in his mouth, Robb continued: "You know, Max. About forty-five years ago on this very street, FDR came by in his motorcade, smiling and waving. He was here for a fishing trip out on the Gulf. Doctors and hospital personnel were all lined along this street. They even rolled out patients in their beds and wheelchairs here. He had polio, you know? Old Frankie once said, 'When you come to the end of your rope, tie a knot and hang on.' He did all right with his handicap."

Max glanced over at the Reagan–Bush couple. The wife was eating her hot dog without the bun, while the husband kept wetting napkins with saliva to remove his ketchup stain.

In the lab, Zag often relayed to Max info he had overheard from Robb's conversations—it was hard for Max to "eavesdrop" because of the phone receiver hiding his mouth. Robb spent a lot of time on the phone. Max once saw him brushing his teeth without using water while talking on the phone, probably to his wife. He didn't spit anything out; just swallowed the toothpaste and kept on talking.

According to Zag, Robb was loud and obnoxious during telephone calls, often with his stockbroker. He was constantly talking about numbers and which companies were doing poorly. Every now and then, Robb would punctuate his tirades with colorful phrases like: "Be-yuleshit!" . . . "Pure masturbatory fantasy" . . . "Thumb fun"—this one was always accompanied by him gesturing a thumb under his butt. His favorite, oft-repeated phrase was: "If you want sympathy, look it up in the dictionary. You won't find it too far from 'sucker.'"

Any time Max posed an insightful question or made a remark about a photo technique, Robb would say, "Now that's what I call fine-grained thinking." The word *grain* seemed important to him. Maybe it was his essential nature as a microscopist—he was interested in the minute details of life, on a cellular level. He did contradict himself at times, though. Zag and Max would argue over whether a photomicrograph was as sharp as it could be. Max would point out to Zag that even though a photograph might look blurry, you could definitely tell its sharpness by looking at the silver gelatin grain on the print. If the grain was sharp, then the print itself was as sharp as it could get. When they couldn't settle their argument, they'd go to Dr. Robb for a verdict. He would abstain and say, "I'm not a grain-sniffer myself. Work it out."

Whenever Dr. Robb was out of town, Max liked to go into his musty office, which was always open. It was a mini-library of eclectic books. The one book he frequently went back to read was *The Savage My Kinsman*, which contained a shocking account with documentary photographs of the murders of five missionaries by a group of tribesmen in the Ecuadorean jungles.

Max couldn't figure out why Professor Robb had not gotten his RBP until the year before he and Zag arrived. He would have expected Robb to have gotten certified years ago. He seemed so knowledgeable about the field of biophotography. He often berated RIT's biomed program, saying they didn't prepare their graduates enough for the real world of medical photography. And then he usually went off into a monologue on the spot: "They focus too much on ethereal assignments like photographing the moon and stars at night or close-ups of mushrooms in the woods. Too much Zen Buddhism crap. I gotta retrain you RBP residents the proper way to do run-of-the-mill copy work, gross specimen photography, black-and-white printing of photomicrographs, petri dishes, and EKG printouts—the nitty-gritty stuff. RIT is the Kodak school, for God's sake!—what are they doing with their heads in the clouds or sniffing around in the forest? Thumb fun!"

There were days at work when Max felt absolutely fed up with being around hearing people all day long, five days a week. Reading lips and watching for visual cues was tiring and gave him headaches. Normally, he got along swimmingly with people who could hear. They tended to like him on a superficial level—he smiled a lot and was friendly and professional, though he was often quiet around those he did not know or who could not lipread well.

In the operating room suites, Dr. Robb introduced Max to the chief of Orthopedics, a doctor for whom Max might get called to photograph one day. The chief asked Robb if Max could speak. Robb led the doctor and Max out of the OR, where they could remove their face masks and talk more openly. Robb told him that Max could talk. Max added that he was not able to understand what people said with their masks on. The doctor quickly remarked that he wasn't able to, either, and chuckled at his own joke.

One morning while Max was poring over some details about inventory for photo supplies with Audrey, a secretary from the Pathology Department came in to chat with her. She seemed excited about something and gesticulated animatedly, completely ignoring Max, who was standing right next to her. Max didn't know what to do—she stood in the way between him and Audrey. Max decided he needed to go to the bathroom, and tried to squeeze his way past the Pathology secretary to leave the lab. Before he could get away, Audrey introduced Max to her with the short explanation that the secretary needed to face Max when talking to him. He couldn't look at the secretary's face to read her lips until Audrey was finished with her introduction. Then Max turned to the secretary to say hello.

Her response was a cold, nervous hello. Then something was said between the two in what seemed to be Spanish. The secretary looked at Max and asked if he could lipread Spanish. She then laughed, and looked at Audrey to see if she liked the joke. Max excused himself to go to the bathroom.

Sitting on the toilet, Max mulled over these forms of discrimination, which had been with him all his life, intentional or not. One Christmas, his aunt gave him Steve Martin's *A Wild and Crazy Guy*, a double album of stand-up comedy routines. He was twenty-three years old and in college when he received it. It bothered him that his own aunt still couldn't conceive of the idea that he had been profoundly deaf since birth. How did she expect him to lipread a goddamn record album?

When he was six, his parents signed him up for a baseball clinic. At the end of the four-week clinic, his Pony League coach gave him a Stan Musial record album with baseball hitting tips. Not quite as bad as his aunt, but just as ignorant.

When his family moved to the suburbs of Baltimore, he gradually got to meet kids near his age in the neighborhood. It was slow work, getting acquainted with them. The kids had been in the

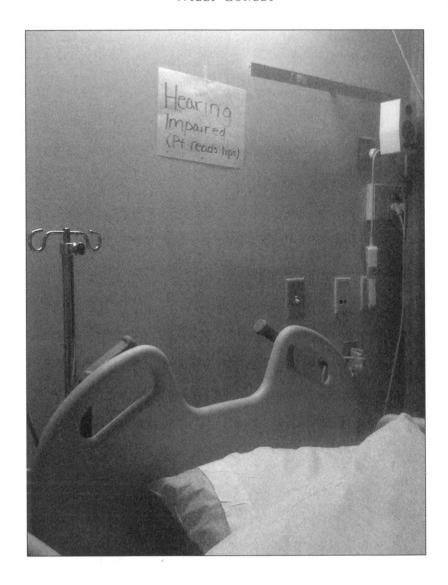

neighborhood all their lives, and then there was the deaf factor, something that hearing kids generally did not take too well.

Sometimes he'd join them to play kickball on the streets or baseball up at the local elementary school. Just as things were warming up, they invited him to hang out with them in the woods or go up to Frito Lay, a potato/corn chip factory in an industrial park that often discarded their rejects into a Dumpster. The kids would climb into the Dumpster to pull out bags of chips. For some reason, it never occurred to them that the merchandise might be dirty or stale. It was free food. It was more about the discovery of unopened products than about satisfying hunger.

One day they saw a billboard with graffiti on it. It said: "Fuck you!" All of the kids gathered around Max and asked: "Do you know what that says?" Max had no idea. He was eight at the time. He had neither seen nor heard the phrase before. He saw that it had the letters *u, c,* and *k,* as in *duck.* So, he just replaced the *d* with an *f* and pronounced it the same. He slowly said, "Fffuck you!"

The kids howled with laughter. Obviously they knew what it meant—as hearing kids always did. They were always as ahead socially as they were phonetically. Max knew where he stood as a deaf person in the hierarchy of hearing people, even in the adult world.

Max flushed the toilet and went to wash his hands. He looked at himself in the mirror and thought, *This too shall pass.* Then he recalled Dr. Yazzie's words from Johns Hopkins: "Stick-it-to-'em!"

9-14-1981
Pirates' Beach

Ahoy me hearties! -- thanks very much for
sending me the hearing aid batteries. I was
really, reallllly deaf for a few days there. My
co-workers couldn't understand why I suddenly
had a terrible time understanding them.

I don't mean to rub it in, but as I write
this (actually, typed what I wrote later) Zag
and I are lying on the beach about twenty feet
from the Gulf. It is sunny out and 83 degrees
(you probably can smell the Coppertone lotion
on this letter). On the positive side (wink,
wink), I did bring my photo books to study for
the written exam. By the way, we got the written
exam date -- it will be on October 15th in the
medical library.

The one thing we have to watch out for around
here are Portuguese man-of-wars. I thought
those jellyfishes were limited to the waters of
Spain and Portugal. Wrong! They're all over the
place here -- half-moon-shaped bubbleheads the
size of a human stomach with tentacles about
five to ten feet long. Knock wood, but we've
not been stung by any. I've heard a sting could
probably put us in the hospital lying on a bed
looking at the other side of some idiot medical
photographer's lens -- heh!

This morning I was reading the front page of
the Galveston Daily News and was shocked to find
this big photograph of a bad car accident with
these captions:

"Vehicles Collide: George Maynard, 34, a
construction company owner who is deaf, surveys

damage to his 1980 Toyota pickup truck after his
vehicle and a Galveston Fire Department truck
en route to a fire collided about 1:50 p.m.
Saturday at 23rd and Market streets. Maynard,
who apparently was not injured, said he had not
heard the siren. No injuries were reported."

Oh brother, don't you just love how the media
perpetuates the myth that us deaf people are
bad drivers because we can't hear a stupid
siren. This guy George must be a major numbskull
probably reading a magazine while driving,
never mind that he's deaf. For anyone with
a good pair of eyes (that are wide open and
looking -- one is driving two tons of metal,
right?), how could one not see a gigantic red
fire truck approaching an intersection? Give me
a break! It's nice to know there's another deaf
person on the island, but I'm not sure I wanna
meet this guy.

Miss the dickens outta ya!

Love, Maxx xoxo

P.S. Have enclosed some photos of the man-of-
war. Looks like a purple empanada, don't it?

Red Fire Ants

Burns We are often called to shoot burns. We shoot them when victims first arrive at the hospital and at various times throughout their stay as their healing progresses. The biggest mistake in shooting burns is shooting too close. Shoot whole areas: arms, legs, torsos, head and neck, etc. Often you cannot get clean shots of burns and you must shoot around people working on the patient. Angle the flash unit to avoid getting bad reflections. Watch your shadows. Be sure to write down the patient's name and that of the staff doctor in charge.

Watching the surgeon's gloved hands crawl into the fetid bowels of an obese patient made Max think of red fire ants. He wasn't sure why. Maybe it was the color red, the hand crawling . . . perhaps it was imagining being burned by the cauterizer that the surgical assistant was using to stanch the bleeding around the incised wound. One of the first warnings he'd gotten upon arrival on Galveston Island was to beware of red fire ants. A photo resident who'd worked before him had gone out on a nature shoot during her first day on the island. She had set up her camera and tripod on a sand dune by the Gulf out on the west end. She was concentrating so hard on arranging the composition of her landscape shot that she hadn't realized her legs were already covered with red fire ants. She didn't worry at first, just brushed them off—until they went up her shorts. Then she felt severe stinging and burning sensations, and ended up getting huge welts all over her legs that took a long time to heal.

Max had lots of idle time to think while waiting in various operating rooms until he was summoned to the surgical table to

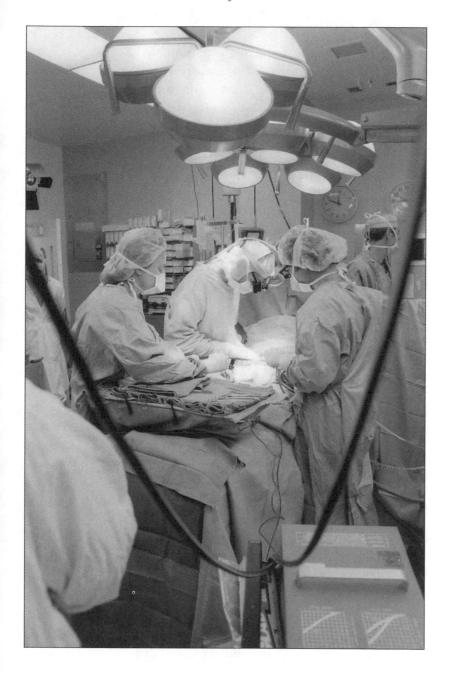

take photographs. He learned that surgeons tend not to call in photographers at the moment they are really needed, preferring to keep these lower-echelon technicians waiting on standby for at least a half hour in the room. In the world of the OR, the doctor is king. As an aspiring medical photographer, Max made damn sure he obeyed the rules of the kingdom.

In the teaching hospital, the senior medical photographers usually got the plum assignments: photographing VIPs, new surgical procedures, or rare scientific discoveries. One time Ken Norton, the boxer, had a brain aneurysm that needed photo documentation. Another time Kenny Rogers had some vocal nodules removed; they needed to be recorded for surgical pathology. Out in Los Angeles at Cedars-Sinai Medical Center, rumor had it that the photographers had gotten into a shoving match over who would photograph Michael Jackson when he burned his scalp during the filming of an infamous Pepsi commercial.

Max got stuck with the prune assignments—venereal diseases, rectal polyps, softball-size tumors, oozing bed sores, and the like. Burns were the worst. The rancorous odor of baked flesh was always hard to take—none of the photographers wanted to do burns. Consequently, burn assignments got relegated to the photo interns, which probably explained why doctors sometimes returned to the photo lab to complain about the poor quality of the photographs of burn wounds.

One day a circulating nurse was kind enough to show Max a solution, literally, to getting past malodorous medical situations. She opened up a cabinet outside the OR and took out a few vials of colored aromatic oils: vanilla, sandalwood, cinnamon, spearmint, patchouli, lilac, coconut—stuff usually seen on a street vendor's table in New York City. The nurse held out a vial of patchouli and patted her heart to show it was her favorite. She suggested squeezing a few drops into the face mask before working with patients. Max picked the patchouli in order to build up a little camaraderie with her, and its woody, hippie smell did help take his mind off the foul circumstances on the table.

"Exploratory Laparotomy, OR 4." When the lab secretary held out the assignment slip to Max, she asked if he knew what it meant.

"Of course!" he said with a confident smile. "Do you think I studied four years of biomedical photography in college to learn how to shoot close-ups of lint in my navel?"

She gave him an affectionate slap on the hand as he took the slip from her. On the way to the operating room he took a quick detour to the medical library to look up "exploratory laparotomy." A medical-surgical nursing textbook explained that it was a procedure involving an incision into the abdomen and exploration inside the bowels for anything out of the ordinary.

While still waiting in the surgeon's court—actually the head resident's court—Max briefly stepped out of the room to put more drops of patchouli into his face mask. Then he watched the resident surgeon's technique for any signs of nervousness or tension, wondering how much of a rookie the guy was in his field. Finally, the surgeon withdrew his hands from the bowels. Seemed nothing abnormal had been found. The surgeon, looking formidable in his sterile getup, proceeded to sew the patient back together. A big grin spread behind Max's mask as he watched the tall egomaniac handle a needle and thread. As the resident stitched up the patient's abdomen, he joked with the shapely OR nurses and then berated the other OR personnel for some reason that eluded Max.

The scrub nurse counted all of the bloody tools used during the laparotomy. She counted again, and then once more. She then gestured to a circulating nurse to come over, and whispered into her ear. The circulating nurse searched under the surgical table and under all of the smaller tables in the room. She looked at the surgical nurse and shook her head in the negative.

The surgical nurse turned to the head resident, said something, and pointed to a gap in the lineup of instruments on her tray. The resident followed her gaze to the large torso, which looked like an old leather medicine ball. He snapped his head and shouted. The circulating nurse ripped off the surgeon's stained sterile outfit and replaced it with a fresh set. He snipped off the stitches that he'd joked over and tweezed out the filament. The gloved hands crawled back in. He cocked his head to the side as if bending down to find keys that had dropped below a car seat. Out came a pair of bloody forceps.

Max could see a collective sigh of relief in the room. The resident shot a glance in Max's direction. Having anticipated this, Max picked up his camera and blew imaginary dust off the lens.

After two and a half hours, Max had still not been called to the table to photograph anything. The doctor certainly didn't want a pair of rusty red forceps recorded on film for publication or presentation. Still following the rules of the king's court, Max stood there and waited until he was dismissed. The new line of sutures made Max think of the red ants marching in line across his own naked abdomen.

Dr. Robb had arranged for Max to live temporarily in a trailer home with a senior medical photographer who was heavyset and secretly nicknamed Bimbo by the other members of the department. When they were first introduced, Max held out his hand. Bimbo just nodded slightly and said, "Yeah." On the first day of his internship, Max followed Bimbo around the lab learning the day-to-day operations—loading film onto developing reels; feeding film through the E-6 color slide processor; operating the darkroom enlargers; pouring chemicals into the Versamat, the black-and-white automatic printer; using the MP4 copy camera on a stand; and keeping thick textbooks open and flat under the camera. Throughout all this, Bimbo never said a word, but Max could tell he was silently enjoying the superiority of having an intern take note of his every move and technique.

After work, Bimbo squeezed into his VW bug and motioned for Max to follow him. Out on the west end of the island where Bimbo lived, Max saw his first trailer up on stilts. The Gulf of Mexico was only fifty yards away down the beach road. Homes there had to be up on stilts by code, or else the frequent storms that came through would flood them.

Inside the trailer, Bimbo disappeared into a back room. Since Max wasn't given a tour of the place and had no idea where he was supposed to sleep, he set his bags by the sofa in the living room. Bimbo never said anything about dinner, and didn't come out from the back room. Max stayed where he was, examining the trailer while trying to figure what to do about his appetite, which hadn't been attended to since breakfast.

The living room opened into a kitchen with food-encrusted pots on the stove. Bags of tortilla chips, corn chips, and potato chips were open, with chips crumbled all over the counter. Everything seemed to be opened, for that matter. Cabinet doors. Utensil drawers. The oven. Even the freezer was partway open, dripping water onto the floor. A curious smell, a mixture of mildew, fried chips, and athlete's foot, hung in the humidity.

Max decided to go across the coastal highway to the convenience store to get a Pepsi and whatever food struck his fancy. He settled for a microwaved burrito and ate his dinner outside, in front of the store, leaning against the wall and watching tanned half-naked people come and go. Crossing back over the highway, Max went down to the beach and watched body surfers chase light brown waves. The surf didn't have that crisp white break that the Atlantic had. As soon as the sun set, mosquitoes came out in droves, forcing him to run back to the trailer. Except for an incandescent light coming through the blinds at the rear window, it was dark. He tiptoed up the steps and slipped inside. He felt around for a light switch and found one by the sofa. A lamp with a Donald Duck shade came on. Just about every piece of memorabilia on the walls and end tables revealed an obsession with Disney: Mickey & Minnie Mouse, Pluto, Scrooge McDuck, Tinkerbell, Snow White and the Seven Dwarfs, and Dumbo. Max unrolled his sleeping bag as a bed sheet over the sofa. He stripped down to his underwear and lay down on top of the bag. As he was about to turn off the grinning Donald Duck, Bimbo waddled into the living room.

"Hey—I, um . . . just got back from the beach," Max said, "watching the body surfers. You surf?"

Bimbo lifted the cover to his stereo turntable and slid on a record. Before Max could say anything more, Bimbo began dancing along the length of the living room and kitchen. All he had on was black nylon shorts. He pranced this way and that, making sharp turns and twists, guiding an imaginary partner through a dance routine—a fat Fred Astaire with doughy flesh jiggling every which way. This went on for twenty minutes or so. Max didn't know if he was supposed to watch Bimbo or ignore him (to allow him privacy to practice, if that was what he was doing). To be safe, Max sat up and pretended to half watch and enjoy the beat pumping through the hollow flooring and Masonite walls. Then, as suddenly as he'd entered, Bimbo exited, leaving the stereo cover open. The needle automatically lifted off the center of the record and rested itself on the side of the turntable. The spinning stopped.

The next morning, Max awoke early with a burning sensation on his abdomen. In the light from the Donald Duck lamp, he could see a thread of red fire ants marching across his stomach toward the kitchen.

9-29-81
Beach House porch

Hey folks!
   Am settling into some semblance of a routine.
Here's a typical day's schedule:
6-7:30 a.m. - rise and shine; breakfast and
watch The Three Stooges (very important for my
sanity)
7:30 - leave the house for work (20-min. drive)
8:00-5:00 - work, work, work
5:30-6:30 p.m. - wack, wack, wack (tennis with
Zag)
7-8 - dinner (Zag's a good cook!)
8-midnight - study for written exam
We'll get our first paychecks soon. I'll be
able to loosen my belt a notch. Work has been
going okay. There's so much I don't know about
this field that some days I feel defeated.
Zag has been real supportive. He's brilliant
that way. I just need to read more, study,
and review. Think all this has to do with me
being an average student growing up in public
schools with no interpreters or note takers,
not getting full access to information. My
processing mechanism is stuck in a primitive
mode or something. Haven't met many people
yet, particularly females. It gets frustrating
because it makes me really nostalgic for all of
the female friends that I had during college.
I'll be fine once I meet a woman to confide in
and for companionship. Don't get me wrong -- I'm
not lost and lonely. Just have to be patient
with myself sometimes.
   Oh -- you asked about the hospital. It's the
largest complex on Galveston Island. Why was it

built here of all places? I think it's because
Galveston was Texas's largest city at one time,
so it made sense to build a hospital. It's grown
little by little over time to the point where
it's now a major teaching hospital. On Seawall
Boulevard, which runs east and west along the
island, are several souvenir shops, fishing piers,
bars, and seafood restaurants. We saw a couple of
shopping centers in the middle of the island where
it's wider. And out west where we are, it's mostly
mobile homes, beach houses, and cottages. Since
summer has been over, there are not many people
around. We see some families open up their houses
for the weekend, and then by Sunday afternoon,
they're gone. That's one mistake Zag and I made
when we picked our house. We didn't take into
consideration that our community would become a
ghost town during the off-season. We're learning
to live with it. Once in a while, a co-worker from
the hospital will drive out and stop by for a beer
or a meal. It's comfortable, pleasant, but just a
little lonely at times.

I hope Grandmom and Grandpop's lives have
eased up a little in spite of all their medical
problems. Keep me updated on their condition.

Took my hearing aids in to the Audiology
Department for a tune-up. Folks seem pretty nice
there. One woman even knows some signs.

Two more weeks till the written exam . . .
gulp! Dr. Robb is going to give us a mock exam
next week. You may not get a letter from me for
a while, as we'll be in a don't-mess-with-us
zone while the big date draws near.

Mucho love,
Your One & Only

Cross-the-Heart

Public Relations   Occasionally, you will be asked to photograph a variety of situations outside of the hospital but within the university system. Examples would be taking pictures of building dedications, public relations photos of a particular setting, grip-and-grin ceremonies, graduations, convocations, orientations, etc. In all situations, be sure to wear your white lab coat with identification. Get to the assignment site early to study the situation to ensure a photographic setting. You might have to move a trash bin or a traffic cone out of the way. Check out the background and the time of day the assignment will happen. You want to avoid noontime shoots with the sun directly overhead. This causes deep facial shadows which makes everyone in the picture look like raccoons. When

talking with the group to be photographed, be lively. Talk it up. Most people are self-conscious about having their picture taken. Reassure them that they look good, even if they don't; find ways to make each person look their best for the shot.

Word spread through the hospital that there was a deaf man working in the pathology photography lab who had graduated from the Rochester Institute of Technology. It was unheard-of on Galveston Island for a deaf person to get any education beyond a deaf-and-blind high school institution. A hospital representative from the Affirmative Actions office had set up an appointment in the lab to meet this man she'd heard about named Dempsey Maxwell McCall.

When it was time for his appointment, Max stepped out of the darkroom and squinted for a minute to let his pupils adjust to the lighting in the room. Out in the hallway he saw a tall African-American woman dressed in a sharp business suit holding a legal pad.

"Hello, I believe I have an appointment with you?" said Max.

"I'm supposed to meet with a gentleman named Dempsey Maxwell McCall," said the woman. "My name is Dotty, from Affirmative Actions."

"Hi, I go by Max. Dempsey Maxwell McCall is my legal name."

"Oh, my Lord. You speak so well for a deaf person," she said.

You talk pretty good for a Southerner, he wanted to say. He'd been told many times by hearing people how well he could speak, sometimes even while other deaf people—with unintelligible speech—were standing right next to him.

"I brought this yellow pad thinking that we would be writing back and forth to communicate. Well, I'll just use this for my interview notes. Is there a quiet place where we can converse?"

"I wasn't aware you were going to interview me. I already had my entrance interview over at personnel. Is this a follow-up for probation or something?"

"No sir, not at all. This is for *The UTmost*, our house organ."

"I'm sorry—your organ what?"

Dotty chuckled.

"*UTmost* is a newspaper created in-house by the University of Texas. My department would like to interview you and contribute a human interest article for the paper," she said.

"Why would the university want to interview me? I've only been here a month."

He checked his watch. Lunch break was coming up soon, and a bunch of the photogs were getting together across the street to eat chicken-fried steaks at Ducky's, a local Galveston joint. He had to finish printing up black-and-white photos of a plastic surgery sequence.

"We are always on the lookout to feature new employees who come from special backgrounds," said Dotty.

A red flag went up in Max's mind. "Special"? As in "Spedz"? He remembered the derogatory label from his school days for students in special ed classes. They were usually slow learners, or mildly retarded, or had some physical disability. Thankfully, he'd never been placed in those classes, but he might have been had his parents not fought so hard to keep him in regular classes. "Don't be a Spedz" was a common refrain among the "regular" kids. Max felt for those in special ed classes, for at times he too had been ridiculed with the name "Spedz."

"Um, what do you mean by 'special backgrounds'?" asked Max.

"Oh, for example, someone from another country, or a person with a unique skill like skydiving, or one with a disability."

"I don't fit any of those categories," said Max.

"Don't you think it would be good for others to know how much you have accomplished as a hearing-impaired person who performs medical photography? You would get your photo in the paper, too."

She had him there. He began imagining cute medical students and nurses stopping by the lab to ask for him. Besides, doctors and scientists would know more about him, which could help alleviate the awkwardness of working with a deaf person.

"Sure, I'll be glad to do the interview. But can we schedule it for another time? I have a photo deadline I need to meet by noon," said Max.

Dotty agreed, and then wanted to know one more thing—if he would be willing to volunteer to teach an informal class on campus in basic sign language to a group of health-care professionals. He accepted, even though he wasn't trained to teach sign language; it'd be a good opportunity to meet some people.

On his first day of class, there were four women waiting, seated in a semi-circle. One of the women was a grandmotherly type, who had been working in medical records for twenty-five years. Another woman was an X-ray technician with two artificial arms with pairs of clasping hooks for hands. *Guess I'll have to excuse her from the fingerspelling portion of the class*, he thought to himself.

The third woman, a big-boned physical therapist over six feet tall, stood up and gave him a firm, pumping handshake. And then there was Annette, brunette and demure, who already knew how to fingerspell her name neatly when introductions were made. She immediately wanted to know how to sign *blood* and *heart*, for she worked as a phlebotomist at the blood bank. While Annette was telling Max and the class about her line of work, he was already thinking about which restaurant to take her to, the clothes he would wear on their first date, the home they would live in after they were married, and the number of children they'd have and their names.

Max asked the class why they wanted to learn sign language. The physical therapist said she wanted to be able to communicate with potential hearing-impaired patients. The grandmother said one of her grandkids was deaf. They watch sign language on *Sesame Street* together, she said, and she wanted to be able to sign as well as that woman on TV who can hear and is very expressive and fluent. Max had to let her know that the woman was Linda Bove, a famous actress who was deaf and a native user of sign language. The X-ray technician began talking and gesticulating but Max couldn't understand her, of course. Annette helped by fingerspelling for her. "B-o-w-l-i-n-g."

Max asked if the X-ray technician wanted to learn sign language because of bowling.

Annette fingerspelled further, "H-e-r l-e-a-g-u-e h-a-s d-e-a-f p-e-o-p-l-e."

He could picture the X-ray technician trying to converse in sign language with her prostheses. He'd seen that before. What he couldn't see was how she could grab a heavy bowling ball and roll it down a lane. Perhaps she had a friend set the ball on the lane and then gave it a nudge forward with her foot or something.

Annette, who always waited for everyone else to reply first, said that she wanted to be a certified sign language interpreter so that she could interpret for some of the deaf parishioners at her Jehovah's Witness temple. Immediately Max stopped playing his planning-the-future game. He proceeded with the strict business of teaching the ABCs of ASL.

A month after the interview, Dotty passed on a message to Max from a woman named Evy who taught a beginner's sign language course in the evenings at Galveston College, the island's community college. She was inquiring if he'd be willing to substitute for her while she went to Beaumont for a workshop. He agreed to do it in the hopes of forming more connections with women from the island—no longer "island women," which conjured up images of women in films set in the South Pacific. Evy said that it would be really good if he signed to the class about himself. They would get a good glimpse of Deaf culture that way.

Max never did get a date with any of the women from his classes, though the experience proved to be the necessary link in meeting someone who would forever change his outlook on life.

One early autumn day, he was finishing up a work request to photograph a series of shots of the university's newly erected lecture hall, a state-of-the-art facility on the outskirts of campus.

Max decided to take a break and walked across Market Street to
a corner store to buy a soda. There, he saw a Hispanic man be-
having in an animated way next to a rusted, beat-up yellow Gran
Torino. The man was gesturing to a woman—who turned out to
be Evy. As Max walked closer, he could see that they were signing
to each other. Max could tell that the man's use of ASL was that
of a native signer. Evy was getting in a sign here and there, but it
was clear she didn't understand in any detail. Her responses were
vague, and Max thought the man accepted her less-than-fluent
signing because he didn't have anyone else to communicate with
outside what was probably a very small circle of deaf friends.

Max wanted to meet him. He had been on the lookout for
others of his kind but hadn't had any luck for two months. Deaf
people were truly part of an invisible culture, and here was a deaf
man, who had come out of the woodwork and into broad daylight.

When she saw Max, Evy threw up her arms in relief. "I want
you to meet a friend—R-e-y-n-a-l-d-o," she said with choppy,
half-formed hand shapes. She was one of those people who hated
to fingerspell, and felt it was a burdensome part of the language.
Instead of working at it to form crisp, sharp letters on the hands,
she had given up and left it up to the viewer to decipher the missing contours of the manual letters.

Max nodded his head to Reynaldo. "My name is Dempsey Maxwell McCall. Name sign—X over the heart—Max."

Reynaldo asked why the cross over the heart.

Evy said, "Yeah! I was wondering about how you got that name
sign."

"Well," Max began, "one time a good Deaf friend of mine was
teasing me. Said 'You should be one of the X-Men.' I used to wear
a big hearing aid box on my chest, wires coming out of my shirt,
connected to my ears. My friend said, 'You look like some kind
of deaf m-u-t-a-n-t.' He had another name for me—'The Deaf
M-u-t-e,' get it? 'Mute,' short for 'mutant.' I told him I preferred
to be branded with an X on my chest. So, that became my name
sign."

Evy let out a burst of laughter. Reynaldo half-smiled, looking back and forth from Max to Evy, waiting for Max to finish his story. Evy said to Reynaldo, "The X-Men, you know? Group of superheroes? They fight the bad guys. You've seen them in comic books." Reynaldo looked at Max, not seeing the connection.

Evy then proceeded to act out the iconic moves of each member of the X-Men team, but it wasn't working. Her gestures and facial expressions were gawky. And it didn't help that she was wearing tinted eyeglasses and a blue polyester pantsuit in a loud pattern.

"The concept of the X-Men is like Superman," Max said. "Know Superman—big *S* on the chest?"

Reynaldo's face lit up. He mimed a cape, big arm muscles, and a curl on his forehead.

"That's it!" said Max. "X-Men—similar idea except different people, different costumes. They make the world right."

Reynaldo gestured an *X* over his heart, almost as if asking: "You promise?"

"Yeah, that's me," said Max, holding out his hand, almost sure Reynaldo wasn't asking if he'd promise to make the world right. "Good to meet you."

10/27/81 (TGIF!) Galveston, picnic table on the
seawall
Hey Mom 'n Dad!

I'm getting a lot of stares from people
walking by on the seawall. Guess they don't
often see someone with a typewriter out here.
Just got back from Corpus Christi. Don't ask
me why they call that place "Body of Christ."
Could be that they're still strapped under
the Bible Belt down there. Zag, myself, and
a few others from UTMB caravanned down to
the local chapter meeting of the Biological
Photographers' Association. Socially, it was a
good experience. Academically, it was literally
nothing to write home about. It wasn't the
most informative meeting. Just a bunch of
grandfathers reminiscing about the good ole
days. We came away feeling pretty good at how
knowledgeable we were about the photo areas
presented at the meeting.

The trip down and back was gorgeous; such
exquisite beauty in the Texas sky, the flat
coastal landscape, and the vegetation. The
simple, natural environment of Padre Island, a
long string of low sand islands made Ocean City,
Maryland look like a cheap little whore. (Pardon
my Texan, Mom.)

Dad, I know how you were fascinated by Mount
Rushmore. You'd be interested in knowing that
there is a Corpus Christi Seawall, designed
by Gutzon de la Mothe Borglum (God bless you,
sniff) the sculptor of Mount Rushmore. I
think he was a little more creative with the
presidential sculptures.

One night we ate at a really cheap Mexican joint with delicious, authentic Mexican cuisine. It was the kind of place where the grandmother cooks in the back, the mother is the hostess/cashier, and the granddaughter is the waitress. The father? God knows where he was or what he was doing. I ordered a combo platter of nachos with jalapeño peppers, tortillas with picante sauce, hot tamales, enchiladas, and burritos. My tongue is getting tamed. All in all, a worthwhile trip.

When we got back, Zag and I found an official-looking letter waiting for us. <u>WE PASSED THE WRITTEN EXAM!!! YAHOOOO!!</u> Cleared the first hurdle. Boy, were we hungover the next morning.

Zag and I have been to Houston a couple of times now. It's only an hour's drive up north. A couple from work took us with them to the Astrodome to see the Astros play the Braves.

The 'Dome was something else. You should see
the scoreboard. Instead of singing "The Star-
Spangled Banner" to a flag we sang it to the
scoreboard with computerized images of the
American flag, bombs bursting, and all that
flash on the screen.

The second time we went to Houston, the same
couple took us to an outdoor theater where we
saw the American Deaf Dance Company perform for
free. I saw some old deaf friends from RIT in
the audience and chatted with them a while. The
dance company was really good -- all of them
were profoundly deaf.

Things are beginning to pick up down here
-- can't complain. Been trying to get rid of a
pestx pesky head cold, hopefully this weekend
so I can get out in the hot sun, rest, run,
and swim in the warm waters of (cue the music)
the Gulf of Mexicooooooooo! Sorry, couldn't
resist while you're probably now getting your
overcoats out of the attic for the winter. Am
looking into cheap flights home for Christmas.
Can't wait . . . Love, Max

The Face of Grace

The Clinical Studio   Patients are shot with the lights set up at 45-degree angles with the flash reflecting off the umbrellas. Positions for lights and patients are marked on the floor. The inpatient lenses are precalibrated. Follow settings on the calibration tape. Use cross-lighting to accentuate lesions or bumps. Always take a few shots with flat lighting. Use blue background for most medical departments except Orthopedics. Mandatory for plastic surgery. Use gray for Ortho and other departments that require full-body shots. Black velvet is for Employee of the Month and student directory/yearbook photos.

Since most biomedical photography labs within a university hospital have a clinical studio, Max elected to serve a two-week rotation in clinical photography as part of his residency. He needed the experience of photographing live human subjects, who mostly stood or sat before a seamless blue backdrop. Once, while on 24-hour call, he was summoned out of bed at four o'clock on a Sunday morning to photograph a patient. When he came in to open the studio, the patient was waiting in the hallway in a wheelchair with an orderly standing by. Most of the patient's nose was gone. When Max read his chart, it said that the nose had been bitten off during a bar fight.

Dr. Robb had warned Max that unusual or shocking cases often came through the studio. About a year ago, he said, he'd had an unusual plastic surgery case where a woman had lost a drastic amount of weight. When she came in, with her clothes on, she looked good. Then she went to undress behind the curtained-off area for patients, and Robb heard all kinds of strange noises, such as grunting and groaning, and rubber hitting the floor. It turned out that she had been wearing a weight-loss suit underneath her clothes. When she emerged, large flaps of loose skin hung down about twelve inches around her waist. Following through on the case, Dr. Robb photographed the plastic surgery team hanging up the excess skin on two IV poles—like skewering a piece of meat— then cutting it off, and then suturing the new ends together.

Sometimes Max took pictures of patients with wounds that seeped fluids onto the floor. He had to delicately maneuver a camera around the patients' bodies and step over puddles to photograph the angles and poses ordered by the physician. Working quickly to reduce the patients' agonies and embarrassments, Max got them back to their stretchers and on their way to where they'd come from. Next, he exchanged the camera for a mop and cleaned up the mess. It felt as though he were photographing so much horror and death, seeing such ugliness wrought upon the human body day in and day out. But it started to feel like the norm—until the day the students arrived.

One day toward the end of his two-week stint, a group of medical, nursing, biotech, and physical and occupational therapy students lined up out in the hallway to have their yearbook pictures taken. Each semester, the photo department arranged an entire day for these "mug shots." It was a nice respite for Max—taking pictures of healthy faces—since he had spent most of his time in the studio looking through the viewfinder at people missing an eye, a leg, or some other anatomical part.

Max was quickly seduced by the hundreds of bright, fresh faces parading through the studio. "Sit here. Straighten your back. Tilt your head a little bit. Would you like a glass of water? You want a comb? Wet your lips—we want to see a little highlight. It'll make you look great!" He made little trivial remarks to keep them around longer. No wonder the lines were so long.

When a nursing student walked in and said, "Hi, I'm Grace," so loud and clear that Max found her easy to lipread, he slowed his pace even more. There was something terribly erotic about a woman who was easy to lipread. It gave him goose bumps watching her lips, tongue, and teeth wrap themselves perfectly around words. To regain his composure, he took his sweet time marking her name off the student roster. Then he fiddled with the camera, making calculations with an exposure meter in an effort to appear knowledgeable. In fact, no calculations were necessary, since all of the exposure settings had been preset and standardized for the yearbook portraits.

Grace knew instinctively how to pose. He snapped a few frames and then mustered the nerve to say, with his best pronunciation, "Stop by the studio and visit us again sometime." Her blue eyes seemed to answer that she would indeed.

A week later, Grace did stop by, to ask Max how her picture had come out. None of the other students had ever stopped by to inquire about anything like that, but he took the time to track down her image. He put on a pair of white, lintless gloves—which nobody used to handle routine, superficial assignments like yearbook pictures—and retrieved a 35mm negative strip out of its protective sleeve as if it were the only documentation of the Holy Shroud of Turin. He displayed the negative on a light box and invited Grace to look through a photo loupe at the five frames of her face—Max had gone three over par on the usual lab protocol of two shots per student.

The cool illumination coming up through the frosted glass accentuated her profile and the long auburn hair spilling onto the light box. She brushed a lock of hair back behind her ear, revealing a nicely shaped nose with a faint sprinkling of freckles. Her full lips almost kissed the surface of the glass. Max stood by her side, blocking the view from co-workers who might happen to walk by.

"How would you like to get together for a barbecue on the beach?" she said, still facing the glass.

Having a hard time lipreading sideways, he said, "I didn't quite get that. Would you please look at me and repeat it? I'm deaf."

"Oh, sure! You know, my father is hard of hearing."

"Cool!" Max said. "I mean—not that he can't hear well. But, cool that—umm—your father and I have something in common."

"Oh, he hears pretty good with his hearing aids. He doesn't need to read people's lips."

"I see," said Max. "Well, I'm afraid I do."

"Oh, that's no problem," said Grace. "What I asked before was if you'd like to get together at the beach for a barbecue." Her enunciation of the word *barbecue* ended with her lips puckered.

Max answered yes to the lips. He hoped his volume wasn't too loud. After work he rushed home to shower and then drove over to Grace's house, following her directions. She lived with her father and brother, who, Grace explained, would be joining them.

"Oh . . . great . . . swell, bring them along," Max said. *The more the warier*, he thought. They all climbed into Grace's car—a Mercedes SL380 convertible, Max noted. She drove down Seawall Boulevard and turned off at a beach access ramp that led to the hard-packed sand of Porretto Beach along the eastern end of Galveston Island. Grace parked the car a few feet away from the Gulf. What Max had grown to love about Galveston was that, even as late as November, the evenings still felt like balmy summer nights.

Grace's father and brother set up the hibachi near the car and lit up the coals. Max could see that her father was wearing a Miracle-Ear hearing aid—about the size of a tiny snail shell, well concealed inside the ear canal. They were good for people with very mild hearing loss, but of no use to profoundly deaf people like Max.

Max and Grace played by the surf, throwing a Frisbee back and forth. He learned that her father was an orthopedic surgeon, a breed he considered the blue-collar workers of operating rooms. They were strong, quiet, and put in long hours doing messy work with hammers, saws, nuts, and bolts. Then it dawned on Max why her father looked familiar—he was the chief of Orthopedic Surgery, whom he had met months ago.

When the sun went down, they stopped throwing the Frisbee. Max moved in closer to read Grace's lips. The hot dogs and baked

beans were ready. He sat on a rock munching on his hot dog while Grace sat a few yards away on a big piece of driftwood with her father and brother. Max could hear their voices, but couldn't make out what they were saying. Grace's face became a silhouette as darkness engulfed the sky. Max couldn't see her lips or her smile. He wanted to talk but couldn't; it would be like talking to the stars. He finished his meal in silence.

Back at her father's house, they had coffee. Her brother went to his room. Max, Grace, and her father looked furtively at each other while sipping from their cups.

As if on cue, her father set down his cup and asked, "Max—do you consider Jesus Christ your personal savior?"

"Uh, no. Not really," he said.

"I see." After a long silence, he said, "Well, Grace, hon, time for me to turn in. Nice seein' ya again, Max. Goodnight, y'all."

Dempsey Maxwell McCall said goodnight—to all of them. He walked out the door and down the steps. He got into his car and rode away with the framed image of Grace's blue eyes and smile forever etched in his mind.

December 20, 1981
Pathology Lab
To my dear family (feel free to share w/ relatives):
    Merry Xmas! Yesterday, the whole Pathology
Department had their annual Christmas dinner
at a fancy restaurant in Galveston. It was a
dressy affair; Zag and I each brought a date.
The whole thing was paid for by the department.
Open bar and prime ribs were the highlights of
the evening -- they were actually better than
our dates.
    I still feel bad & guilty that I'm gonna miss
the holidays with you all for the first time
in my life. As I mentioned over the phone, most
everyone here will be gone for two weeks. That
means we get the lab to ourselves to totally
focus on developing our portfolios and not have
to worry about the day-to-day operations of the
lab. No interruptions. As Zag would say, "We
gotta bang this sucker out."
    Made a little something for you since at the
present time I can't afford lavish gifts. I
gathered a bunch of slides, some mine and some
Zag's, and put together a slide show with a
script. I've enclosed a slide carousel since I'm
not sure if I left one behind at home for you
when I left. The slides are all in order -- every
time you get to the next number on the script,
all you have to do is advance to the next slide.
This show revolves around bits and pieces of the
life that I lead down here. Not all parts are
represented because I don't have a photographic
record of EVERYTHING I do. If I did, you all
would keel over from shock [FLOP] . . .

After the show you are probably going to think, "Does our son ever do any work, or is he ever serious about life?" Yes folks, he studies hard, works hard, has a serious side, but doesn't want to bore you with that part of him.

OK, hit the lights . . .

SCRIPT:

Slide #1: here's a little tour around Pirate's Beach where Zag and I live. This is the entrance to our beach community. The road we're on is Pirate's Beach Boulevard. Legend has it that pirate Jean Lafitte buried some of his plunder here between 1817 and 1820. To this day it's never been found.

Slide #2: folks, this is it! Home Sweet Temporary Home, the place where two aspiring medical photographers are developing their exquisite talents, and are on their way to fame and fortune. You can't quite see our backyard,

but every now and then Zag or I take a shovel
and dig into the grass and lift up a hunk of sod
to see if we can discover Lafitte's treasure.
Hey -- can you blame us?? The yard looks a
little funny, like it's been raided by a family
of groundhogs with all those little mounds
everywhere. We'll flatten the yard out one day.
(Don't tell our landlord -- wink, wink.)

Slide #3: this is the site of the "Battle of
Three Trees," ignited when Lafitte's men stole
an Indian squaw. The cannibalistic Indians
avenged the kidnapping by devouring four of
Lafitte's men. Hmmm, wonder if that's how Texas
got famous for its barbecue . . .

Slide #4: our beloved TV which we turn on every
morning at 6:30 Monday—Friday to watch *The Three
Stooges* for half an hour. We caught one episode
where the Stooges played photographers. They
were developing film in a darkroom. Here's a
snippet of their actual dialogue:
Larry: I can't find the negative.
Moe: How about the positive?
Curly: I'm positive about the negative, but I'm
a little negative about the positive.
Moe: Oh, negative, eh?
Curly: No, I'm positive the negative is in the
developer.

They're a great waker-upper and keep us from
going off the deep end.

Slide #5: now for a look at the beach . . .
occasionally we see horseback riders galloping
up and down the hard-packed sand we have here.
It's a beautiful sight, but you have to watch

where you step, especially if you're barefoot
[SPLAT! arrrgggh!! #@%$!!!]

Slide #6: there are many beautiful homes along
the beach. Here is one that I especially like.
It looks like one of those fancy restaurants
that is partway over the water. I've heard
they've called this whole area a "playground for
alcoholic playboys of the Houston rich."

Slide #7: self portrait in front of a broken ice
box.

Slide #8: these are a couple of the buildings on the campus of the University of Texas Medical Branch. The university has a nice mixture of old and modern buildings, both with beautiful architecture. The main building you see here is "Old Red," done in Romanesque Revival style with its round arches and rows of bricks and stone. Up until 1922, Old Red was the only classroom and lab space for medical students. Now the university has about 60-some buildings.

Slide #9: the back entrance to the Pathology Building where we work. Notice how small the door is? Only 4½ feet high. It's for when they wheel donated bodies up the ramp and through the door to the anatomy morgue, which is right down the hall from us. You don't want to see a photo of that. We call this the Leon LeBeau Door. Named after a diminutive microbiology professor who occasionally comes to lecture to the photo residents about aspects of medical photography. He can walk through the door without having to duck his head.

Slide #10: this is the photomicroscopy room, where we do a lot of our work. When anyone starts bothering me or is trying to feed me a lot of stuff, I hold up this sign with Hebrew

writing on it. It means "Bullshit!" Zag is
Jewish and he feels at home when I hold up this
sign.

Slide #11: the copy area (not Xerox kind of
photocopying); a lot of doctors bring in these
thick medical textbooks that weigh about 20
lbs. apiece. Usually they'll want us to copy a
chart or an illustration out of the book to make
a 35mm slide for an upcoming lecture. We have
to crack open a book to page 1,469 or something,
and the edges of the damn charts are almost
always near the binding. Have you ever tried
holding flat a thousand-page book? Good night!

Slide #12: Happy birthday, Mom! I'm holding a
piece of Texas sheet cake (chili powder is one
of the ingredients) with a lit candle in your
honor.
   The End.
   Let me know what you think. Miss all of you
very, very much.
Mucho love,
Max
P.S. Please save the slides -- a few belong to
Zag and he'd like to have them back someday. No
hurry.

New Year's with Reynaldo
(or, Death Never Sleeps)

Autopsy Photography This situation is relatively similar to shooting in the OR (see Surgical Photography). The main exception is that you do not need to be sterile or wear scrubs. You should wear the shoes you designated for autopsies only. Feel free to move the surgical light around to suit your shooting situation, or turn it off and use your flash. Ask the pathologist what he or she needs, and whether black-and-white or color is needed. If the field is messy, ask the pathologist if you can outline the perimeter with clean gray or blue towels. It will make the photos look nicer for lectures and publications.

Using his streetwise wiles and pseudo-innocence, Reynaldo somehow convinced Max to join him for a New Year's Eve party in Houston hosted by the deaf association there. What it really meant was that Reynaldo needed a ride to the party. Max figured since he didn't have any plans for New Year's yet and it was already the 29th, why not humor Rey and give him a lift. Max asked Zag if he wanted to come along. Going anywhere with Reynaldo meant an odd adventure was in the works. Zag had no plans except to stay home, drink Lone Star beers, and watch the ball drop at midnight on TV. He had been homesick for New York City, and watching the New York revelers would be the next best thing to being home.

Max told Reynaldo he'd pick him up at his apartment at 8 p.m. on the 31st. That night Max and Zag worked in the lab until 5:30. They were the only ones left, and the place was starting to feel lonely and spooky. Two doors down from the basement-level lab

104

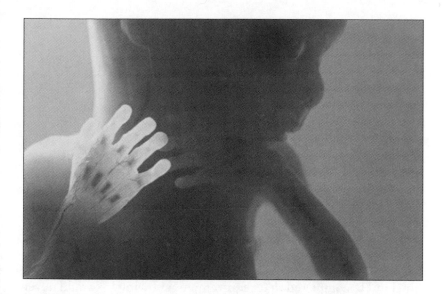

was the anatomy morgue. Next door, on the other side of the lab, was where human anatomical specimens were stored in large pickle jars. A cheerful hospital staff member named Bob was the curator of this anatomical bank. Max always wondered how the man could remain so upbeat, day after day, amid a room full of dead body parts. Every time Max passed Bob in the hall, he always greeted Max with: "How're y'all doin'?"

Bob once gave Max a tour of the bank. The room was set up like library stacks, with rows upon rows of human body parts—a macabre dime museum. So this was the kind of place from which his old biology teacher, Mr. Orendorf, had acquired his syphilitic heart for class. What shook Max to the core were the jars of fetuses. Their miniature faces looked like the faces of grown men sleeping upright—some without brains, or a hole where the nose should be, or a jaw missing, or one with two arms but no legs. Robert Ripley would buy out this whole place for his believe-it-or-not museum, if he could.

On the wall was a piece of paper that read, in large block letters: ALL SPECIMENS MUST BE TREATED WITH DIGNITY. DISRESPECT

FOR SUCH MATERIAL THAT WAS ONCE A PART OF A LIVING BEING WILL NOT BE TOLERATED.

"Let me know if y'all have any questions. If y'all see something y'like, just holler, and I'll git her down for y'all," said Bob. Genuine customer service with a smile. Bob gave Max a pat on the back and left him alone to scan the shelves of jars.

One of Max's portfolio requirements had been a photograph of a gross anatomy specimen documented with the proper background color, exposure, and scale. Max had to produce one color slide and a 5x7 black-and-white glossy print. After a half hour scanning the shelves, Max settled on a kidney that was sectioned longitudinally in half. He didn't want to pick something that was round or slimy. A good, firm kidney with one flat side to prevent it from rolling around on the table would help get the job done quickly. He completed that requirement, knowing he would never again have to visit the bank and experience the eye-burning smell of formaldehyde and the odd assortment of human deformities.

As part of Max's orientation to the Pathology Building, Bob had also given him a tour of the anatomy morgue. This place was a horror film set, with the stereotypical white-tiled floor and walls, fluorescent lights, autopsy table, Frankenstein-esque lamp, weight scale, and stainless steel sinks. A large, raised rectangular block with a metal cover, the cadaver-immersion tank—like a tub from an old Russian bathhouse—sat in one corner of the room. A technician came in and lifted off the cover. Strong formaldehyde fumes hit Max. Two bloated bodies floated in the amber fluid. The technician got a long wooden stick and stuck it in the bath. To ensure that the bodies would be well preserved, he turned them over one at a time so that they faced down. And then he replaced the cover.

Zag tapped Max on the shoulder, startling him out of his trance. "I'm hearing strange sounds next door, Max. It's creeping me out."

"Yeah, I'm getting a little spooked myself," said Max.

"We're probably the only ones working late in the building on New Year's Eve."

"Except for the anatomist that turns over bodies in the immersion tank next door. Maybe that's what you're hearing? The splashing and plopping sounds."

"How would you know how that sounds?" said Zag.

"Oh, I don't know. I'm just guessing."

"Let's get the fuck outta here, boss. I'm ready to celebrate New Year's Eve."

They cut out for home, exiting up the ramp and ducking through the little Leon LeBeau door where donated bodies were wheeled in. Back home, Max and Zag quickly got showered, shaved, and dressed. Max turned on the stereo and played the album *John Barleycorn Must Die*. Since their move into the beach house, all he had wanted to listen to was music by Traffic, which Zag had introduced him to. Both munched on a bowl of pretzels and popped cans of their first Lone Stars for the night. Max wanted to hear the song "Every Mother's Son." Zag had written out the lyrics the other day, and Max was starting to memorize them—his way of being able to follow music:

"Once again I'm northward bound, on the edge of sea and sky . . ."

The great thing about Zag was that he had no qualms about cranking up the volume to compensate for Max's hearing loss. Zag loved concert-level amplification. Max could really feel the bass and drums through his housemate's powerful Harman Kardon stereo system. And it helped to be in an all-wood beach house on stilts where you could feel the vibrations throughout the whole house—even while sitting on the toilet.

At eight o'clock, they rolled up to Reynaldo's shotgun shack facing an alley on Avenue E; he wasn't outside waiting. Max went up to the door. There was no doorbell or doorbell light button to press. He tried the doorknob and found the door open. He stuck his arm in and waved—a courteous way to inform a deaf person that someone is at the door. No response. Max opened the door further and peeked in. The place was a rat hole smelling of mildew, cat piss, and unwashed socks. Then the bathroom

door swung open, and out came Rey. Each was startled to see the
other. Rey burst out laughing and gave Max a bear hug. He had a
floppy cowboy hat on his head and was dressed like a zoot suiter
in secondhand clothes. He looked as out of place as a surfboard in
a subway, but Max didn't want to say anything about his attire. It
was obvious that this was a big night for Reynaldo.

"Scared me, you!" said Reynaldo. "Me thought my ex-brother-
in-law."

"Does he scare you?" asked Max.

"Sometimes he come . . . beat me. If me not pay money to ex-
wife."

"That bastard beats you?!"

Reynaldo nodded and toed aside an empty pizza box on the
floor. On the cover was the proverbial mustachioed, smiling chef
with a wink and the classic Italian gesture of "magnifico."

"Aw man, that burns me! We gotta do something about that."

"No, no, no—don't. Make worse—leave it," said Reynaldo.

"Leave it alone? How? Your ex-wife and her brother are taking
advantage of you."

"My ex—M-R, little bit, remember?"

"Yes, I remember she's a little retarded. You showed me a picture of her one time," Max said. It was a tattered wallet photo,
but Max could see in her eyes and the way she hung her head
that there was some level of mental retardation. In her arms was
an alert and beautiful half black, half Hispanic baby boy about a
year and a half old, the subject of much angst and financial strife
for Reynaldo.

"My son . . . me don't want turn everything upside down. Keep
peace," he said. "Brother-in-law hits like a pussy—no hurt me."

"OK, let's go. Zag is waiting out in the car."

"Jew Man's here? He coming with us?"

"Oh yeah! He wouldn't miss this for anything." Reynaldo loved
Zag, for some weird reason. Observing the two of them communicate was like watching a good mime trying to gesture to a bad
mime. Zag thought he understood most of what Rey said, but
often Max had to interject and clarify what Rey had really meant.

Because Zag was hearing, and good-natured, Rey put him on a pedestal, which told Max that Rey's past contacts with hearing people had rarely been positive.

Reynaldo climbed into the front seat and turned around and gave Zag a big smile. Both gave each other a hearty handclasp. Zag gestured a J on his chest and held both arms straight out, as if he were flying like Superman.

"Jew Man's here and he's gonna fly!" Zag tried to say.

Reynaldo let out an ear-shattering deaf laugh. Zag handed him a can of Miller Lite.

"Sorry, no Tecate tonight. We're poor like you," Max said.

"Lemon, salt—where?" asked Reynaldo. Max pointed to the glove compartment, where he kept carryout salt packs and a lemon-shaped container of reconstituted lemon. Zag slapped Max on the back of his head. Max turned around.

"Don't tell him stuff like that," said Zag, while Rey was rimming his can with salt and lemon juice. "We're not as bad off as he is."

"Sorry, but sometimes I need to put him in his place," Max said without signing his words. "Did you see the look he gave you? As if he was disappointed that you didn't have expensive Mexican beer."

Reynaldo looked at Max and held out the salt and lemon, gesturing to see if he wanted his beer Mexicanized. Max nodded and handed him his beer can. Zag held out his can so Reynaldo could dress his beer as well.

"What's with the lemon and salt?" asked Zag.

"Rey told me that in Mexico and South America it helps to improve the taste of shitty beer."

Reynaldo handed Zag back his lemon-and-salt-laced beer. Zag took a big swig and gave a facial expression of pleasant surprise. He signed, "Shit, thumbs-up!" Reynaldo roared with laughter at Zag's clever sign play.

The men drank in silence. Mexican fan palmettos swayed to and fro along the alley. The humid summer-like breeze off the Gulf of Mexico made it hard for Max to believe that it was late December. He felt he would be perfectly happy not going anywhere, just sitting all night in the car sipping beers and enjoying the warm Gulf air waft through the car. Yellow pools of light from the sodium-vapor street lamps lined the alleyway, seemingly all the way to infinity.

Zag tapped him on the shoulder and gestured, "Let's go." Max started the car and put it in gear, but before taking his foot off the brake, he asked Reynaldo where they were going.

"Over bridge, Texas City," said Reynaldo. "Pick up friend—woman."

"He wants us to stop off in Texas City to pick up a lady friend," Max told Zag. "Sorry, I thought it was just going to be the three of us."

Zag leaned over to the front seat and looked at Reynaldo before gesturing, "Big boobs?" Reynaldo nodded eagerly. Zag rubbed his palms greedily together and smacked his lips. He held out his hand for another bro-style handclasp. Reynaldo let out his patent deaf roar of laughter. Max let go of the brake and eased the car onto Broadway to head toward the causeway.

Reynaldo guided Max through the suburban blue-collar communities of Texas City. In the background, the oil refineries, basked in bright orange floodlights, were smoking and going full blast into the new year. Max parked in front of a split-level house that had seen better days. An airboat sat on a trailer on the front lawn. An old Chevy pickup with its hood up was in the driveway. A redheaded deaf woman whom Reynaldo introduced as Oma Dell—name sign *O* on the chest—met them at the door. She welcomed them into her house. Max turned to Zag and secretly gestured two *O*-shaped nipples.

"Her name is Oma," Max said. "Two *O*s like this."

"Get outta here!" Zag said. "I saw just one *O* on the chest."

"Maybe she only has one tit," Max said.

They sat in the living room, which smelled of motor oil. A bald man in his fifties had full reign over the sofa. He was cleaning out a carburetor on his lap. On the coffee table were auto parts, hand tools, and dirty rags.

Reynaldo said, "That Cooter, Oma's boyfriend."

Zag and Max made a move to shake his hand. Cooter looked up and just lifted his eyebrows to acknowledge them, while still wiping his rag through the carburetor shafts. Oma asked if they wanted something to drink. Her right eye constantly blinked, seemingly from a nervous tic. Although she was probably in her fifties, she looked older because of the wrinkles on her hands and face. She voiced and signed everything she said, apparently knowing that Zag was hearing. To Max, her voice sounded like his grandmother's. He was mentally laughing his ass off at Zag's anticipation of her being a sexy woman with big breasts.

"Dr. Pepper, milk, or water?" asked Oma, and then added, "If Cooter is in a good mood, he might let you have some of his beer in the cooler over there."

Max and Zag said "water" in unison, almost too quickly. Reynaldo said "beer" and went to the cooler beside the sofa to help himself. Before he lifted the lid, he looked at Cooter, who gave him a slight nod of approval.

A pale-skinned, plain woman with long black hair entered the living room. She was obviously a hearing person because of the way she enunciated her words, slowly and clearly, to Oma. "I heard you talking to someone."

"This is my friend Lenora. We work together as secretaries over there at Union Carbide." Max looked through the plate glass window to where Oma was pointing. He could see that her living room had an unobstructed view of the chemical plant, with its large cluster of buildings, pipe work, and smokestacks surrounded by a high chain-link security fence. Reynaldo got up and walked over to give Lenora a bear hug. He thought that everyone deserved a bear hug—part of Deaf culture, he always said.

"Hi Rey," Lenora said, patting his back. She touched his coat lapels. "Nice duds." Reynaldo introduced her to Max and Zag— the Jew Man, with the help of Oma voicing for him. Lenora giggled, and held out her hand for them to shake.

"Nice to meet you, Lenora," said Zag. "I'm hearing, by the way."

"Oh, good! I thought I was the only hearing person here," she said.

"Is it OK if she comes with us to the party?" asked Oma. Her winking was getting excessive. Max had to remind himself that she wasn't winking to get him to say yes to go along with some joke she had in mind. She was serious, her left eye looking straight at him, unblinking. Max looked sideways at Zag and then at Reynaldo to see whether it was OK with them for Lenora to join this ever-expanding New Year's expedition to Houston.

"Of course," said Zag. "The more, the merrier." He turned to Reynaldo: "Jew Man wants to fly!" He struck a superhero pose and aimed for the door. His outstretched arms made Max think about Zag's parents, and how much their son and thus their lives had evolved—for better or worse—since the days when they had settled in the United States as survivors of Auschwitz. He never forgot how embarrassed he'd been the first time he met them in their tiny Brooklyn kitchen.

That morning, Zag's mother had made strong European coffee. When she'd set their coffee cups on the table, he saw that she had a tattoo of a row of numbers on her left forearm. Zag's father was doing a crossword puzzle, and Max noticed he had a similar tattoo in numbers on his left arm.

"Hey, Reuben!" Max had said. This was a month before they'd ended up in Texas as medical photography interns and Reuben had shortened his name to Zag. He was much happier now—he'd hated being associated with Reuben sandwiches.

"I think it's so cool that your parents have tattoos!" Max had said. "Mr. and Mrs. Zagruder—you two were ahead of your time!"

For a moment, none of them moved. Zag rubbed his hand over his eyes to gather his thoughts. His parents stared into their coffees. Then, for the rest of that morning, the three of them gave Max a proper education about the horrors of the Holocaust.

Reynaldo gulped the rest of his beer, then slammed the bottle onto the table next to Cooter's carburetor parts. He copied Zag's Jew Man flying pose. Cooter flicked his towel at Reynaldo's butt.

"What the fuck are you doing? Is that some dumb spic move?" said Cooter.

Reynaldo sat next to Cooter and gave him a bear hug, knocking the carburetor to the floor.

"Love Cooter! He cool. Talk honest!" said Reynaldo to Max and Zag. He picked up Cooter's carburetor and blew off whatever dirt it might have picked up.

"Sorry."

"Thank you," said Cooter, "but back off—can't you see I'm working here?"

"Is that for your pickup out there?" asked Max.

"Airboat," said Cooter.

"He works for an airboat manufacturing company over in Bayou Vista. Got an old, broken-down boat the company thought was no good. He's fixin' to get it up and runnin'," said Oma.

"You gotta tell 'em everything? Why don't you tell 'em what kinda underwear I got on?" said Cooter.

"I'm just being social. We got guests in the house."

"I didn't invite 'em." He scratched his ear, getting grease all over it.

"I'm ready to go," said Max, heading for the door. He turned around to Cooter. "Nice to meet you."

"Same here," said Zag. Cooter lifted his eyebrows and went back to carburetor cleaning.

Reynaldo gave Cooter a friendly punch on the shoulder, and took another beer out of the cooler. Cooter gave him a thwack with his rag before Reynaldo escaped out the door.

In the car, Reynaldo sat in the front seat with Max to give directions to the party. Zag looked content to sit in the back between Oma and Lenora, juggling conversation between a deaf woman and a hearing woman. Reynaldo guided their way toward the Gulf Freeway to get to Houston. After fifteen minutes of wending through the suburban communities of LaMarque and Hitchcock, they ended up on the graveled grounds of Baywinds Mobile Homes. Repossessed trailers and double-wides lined the two lanes of the trailer park. On one of the lots were the charred remains of a trailer that had burned down. All that was left was the refrigerator and stove.

"Doesn't look like Houston to me," said Max.

"That!" said Reynaldo. "See burned-down trailer? Live next there."

"Who?"

"One more friend, pick up."

"What?!"

"Name's SV."

Zag leaned forward over the seat: "What's the matter, guys?" Max let out a long, disappointed sigh.

"Rey wants to pick up one more friend."

Zag looked sternly at Reynaldo. He subtly gestured: "Nice boobs?" Rey showed him an hourglass figure with his hands, and then blew on them to cool them off.

"C'mon, Max—one more won't hurt," said Zag. "You've got room up front here."

"Yeah, and maybe two more for the trunk if this keeps up," said Max. "Before you know it New Year's has come and gone."

"There she! SV!" Reynaldo exclaimed. He quickly got out of the car and met her as she came down the steps. She was wearing a gold miniskirt, a tight black top with spaghetti straps, and a faux leopard fur coat hanging over her shoulders like a shawl. Reynaldo gave her a big hug, lifting her off the ground. The coat fell onto the gravel. He picked it up quickly and brushed it off. Then he put it on himself like a pimp and sashayed to the car to open the door for her. She followed him, trying to ford the river of gravel in high heels. Then she ducked her head through the passenger window to see who was in the car.

"Hi, I'm SV. Oh, hello, Oma, I didn't see you back there!"

"Hi darling! Good to see you," said Oma. "Her name's Svetlana. We call her SV."

Playing the debonair doorman, Reynaldo wrapped the leopard fur around her shoulders and invited her to sit in the middle.

When SV sat down next to him, Max smelled a mix of cigarettes, vodka, and cheap perfume.

After a forty-five-minute drive, Max's Blue Baby Special pulled into the downtown parking lot of the Houston Association of the Deaf. The club was on the third floor of a nondescript building. When they entered the clubroom, they were hit by a wall of rock music blaring from a DJ station. Zag and Lenora, both hearing, were struck by the extremely loud volume coupled with an unfathomably deep bass. They huddled close together, stranded on an island in an ocean of gyrating deaf people. Reynaldo and SV were already on the floor dancing out of sync with the driving rhythm of Bad Company's "Burnin' Sky." Max tried to avoid eye contact with Oma, knowing she was standing around looking for someone to ask her to dance, hoping it would be him. He was about to head to the bar to order a beer when Oma stepped into his path.

"I'm a little ashamed to be asking this, but would you care to dance?"

"Uh, sure, fine," said Max, kicking himself for walking into that trap. He was going to get Reynaldo back for this. Oma and Max danced perfunctorily while eyeing other people's moves. When the song ended, Max said he was going to get a beer.

"You mind getting me one, too?" said Oma. She kept winking at him, and this time it was full of nasty hints. At the bar, he tried to strategize a way out. He looked around for a familiar face, but since he was new to the area, he didn't see one. Eavesdropping here was easy—everyone conversed in ASL, a language for all to see. There were no secrets, no privacy. Perhaps this was why deaf people were so blunt with each other. Unfortunately for Max, the conversations around the bar and on the dance floor were banal. How could he get excited over dull topics like what people were wearing, or how to irrigate a dry lawn? The bartender took his order for a couple of beers. It felt nice to simply request his drinks in ASL and not have to shout in the ear of a hearing bartender.

About a half hour before midnight, a strategy fell into Max's lap. Zag came up to him, Lenora trailing behind, her face ashen.

"Hey boss—we oughta split this pop joint. It's a madhouse. We're literally going deaf here. The music's so fuckin' loud, my ears are gonna bleed any minute."

"Huh? What did you say?" said Max. He tried to stifle a smile.

"I said we should—"

"I know what you said. I can lipread, remember? I was just messin' with ya." The first time Max and Zag had hung out together was at a noisy college bar in Rochester. Zag couldn't believe how well Max could lipread various conversations going on around the bar. Zag would point out specific people and want to know what they were saying. Over half the time, Max could pick up on the gist of the conversation. Zag was floored; he said he felt like he was with a CIA agent. As for the rest of the time, for people whose lips were blocked by a drink or a moustache, Max just invented juicy data for Zag to swallow. There was no way to verify the accuracy of his lipreading skills, so Zag took his word for it.

"I'm serious, boss. This place is killing us. Lenora is miserable. What's more—this deaf DJ sucks. He played this one song and the record needle kept skipping over and over. Longest fuckin' song I've ever heard. We're the only hearing people here—I don't have the nerve to go up and inform him his records are skipping. And, don't say 'Huh? What?' or I'll smack you."

"Wwwwell, to tell you the truth, I'm dying to get outta here myself. The trick is convincing Reynaldo to leave," said Max.

"Can't he find a ride home with somebody else?"

"I'm ready to say 'tough shitsky' if he can't."

It turned out that all it took was some coaxing for Reynaldo to understand Zag's situation. SV was high as a kite and willing to float along whichever way Rey pulled her string. The six revelers ended up back in Max's car on the Gulf Freeway heading to Galveston. Zag had cooked up a plan to celebrate the new year at the beach house. Max reluctantly gave in; at least he would have something to do that did not involve Oma, and would soon be home. In the rearview mirror Max could see the silhouette of Zag with his arms around Lenora. Oma was next to them, arms crossed, looking out the window. In the front seat, Reynaldo was necking with SV while snaking his hand up her skirt.

Max kept his eye on the speedometer. He was sure that state troopers would be all over on the lookout for speeders and drunken weavers. Up ahead he saw a long line of cars backed up. He slowed down and joined the train. Inching along after a couple of miles, they passed the reason for the backup—a three-car accident in which one of the cars had been flipped onto its roof. As they slowly passed the crushed metal, glass, flashing lights, cop cars, and people crying, Max saw a body covered in a sheet lying beside one of the cars.

Suddenly Zag tapped Max on the shoulder. Max reached back to turn on the overhead dome light so he could lipread what Zag would have to say.

"Pull the car over!"

"Why?" said Max.

"Lenora is gonna get sick."

Max fought the urge to groan: "Now? It'll take forever to merge into this growing line of cars and get home." He quickly eased his car over to the right shoulder and put it in park. In the side-view mirror, he saw Zag rubbing Lenora's back as she heaved up and down. Reynaldo and SV continued to make out, oblivious to what was going on. Oma was kneeling on the backseat looking out the rear window, as if it were fascinating to watch a human vomit.

Once Lenora felt better, Zag helped her back into the car. Max offered her a stick of gum, which she gladly accepted. Back on the slow-moving train of cars, Max wondered if he would soon be called to the morgue to photograph the body he'd seen on the road. The numerals in the car clock turned to 12:03. He thought, *Will this night ever end?*

February 2, 1982
Happy Groundhog Day,
UTMB, Moody Medical Library

Dear Mumsie and Dadsie:

I'm pissed at myself for not writing sooner.
Have had some kind of a brain-lock clasped on
and couldn't find the keys. This will probably
be a long one. I've been holed up in the lab
pretty much for the month of January. Adopted
a tunnel-vision mentality to prepare myself
for nothing but the most critical phase of my
certification -- the portfolio. I swore off all
social contact, including Reynaldo (remember my
Deaf Mexican friend?), warning him that I was
not going to be available at all for a while.
Surprisingly, he was okay with that. He said he
was going to visit a friend in Seattle for a few
weeks who might help him find a good job.

Well, he's back in town already. It seems
the job situation there wasn't good for him.
He wasn't eligible for welfare and couldn't
find a job. He has yet to get his green card
so he's still an illegal alien. He got his old
part-time job back at the tackle factory, but
he's talking about going back to Mexico to find
what's left of his family (parents, relatives).
He doesn't seem to be too happy here. He plans
on leaving sometime this summer. What a sad case
-- depresses me sometimes when I see him.

Actually today was the first day I saw him
but the old feelings of pity for him returned.
I don't show it to him of course and I try to
encourage him to do things or give him direction
that will guide him the right way. He just sort
of half takes it all in and then forgets about

it or doesn't care. Except for his little boy,
Rey's mind seems to be concerned with what he
considers the finer things in life, like a big
beautiful house and a car, and earning lots of
money. He doesn't seem to understand that he is
uneducated and illiterate, and therefore his
choice of jobs is very limited. He works at a
place for a while and quits, comes back and asks
for his job again, then quits, and round and
round and round it goes. He came to me once with
a note from UTMB Housekeeping saying that they
couldn't hire him anymore because he had quit
twice already.

The tackle factory pays Reynaldo quite well
in spite of his shortcomings, but he doesn't
realize how well Junior (his employer) has been
treating him, and how Junior goes out on a limb
for him. And now Reynaldo wants to split for
Mexico. I can't half blame him, because of his
immediate family -- the retarded black girl with
whom he has a son and who won't let him see the
boy. And her brothers who are protecting her and
acting as physical barriers, I mean physical
-- like with guns and knives. It seems that Rey
is barely going to have enough money saved up
to buy a one-way ticket to Mexico. Who knows
what'll happen to that guy.

Meant to tell you in my last letter about this
other deaf guy that I met, though I don't know
him that well; kind of keeps to himself. He
works for UTMB's Groundskeeping department. I
happened to meet him while he was out trimming
around trees with a weed whacker. He had taken
a break and was talking to himself in signs.
At first it didn't make sense because he was
wearing soundproof earmuffs. I went up to him

and signed, "Excuse me, you deaf?" He signed
back that he was. Introduced myself and asked,
if he was deaf, why was he wearing earmuffs. He
said he wasn't totally deaf -- had some residual
hearing. A doctor had advised him to use
earmuffs if he wanted to preserve what little
hearing he had left. Interesting idea. I never
thought of that. All the years I grew up cutting
grass, whacking weeds, listening to Bad Company
at full blast was I making myself deafer? Ahh --
water over the dam. I'm fine, give or take a few
decibels.

   When I got back to the lab, I told one of
the other photographers, who has been at UTMB
a long time, that I'd met a deaf employee who
works with the grounds crew. He said, "Oh yeah,
obviously you met Kelvin. He came to the lab
once and asked for some money. I was working
the front desk. I noticed he was deaf because
he wrote his request in bad English on paper.
He was wearing his UTMB ID tag, which told me he
was employed by the university. I felt sorry for
him and gave him a couple of dollars. A couple
weeks later, I get called to the front desk. I'm
told, 'The guy who begged some money from you
is here.' He asked for some more money because
he was saving up to go to some big conference
to learn something. I gave him another couple
of dollars. Thought that'd be the end of that.
And then he came back to beg some more." The co-
worker cut him off when he learned from a buddy
of his in Groundskeeping that Kelvin hadn't gone
to any conference. Kelvin had been scamming
him by using the money to pay for a number of
children he'd fathered with several women. My

colleague said it was hard, but he'd had to put his foot down and say no to Kelvin.

My co-worker said he sometimes sees Kelvin down at the donut shop, but avoids eye contact whenever he passes him. "He was a user -- used his disability the wrong way. So, watch out for him," my colleague warned me. "Don't get caught in his web of deaf deceit." He feels bad. He would've liked to have signed to him, maybe somehow he could've helped him.

You won't believe this . . . last week I was sent to the Ear, Nose, and Throat Clinic to take some public relations pictures with a Dr. McCovey who has been at UTMB for 25 years. I really wanted to do a great job, as I don't often get public relations assignments. As I was setting up the lights around McCovey, and careful not to create bad shadows, I noticed that she wore two behind-the-ear hearing aids. I politely asked if she was Deaf. She said no, hard of hearing. She did not have to lipread to understand people, which confirmed she could hear pretty well. I told her that I was profoundly deaf, and wore hearing aids too. McCovey said she'd noticed by the quality of my voice. Said I clipped my words. I wasn't sure whether to take that as an insult or not.

I then asked if she knew sign language. Said she didn't need to. Grew up speaking all her life. She would have liked to have learned some signs but "you can't teach an old dog new tricks." I didn't believe that, because someone had told me that she was a member of Mensa (the high IQ society), and that she'd just gotten certified to be a licensed instructor in flying.

While I was rigging up the flash units,
McCovey mentioned that she liked to collect old
cameras. She never wanted to buy new ones. She
opened a cabinet nearby and asked if I could
shoot her PR pictures with an early 1900s camera
that she held out. It was one of those Kodak
box cameras, a Brownie Hawkeye. Told her that I
was sorry, but I didn't carry size 127 film for
that camera. It's 46mm film -- all we deal with
mostly are 35mm films. McCovey looked genuinely
disappointed with me. I thought to myself,
"Well, I'm disappointed with you!" She didn't
show a glimmer of interest in the fact that I
was deaf and working as a medical photographer
in the very same hospital where she worked.
Incidentally, the PR shots turned out okay --
they weren't that great. I wonder why? . . .

It's interesting that these deaf people are
starting to appear out of nowhere. Must be "Deaf
Emergence Month."

Am running out of news and my hands are
getting tired from typing. Need to get back to
work. Write me sometime to let me know what's
been happening on the home front.

Take care and stay healthy.

Love y'all!
Dempsey Maxwell, RBP-To-Be

P.S. Did I tell you that Aunt Bev and Uncle
Joe sent me a nice, bright blue Izod alligator
sweater for Christmas? Unfortunately, it was
too big for me. They must have the impression
that I'm 6'4" and weigh 195 lbs or something;
I'm still 5'7" and around 155 these days. I'm
looking for someone to sell it to.

The Deaf Heart

Surgical Photography When called to an operating room, go to the locker room and put on scrubs: shirt, pants, hat, mask, and booties. You do not have to scrub your hands. Once in the room, do not touch anything that is sterile, and that includes: surgeons, scrub nurses, instruments, patients, surgical table, surgical light handles. If you accidentally touch something, make sure you tell the circulating nurse. It is better to get into trouble than to risk infecting the patient. DO NOT WASH THE CAMERA! Ask the surgeon what shots are needed, how many are needed, and what field of view. If you shoot a close-up, also shoot a backed-off shot for orientation. If the field is bloody, ask the surgeon if he or she would like it cleaned up. It will make the photos look better for lectures and publications.

Max rushed into the OR staff room and found an empty locker. He went to a shelf of clean, folded surgical garments and grabbed a pair of pants and a scrub shirt labeled "medium." He sat on a bench, removed his clothes, threw them into an empty locker, and shut the door. He tucked in his scrub shirt and tied together the drawstrings of the scrub pants. Next he slipped on the surgical hood and fastened the strings of his face mask over the hood. As he bent over to snap on the disposable, anti-static booties that covered his street shoes, sweat dripped down one of his legs, looking like dark drops of blood.

Check the Nikon. Make sure the Kodachrome's sprocket holes are caught on the pins of the take-up spool. The film advanced twice, the counter showing "1" through the tiny window. *Motor drive's working fine. Turn on the flash unit. Hope the batteries are juiced up. Pull out*

some extras from the bag and put them in the back pocket, just in case.
The flash went off in his face. *Sucker's loaded all right.* Everything
in the room lost its color and went blind-white. He blinked at
ghostlike negative images floating in circles before him. Lockers.
Fluorescent lights. Wooden benches. Soiled towels. Max backed
up until his legs touched the bench. He smacked the flash unit for
misfiring and sat down, closing his eyes.

He had been at the library studying a clinical photography
journal when the call came. On a nearby wall hung a large artwork
showing the vast network of organs, muscles, and veins of the proverbial medical-illustrated man, who seemed to be looking down
on Max. Suddenly, while he was looking at a photo composite on
lighting techniques for facial abnormalities, his beeper vibrated
across the table. He slammed his hand over the beeper before it
fell on the floor. Doctors at nearby tables looked up at him. The
only ones not looking were those wearing headphones seated at
carrels watching medical videos. He felt blood rush through his
face.

Collecting his books and papers, Max had dashed for the library
exit only to be stopped cold by a locked turnstile. He handed the
journal over to the desk clerk, who tripped a switch to let him
through. He ran to his workplace to find the door with the department's nameplate on it—PATHOLOGY PHOTOGRAPHY—locked.
The secretary had taped a handwritten note to the door that said,
"Max, take OR call—it's an open heart case. Other photographers
tied up. Am on lunch break now. Good luck, Audrey."

All of the lights in the lab were off. No one was in the darkrooms. He quickly threw some camera equipment into a bag,
fumbling films and lenses onto the floor in the process. Before he
left, he snatched a couple of paper towels from the wall dispenser
and wiped the sweat off his brow. He crumpled the paper and in
basketball form shot it into the wastebasket, thereby gaining a
little confidence.

In the elevator lobby, he'd paced the perimeter of the room,
waiting for a car. When one of the elevators opened, Max saw that

it was empty and walked into it. He pressed the button for the fourth floor. The doors closed and the "up" arrow light went on. The car started to move. He closed his eyes and rubbed his face. Then the car stopped, but the doors didn't open. Max looked up and saw that he was on the second floor. An arm reached over his shoulder and pressed the fifth-floor button. He jerked around to find that the elevator had opened a set of rear doors, allowing a group of doctors and nurses to file in. He swallowed hard. *Why do I keep forgetting about that rear door?*

Now, when the aftereffects of the flash cleared from his vision, Max stood up to check his reflection in the full-length mirror to make sure everything looked to be in place. He saw himself as a tense, green alien being with white fluorescent tubes coming out of his head. It made him think of something that his junior high school teacher once wrote in his yearbook. "Emulate the turtle— to go places, you must stick out your neck." The teacher's name was Mr. Light.

Rings of perspiration formed at his armpits. His stomach churned and his scrotum shriveled, one controlling the other. *Relax, boy. Deep breaths. You're acting like you're about to undergo brain surgery.*

He walked out of the locker room and into a vestibule with double doors. A faded sign on the door warned him, "Surgical attire must be worn beyond this point!" *No shit, what do you think I'm wearing, my birthday suit?* He waved his hand past the electric eye's vision, and instantly the doors swung open. *Welcome to Wal-Mart! Where are the shopping carts?*

As he walked along the glistening, white-tiled corridor of operating suites he held fast to his camera and flash unit so that they wouldn't sway and bang against things. He imagined how weird it must be for the patients, drugged, lying face up, slowly rolling through the hall with each row of ceiling lights ticking down time till the first incision.

Several OR technicians turned the corner, one carting a portable X-ray machine. *Excuse me, sir, is there a sale on the X-ray machines today?* One of the technicians pushed open the door to the patient-holding room, lined with beds and IV infusion pumps attached to wax-like figures. *Damn! Wish I had time to have that pre-op discussion with the surgeons in no. 3. They're not gonna know about the set of hand signals and gestures I've developed. Gotta convince them I take pictures just as well as anyone in my profession, sometimes better!*

Someone from behind nudged Max out of the way, signaling for him to stay off to the side. She pulled a gurney with a motionless figure on it into an operating room. After standing with his back against the wall, recovering from the surprise, Max moved on to the window of the central OR nurse station and held up his camera equipment for the desk clerk to see. She flipped through a log, found the room number, and showed three fingers up to the glass. *Gotta be sure it's the right room . . . so easy to get numbers mixed up around here.* He gestured "OK" and continued down the corridor.

At the first set of operating suites, he noticed white surgical tape with handwritten labels slapped on each door.

OR no. 1: APPENDECTOMY. *There's Dr. Thompson . . . I remember taking photos for him. He's pretty cool; gestures a lot when he talks. He's doing a very simple operation to shoot. Small working area, easy to get to, crank the lens all the way out, focus one-to-one at f /16. Bam, bam, bam. No sweat. I'm outta here. Will send you the slides, Doc. Thumbs-up!* A nurse opened the door and dropped a bundle of green sheets, splotched with a burnt sienna color, on the floor to be picked up and laundered for the umpteenth time.

OR no. 2: DOUBLE-BARREL COLOSTOMY. *Well, let's take a peek through the window to see if, by chance, they're rebuilding the double-barrel carburetor of a Chevy, heh heh!* The camera slipped out of his hands and knocked against the door. Immediately the OR crew inside stopped and looked in his direction. *Duck! And keep walking! Geez, this feels like a Groucho Marx walk.* A surgeon scrubbing up at a nearby wash station glared down at Max. Brown antibacterial soap lathered down his arms and dripped onto the floor.

Max straightened up and nodded as if he were passing someone he knew on the street.

OR no. 3: CORONARY BYPASS. His stomach gurgled. *Breathe, boy . . . either you walk in and suffer the consequences, or the department gets a bad reputation for not sending in a photographer . . . exhale . . . inhale.* Paper fibers from his face mask stuck to his tongue.

When he walked in, cold air reeking of antibacterial disinfectant hit him. He stifled the urge to pull down his mask to spit out the fiber. The Simplex clock on the wall indicated 10:29. *Time's not so simple.* A team of three cardiac surgeons, an anesthesiologist, a scrub nurse, and a circulating nurse huddled around the coronary-stricken patient. Another person on the sidelines sat on a stool adjusting a complicated contraption of dials, switches, wires, and plastic tubing—the heart-lung machine.

No one looked back at him. It reminded him of his twelve years in public schools, living in a shell. Nothing he had said or done had ever really interested anyone. It had only made him shyer, and easily intimidated—to the point where he'd stopped talking. Kids made fun of his hearing aids—the type that looked like a Walkman with two wires connected to earplugs, all held up with a bra-like strap. If he were to wear them today, he would probably be in vogue, since a lot of people wore Walkmans with all sorts of wires, headphones, and earplugs.

"Hey Stereo, what's the score of the World Series? Ha ha ha ha! . . . We have a—baaahhhhhrnmmm! Attention! This is a test of your emergency broadcast station . . . Knock knock, hello? Hello? Anyone in there? . . . What planet are you from? Ha ha ha!"

"OK, Mr. Popular Jock Strap—nice perfect white teeth you have . . . WHACK! Oooh, that was a good backhand, Max! Awww, now Mr. Jock Strap's on the ground crying with ugly red teeth."

[Deep breath.]

Two of the surgeons had blood splatters on their sterile green frocks . . . *praying mantises with swollen mandibles chewing on their prey. Or is it* preying *mantises?* The chief surgeon's caterpillar eyebrows backed away from each other, jumping an inch when there was a change in the procedure. Max couldn't tell if the doctors were telling him to get ready, discussing the faulty coronary artery, or shooting the breeze about the weekend. *Snap out of it! Warm up the flash unit. Attach the sync cords to the camera body.* His hands became sweaty. The muscles in his fingers twitched involuntarily. Simplex said 10:45. *Keep breathing, dude.*

The circulating nurse left the huddle. She looked over at him, appeared to be chewing on something . . . *Is she chewing gum? Is she saying "How are you?" Or is she asking, "What's that you have there?"* He smiled and nodded in the hope that the gesture would satisfy her questions, if they were questions. *Did she see me smile? You turkey! C'mon, you have a mask on.* He wanted to say something but was afraid of getting into a conversation he could neither continue nor understand. *Maybe I should just wave? Nah, that's absurd . . .*

The nurse shrugged, turned around, and filled the gap she'd left in the huddle. The heart-lung specialist eyeballed Max.

Max looked under the surgical table at the drops of dried blood and disposable plastic wraps from syringes and surgical whatnots. A bottle sat on the floor collecting fluids being siphoned from the top of the table. And amid all this were the feet. A pair of Nike high-tops tapped to some musical beat; the sides of the shoes hung loose and their big tongues stuck out—*"Hey, man, did you catch the Dead concert last weekend?"* Another pair of feet, in Docksiders, scratched a leg.

"No, I went down to the shore. Damn mosquitoes sucked all the blood outta me."

A third pair of feet, in wooden clogs, stretched themselves up and down.

"You know, I read in National Health Magazine *that if you do this every day for fifteen minutes, it'll build up your calf muscles. You won't get so tired standing all day."*

Max walked around to get a better glimpse of the patient. Hands and tools were busy going in and out of the chest cavity, which had been racked open. He could see the rib cage and part

of the heart where they were cutting away the pericardial sac. One of the surgeons, holding an electric wand—a cauterizer—burned the ends of blood vessels to stanch the bleeding.

Max moved around to the anesthesiologist's station behind a sterile cloth barricade and watched the rhythmic LED readout of the EKG. Fresh blood and fluids dripped from hanging plastic bags. The anesthesiologist took a blood pressure reading from the patient's arm, and then, with a syringe, injected a drug into the IV line. The doctor adjusted the flow from the bag of donated blood. He checked the patient's eyes with a penlight for proper dilation. Having seen enough, Max walked away and found a stool by the wall. He sat and waited, idly looking at the clock: 11:15. He started toying with the drawstrings on his pants, then the dials on his camera. Working a finger under his face mask, he tried to dislodge something from his nose. The flash accidentally went off, just as it had in the locker room. Everyone looked at him. Immediately Max pretended to work on the flash unit, shaking his head as if something were wrong with it. Once he felt that all eyes were off him again, he looked up and rubbed the cold out of his hands. Finally getting the sense that they were just not quite ready for him, he took the camera and strap from around his neck and rested it on a small table next to him. He leaned back and stared at the wall: 11:30. All of the colors in the operating room turned gray under the fluorescent lights.

Colors . . . Max remembered that when he'd been three years old, he'd played with Tinker Toys, putting colored pegs into pieces of wood that had holes drilled into them. He made buildings, animals, and machines into all sorts of odd configurations. One day he'd gotten bored with his construction work. He'd plucked out one of the pegs and looked up at his father's ten-gallon aquarium, which contained tropical fish. He wanted them to come out and play, so he held the peg like a knife and shattered the glass. All kinds of wonderful colors came out—blues, reds, blacks, and greens—doing flips on the carpet, all having a fantastic time. Wheeee! He had never seen fish as excited in the aquarium as they were outside of it. Finally, he had figured out a way for them to come out and play. Unfortunately, they could only play for one afternoon, and then he never saw them again.

The clock read 11:47. The huddle broke. Excess fluid was siphoned out of the chest cavity. The area around it got wiped up and the bloodied towels were replaced with sterile ones. A stool was pulled up to the operating table . . . *ah, there's the cue.*

A surgeon beckoned slightly with one of his bloody appendages for Max to come over. Max's stomach tightened. *Camera! Flash unit! Sync cord! Be careful the equipment doesn't tumble onto anything sterile.* The surgical team watched with laser-sharp stares. *The swivel stool! Get up on it. Wait wait wait! It's unsteady. Get back down.* He twirled the seat all the way down until it locked tight. *Now get up and focus that damn camera.*

Under the hot OR lamp, his neck broke out in sweat. He looked around to make sure nothing of his had come into contact with the sterile field. With his index finger hovering over the shutter release button, Max held his breath. He saw the quiet heart way down in the bottom of the cavity, paying no heed to its surroundings. The hollow, muscular organ was not beating, because it was now being bypassed. *The praying mantis chews in big chomps and points at it. Oh my God! What kind of photographs does he want? Macro, normal, or wide-angle shot? Color or black-and-white? How many of each view? What region?* Max's own heart pounded hard against his rib cage. His right eye strayed from the viewfinder to the huddle.

He spurted out, "Doctor—I'm deaf! I have to lipread you and your mask is in the way. Please pull it down for a minute and tell me what kind of shots you need."

The chief surgeon responded with an angry, vigorous head jerk. He pointed again to the chest cavity. The heart—momentarily deaf to the world of green-draped aliens, piercing lights, and cold stainless steel—remained still.

The anesthesiologist left his station and came around to Max with a clipboard and pen. He gestured to Max to step down. Writing quickly, he interpreted for the doctor, "Who sent you here? Never mind—give me a shot of the entire heart and a close-up of the coronary artery. Two color slides of each view."

Max nodded and made mental exposure calculations. He climbed onto the stool again. *Focus. Expose. Advance. Bracket like hell—shoot a few stops over normal exposure and a few stops under. Shoot the entire roll for that matter. Insurance against Murphy's Law.*

The anesthesiologist held up the clipboard to Max. "That'll be all. Send the slides to Cardiology after they're processed."

As he stepped down, he could almost feel the hot stares on his back. He made a mental note to somehow thank the anesthesiologist. It was 11:57.

In the locker room he peeled off his wet scrubs and took a shower. *Were the pictures focused sharply enough? Were the exposures correct? Was the flash output bright enough? Man, I hope my credibility as a medical photographer isn't ruined just because I happen to be deaf. Gotta think of a foolproof way to prevent this from happening again.*

Max stepped out of the shower and put on his street clothes. After tying his shoelaces, he stood up and noticed a heart-shaped sticker with a smiling face stuck on the inside of his locker door. It was the sticker that the blood bank gave out to donors that said, "Smile! I gave blood today!" He closed the locker, gathered up the soiled scrub clothing from the floor and shot it into a laundry basket by the door. On his way out, Max slung the photo bag over his shoulder and began to smile.

March 4, 1982

Ducky's BBQ Joint

Howdy y'all!

Last Friday after work Zag, Joanie (nursing
student/friend of Zag's) and I went to this bar
near the hospital called the Recovery Room. It
so happened that there was some kind of quiche
cook-off going on. Surprisingly, a lot of men
were there eating quiche -- real men don't eat
quiche, do they? Ha! Well, we didn't bring any
but we sure perused the samples they were giving
out. They were all really good and tasty -- what
a way to get a free dinner!

Afterwards we all went to another bar, the Kon
Tiki, where we'd heard the Texas Entertainer
of the Year was going to perform. I envisioned
it would probably be some cowboy or redneck
telling jokes and stories while doing creative
things with a lariat or something. You know
what was going on? A drag queen contest. What a
sight! Of course there were a lot of gay people
around and stuff. It was really fun to watch.
For some of these people, it was a way of life.
My God -- I sometimes worry if some of the girls
I ask out are actually guys. The drag queens at
the bar really looked feminine and their facial
features, bodies, and movements were so much
like a female. Zag was flabbergasted. Joanie,
who's a little older than us, wasn't even fazed.
She's seen it all back in California where she's
from. As you know, Zag's from New York City. He
thought he'd seen it all himself and could tell
right off whether they were men or not. He still
refuses to believe that these "women" were men
underneath.

We learned that UTMB is one of the few hospitals in the country that performs sex-change operations. One of the photographers who regularly works in the clinical photo studio told us that he often has to photograph before-and-after shots of men becoming women. Well, that sort of explains why the Kon Tiki does such good business on the island.

When I was doing my rotation in the operating room, I had to photograph one rare case where a baby's outer genitals did not have the appearance of a boy or a girl. It's called "ambiguous genitalia." This baby had what looked like both sex organs. And you know what's weird? The surgeon had to make a decision on the table as to what gender to make the baby. In this case, the baby was "fixed" and made into a girl.

We're almost done with the portfolio phase of our certification. Our portfolios have to be well packed since they're going to be shipped five times around the U.S. to five different board examiners. Once we ship them off to the examiners, then it's on to prepping for the orals.

What a day! Time to call it quits. Enjoyed your last letter imexxx immensely -- keep 'em coming.

Tons of love,

Max

P.S. Sorry about the brown smudges all over the letter. Such good Texas barbecue sandwiches here.

LeRoy Colombo's View

Witnesses You should obtain written authorization before photographing patients for medical education, teaching, or publicity. The patient, or his/her legal representative, should sign and date the authorization form. Anyone besides the patient who has legal authority to sign should identify his/her relationship to the patient. The signature must be witnessed, and the witness's signature must be included on the authorization form. The signed authorization form must be filed with the patient's health record.

If you're a male, whenever you shoot a picture of a female clinical patient who must disrobe, you must have another female in the room as a witness. This is for your protection. Do not use a staff member from Transportation or Housekeeping. For cases involving suspected child or domestic abuse, be sure to call in a witness as well.

In late February Max received a fancy party invitation in his box at the photo lab. The Old English lettering was printed on ivory-colored card stock along with handwritten notations:

To the biomedical photographers of the
University of Texas Medical Branch:
You are cordially invited to the grand re-opening
of the Tremont House Hotel on the Strand.
We will celebrate Mardi Gras style
with a masquerade ball
Tuesday, March 6, 1982
4–6 p.m.
Please come and take photos at our event.

135

All submitted photos will be reviewed
for a booklet on the historic Tremont House.
Selected photos will receive cash prizes and book credit.
Please show UTMB identification to doorman.

The hotel was in the old financial district of downtown Galveston, along the bay, known as the Strand—the "Wall Street of the West." Thinking he would have no time for the party, Max almost threw the invitation away when an idea came to him. For his Registered Biological Photographer portfolio, one elective assignment was left open to the applicant to decide about, as long as the process and results were somehow related to biophotography and to the photographer's current workplace. He had been working on his portfolio in preparation for getting his certification, experimenting with black-and-white infrared photography, on foliage and people. Subjects must emit heat for results to come out well on film. When taken with a special red or black filter, the images turned out grainy, dreamlike, and sometimes even lurid in appearance. The green in trees and grass turned white, and the sky was often black. Human skin appeared soft and milky white.

Max had the idea of photographing portraits of the people at the party in their Mardi Gras outfits and masks, except that he would not ask them to sit and pose. Instead, he would rove around and catch them on the fly using his flash unit with a black filter over the strobe light. That way, the hidden flash would not distract people or make them self-conscious, as sometimes occurred when they sat for portraits. Model releases and witnesses wouldn't be necessary, as with masks on everyone would be unrecognizable. All of this, he thought, would satisfy his elective requirement—the use of special film (black-and-white infrared film) often employed in biophotography and in a setting involving medical personnel (a bit of a stretch, but UTMB employees were invited). The potential cash winnings also got Max's juices going.

Max knocked on the darkroom door to summon Zag, who came out squinting from the bright lights in the hallway. He read the invitation and told Max he wasn't interested. Zag had been working on printing up a critical series of photomicrographs for a very demanding pathologist, yet he was over-accommodating the doctor because he wanted to mooch copies of the photos to satisfy one of his own portfolio electives. Max had hoped Zag would come along to help with the communication in a noisy environment and to share the burden of carrying around the photo equipment.

During his lunch break, Max took off for the Strand to locate the Tremont House. He walked along Avenue B with its rows of nineteenth-century Victorian buildings, and easily found the grand hotel off Ship Mechanics Row. It occupied the entire block. He could see that a lot of money was riding on the renovations. On his way back to the hospital, Max stopped by the fish-tackle factory where Reynaldo worked part-time. When Max walked in, he saw Reynaldo on the lower level pulling out a large ladle from the kiln and pouring lead into molds to make fishing sinkers. He wore asbestos gloves and a disposable paper mask over his nose and mouth. Max waved to him. Reynaldo gestured for him to wait. Max went over to Junior, Reynaldo's boss, who was sitting at his desk pecking away on a calculator.

"Hey, Junior. How're things?" said Max.

"Howdy, Max! Same old, same old. Reynaldo is down there working the molds."

"Yeah, we saw each other already. How's life in the tackle business?"

"It's sinking."

"That bad?"

"A joke! Our business is making fishing weights that sink, get it?" He scratched his forearm, which had the classic Popeye tattoo of a boat anchor.

"Ah, you got me," Max said, rolling his eyes.

"Thought you was a college boy."

"Eh, sometimes. Other days I'm a high school dropout."

Junior laughed and took a cigar out of his desk drawer. He offered one to Max, who declined. After biting off the tip and spitting it on the floor, Junior one-handedly flipped open his Zippo lighter and rolled the flint wheel to light his cigar.

"Speakin' of dropouts, I need your help translatin' sump'n to Rey for me," said Junior, after a succession of quick puffs to get a good burn going.

"Sure, glad to help, as always," said Max. To himself he said, "I'll bail Rey out once again, as always." Last time he'd done so was a few weeks earlier in the hospital. Dotty, the hospital's Affirmative Actions rep, had called the Pathology Photography Department asking for Max. She'd wanted him to meet her right away in Urology. On the way there, Max had racked his brain trying to come up with a possible reason why she would want to meet him in an area that dealt with human genitals. Upon entering the doors to the department, Max instantly had his answer. Standing next to Dotty with a big smile on his face was Reynaldo. Dotty asked Max to please help interpret in sign language between the doctor and the patient. Somehow Reynaldo had gotten in to see a doctor about a problem he was having. Dotty, clueless that the two men knew each other, thanked Max and left them to sit in the waiting room.

"Did you just walk in here and ask to see a doctor?" Max asked. His signs were firm but under control so as not to attract too much attention.

"Yeah, why not? Doctor here, what for? Help people, right?" said Reynaldo.

"Calm down, no need to make a big scene."

"Me not. My normal talk," said Reynaldo. "Doctor for-for? Help people, right?"

"Yes, but you have to make an appointment. And, you need to have insurance," said Max.

"Me poor. Hospital take-care poor people. Me here before for bad cut—need sewing. Twenty thread sew. Free!" Reynaldo pulled up one of his pant legs to show a scar on his shin.

Max could see that people in the waiting room were staring at them; so much for signing quietly.

"But you can't barge in here in front of these other people," said Max. "They have appointments. Is this an emergen—?"

Reynaldo pointed to a nurse. She came forward and beckoned them into an examination room.

Soon after they sat down, Max was about to ask Reynaldo why he'd chosen this medical department to fix whatever problem he had when an Asian urologist walked in. Max explained that both of them were deaf and that he was here to help interpret for Reynaldo, who couldn't speak for himself.

"OK, what's the pwoblem?" asked the urologist. Max relayed the question to Reynaldo.

Oh boy, thought Max, *here comes another foreign accent lipreading challenge*. The last big challenge he'd faced had been with an RIT photo professor from Sicily, who'd said things like: "Dot photohgroff eez a leetle too moch cun-trahst—it hos too moch bleck-n-white. Nah-thing glllay in beetween—ya need glllay for bah-lunce in dee cumposeetion. Udder-vise, eet loook ahmateur."

"I don't know yet. He hasn't told me," said Max.

"Problem what? Dick," said Reynaldo, pointing to the specific area in case the doctor might not know where the penis was located.

"Aha, and what is the pwoblem with the penis?"

"Dick hurts," said Reynaldo.

"OK, dwop your pants," said the doctor. Max was shocked at how big Rey's member was. He couldn't reconcile the large size with Rey's small stature, or with the fact that he was poor and illiterate. In a strange way, it made Max feel inferior.

"What kind of hurt?" asked the doctor. "Stinging when uwinating? Ache in the scwotum? What?"

Reynaldo said white fluid was oozing out of his penis.

"Aha—sooo, a dischahge. Can you show me this dischahge?" said the doctor, holding his hands out in a questioning gesture. Max signed "discharge" as in seepage; a leak.

Reynaldo nodded his head and gestured, "Wait a minute." He began to stroke himself, a grimace forming on his face. After a long, agonizing minute, the doctor finally realized what Reynaldo was doing.

"No, no, no—I am not asking him to mahstubate," said the doctor to Max, showing an odd gesture that Max assumed was probably his personal technique. Max told Reynaldo to stop jerking off. He tried to rephrase the doctor's question about a discharge, thinking how best to put this visually without involving masturbatory gestures. Finally, Max's interpretation of the doctor's question into ASL brought about a diagnosis and a remedy. Reynaldo had a common urinary tract infection and was sent home with some antibiotics.

Reynaldo was scratching his groin as he walked up the iron spiral staircase to the first floor of the factory, where Max was chatting with his boss.

"Hot work?" said Max, wondering if Reynaldo's urinary infection was still bothering him.

"Not bad. Me used to hot—before live Mexico, remember?" said Reynaldo. "What's up?"

"Want to talk to you about a part-time job idea I have for you," said Max, signing without voicing. "But first your boss wants to say something to you. He asked me to help interpret." He motioned to Junior to go ahead. Junior stood up, cigar in mouth.

"Rey, Ixoiurysosgbwrmxysfhhs—"

"Junior, I'm sorry to interrupt, but I can't read your lips. The cigar—it's in the way," said Max.

"Oh, stupid-ass me." He rested his cigar on a ceramic fish ashtray on his desk.

"Rey—I just wanna say I really like the work you do for me *when* yer here. You work hard and gimme a hunnert percent . . ." Junior began.

Max tried to give the sign for *when* in a big way to carry over Junior's emphasis on the word.

". . . but," continued Junior, "ya gotta show up on time, man . . . on the days that you 'n I agreed on. Ya can't just not show up when ya feel like it, or stroll in two hours late to start yer work."

Max fumbled over translating the double negative of "can't just not," taking time to rephrase the concept in more concrete terms. Junior took back his cigar and pursed his lips, letting out a thin, steady stream of smoke to underscore his remarks.

"Some days me can't come—problems with ex-wife or my boy. How me call you?" Max voiced what Reynaldo had signed.

Junior took his cigar out of his mouth and used it like a pointer, "Not—my—problem!" Ashes fell to the ground. "Ya gotta find a way to lemme know. I don't care if ya need to miss a day or show up late, but I gotta know so I can make other arrangements, ya know what I'm sayin'?"

"How me let you know?" repeated Reynaldo. "Me deaf and don't have phone."

"I know that, I know, but figger out a way to lemme know. Stop by the factory aforehand to lemme know or git a hearing neighbor or friend to call me. Hell, find a carrier pigeon to send me a note. But, ya gotta lemme know—bottom line."

Reynaldo gave Max a quizzical look about the carrier pigeon. Max signed to Reynaldo, "Forget the bird, I'll explain later. Show up on time or let Junior know somehow. Just say you will. You don't want to lose your job."

Reynaldo nodded his consent to Junior. He held up his hand and crossed his heart with the other hand to show that he promised to do that from now on. Junior held out his hand for a gentlemen's shake. Rey shook it and then gave Junior his classic bear hug.

Max asked if he could have five minutes to talk with Reynaldo. Junior gestured with the cigar to go ahead.

"Next Tuesday, I'm going to a really fancy party to take pictures for my work. Right up the street from here at that big hotel— Tremont, you know it?" asked Max.

"Yeah, white horse carriage in front," said Reynaldo.

"Right, that's the one. I want you to be my assistant. Carry my equipment and hand things to me quickly when I need them. Help me for two hours. I'll pay you twenty bucks."

Reynaldo eagerly agreed. Max told him the time and date, and where to meet.

"Oh, one more thing," said Max. "You need to dress up."

"Not have nice clothes same you," said Reynaldo.

"Tell you what. I'll come by to pick you up at your place with some of my clothes that I think will fit you."

"Me not live there anymore."

"You're not at your apartment anymore?"

Reynaldo shook his head and scratched his groin again.

"What happened?" asked Max.

"L-L kick me out. No money pay."

"Aw shit, your landlord evicted you? Where are you staying now?"

"My car," said Reynaldo.

On Tuesday, the afternoon of the Mardi Gras soiree, Max drove along the seawall to meet Reynaldo in his Gran Torino, which was parked by the Gulf of Mexico near 53rd Street. Reynaldo said that he liked to park on the seawall there because of the IHOP restaurant nearby, where he could go to the bathroom, wash up, and get a cheap pancake breakfast with coffee. Max handed him a pair of khakis that were getting too small for him and a light blue oxford shirt. Reynaldo took the clothes and crossed Seawall Boulevard to change in IHOP's bathroom.

Max got out of his car to get some fresh air. He watched a couple of surfers riding the waves, and happened to notice a block of concrete on the seawall. A plaque bolted to the block read:

In Memory of LeRoy Colombo
December 23, 1905–July 12, 1974
A "Deaf-Mute" who risked his own life repeatedly to save
more than a thousand lives from drowning in the waters
surrounding Galveston Island.

Max felt a chill run along his arms. He had never heard of this heroic deaf man from Galveston. Scanning the breaking surf up

and down the beach, Max imagined how hard it must've been for Colombo to visually detect drowning victims. When Reynaldo returned, Max pointed excitedly to the plaque. Reynaldo shrugged.

"Rock, special?" he said.

"This says a deaf lifeguard saved over a thousand people from drowning in the Gulf," said Max.

"Deaf, really? In Galveston? Man where?"

"He's dead now. Died in 1974. I didn't know Galveston had a famous deaf person," said Max. "Makes me feel proud!"

"Why rock? Should big lifeguard statue." Reynaldo put his hands on his hips and struck a heroic pose looking out over the water. "Man buried under rock?"

"No, it's just a memorial plaque," said Max. "Let's go, I don't want to be late."

Reynaldo put his foot on top of the memorial block to tie his shoe. The surfers were getting out of the water and peeling off their wetsuits. A couple on roller skates wheeled by, holding hands. Max made a mental note to look up Colombo in the local library one day. Reynaldo straightened up and indicated he was ready.

"Here, put this on," Max said, handing Reynaldo a white lab coat. "I think that's your size."

"Wow! Me feel like doctor," said Reynaldo.

Max got into his LTD while Reynaldo climbed into his current home. Both drove along the seawall heading east toward the Tremont House.

Max clipped on his UTMB ID card. He had made a fake one in the lab for Reynaldo. It was easy to do, what with all the copy apparatuses around and the darkrooms. Under Reynaldo's name, Max had printed the title: "Medical Photography Assistant." He told Reynaldo he wanted the ID card and lab coat back after the job was done. Knowing Reynaldo, he would abuse this privilege around the hospital, leading to all sorts of trouble—for both of them.

Before they went into the hotel, Max explained that he wanted Reynaldo to carry his camera bag with infrared loaded Nikon camera bodies and individual lenses of various focal lengths. When he ran out of film, Reynaldo was to hand him a camera body and put away the one Max gave him. If Max needed a specific lens, he would sign 28, 55, or 105, and Reynaldo would take out the specific millimeter lens that Max was requesting. One last piece of instruction—both were to play "deaf," meaning that Max was not going to use his voice at all with anyone at the party. It would be impossible to understand anyone wearing a mask. If a situation arose where someone wanted to talk to them, they were going to use the power of gestures. In essence, they were going to be mimes—perfect for a Mardi Gras celebration.

With his black-filtered flash unit mounted on a bracket connected to his Nikon, Max, with Reynaldo in tow, began to mingle among the masked partygoers, snapping random shots of costumed individuals and couples he thought looked interesting. Only one other photographer had shown up for the evening—Bimbo, who had a fixed portrait setup in one corner of the hotel ballroom, with a painted backdrop of palm trees and the ocean with a full moon shining on it. Two big strobe lights with reflective umbrellas were set on stands at 45-degree angles facing the

background. A camera on a tripod stood in the middle, between the two lights. Bimbo was chatting people up, trying to convince them to get their pictures taken in front of his cheesy, clichéd set, which had nothing to do with Mardi Gras.

Meanwhile, Max and Reynaldo, a pair of circus clowns, were having fun gesturing to people, putting them at their ease so they'd show off their costumes and masks for pictures. Max went through four rolls of thirty-six-exposure film. He told Reynaldo they were done, and that he could help himself to food and drinks. Max watched Rey head straight for the food table, where he stuffed rolls into his pockets, making it look like he was wearing bulky clown pants. Bimbo had deserted his photo setup; he was dancing in the ballroom with a lady who looked like a peacock.

Max picked up a flute of champagne and leaned against the bar, taking in the moving montage of revelers, feathers, and colors. He thought of LeRoy Colombo and imagined what LeRoy might do if he were alive, at his age, in a place like this . . .

What was waiting in the library for Max to discover was that Colombo probably wouldn't have been caught dead at a Mardi Gras party. A loner who didn't socialize much, he liked to patrol the beach between 50th and 60th streets. Stricken by meningitis at age six, Colombo had become deaf and paralyzed in the legs, spurring him to a lifetime of swimming, beginning at the Texas School for the Deaf's indoor swimming pool, where he regained enough strength in his legs to walk again, to build up his body and stamina. He was poor and was hardly treated as a hero at the time. A dog owner gave him twenty-five dollars for rescuing her poodle from drowning; an elderly woman gave him thirty dollars to retrieve her false teeth from the surf; a father gave him a couple of cans of beer for saving his two daughters from drowning; bystanders took up a meager collection of a dollar after witnessing him rescue a newsboy. He was always alert for anyone who needed rescuing, whether they were grateful afterward or not. Colombo couldn't yell, so he would blow on his whistle and pound his chest to get the attention of swimmers who wandered too far out in the water. He once swam out to the shrimp boats in Galveston Bay and picked up ten pounds of shrimp. He backstroked to the shore with the shrimp on his chest. One of the first to ride surfboards at Galveston beaches, he'd taught surfing to Dorian "Doc" Paskowitz, who'd gone on to become one of the most famous surfers in the world. Colombo had retired at age sixty-two because of a heart condition, yet continued to swim every day, practically until the day he died.

After downing his champagne and setting the glass on the bar, Max picked up his camera equipment and went over to Reynaldo, whose mouth was full of meatballs. Max took Rey's lab coat and badge, and told him he was leaving. He needed to get back to the lab to process his film for his portfolio. He gave Rey a twenty-dollar bill and a slap on the back. Reynaldo asked if he could stay longer. Max said it was up to him, and that he was on his own to float among this vast sea of hearing people.

April 2, 1982
Saturday, Carl's Lazy Bend Lounge
Dear Daddy-O & Mumsie:

Sorry to take so long in writing back. All's okay here. Just keeping nose to the grindstone with my oral exam preparation. Yep -- you read it right. That means I passed the portfolio portion!! WOOO-WOOO!! Would've called last Friday with the news but our phone has been out of order.

My evaluators rated my portfolio with a number score, which fell in the B grade category. I'm not too bothered by that. It was done under such a huge time crunch, and some of the required portfolio assignments were stuff I had never done before or learned at school -- like "demonstrate a comparison of infrared or ultraviolet differentiation versus conventional techniques of the same subject; e.g., chlorophyll distribution, blood oxygenation, or document alteration." So -- a lot of new, on-the-spot learning while actually doing the requirements to make them look like I knew what I was doing. An A would've been nice, but as long as I passed, I get invited to the orals -- the final part of the certification process.

Hey, guess what? A photo of mine on the historic Tremont House in Galveston got picked for publication. I'll be getting photo credit plus fifty bucks. Notta bad, huh?

I'm writing at a picnic table from one of my favorite places on the island near 10 Mile Road -- only a couple miles from our beach house. Near the entrance a sign reads: "Turkey shoot, every Thursday." Next to me, providing a huge

umbrella of shade, are three oak trees, one
with a tire swing. On the lawn is a homemade
horseshoe-pitching court with rusty horseshoes
in the sand pits. Not too far from that is a
wooden seesaw. A real Norman Rockwell country
setting. This old man named Carl runs a bar out
of his home. You go in there and it looks like a
big family room with leather sofas, armchairs,
dining table, lamps, a bear rug, mounted
alligator heads, Civil War rifles on the wall,
paintings of cowboys and Western landscapes,
a wet bar, a pool table, a dartboard, and some
pinball machines. Can't get any more Southern
than this. His menu was handwritten on a piece
of lined loose-leaf paper. I ordered a barbecue
sandwich and a beer. While waiting for my order,
I saw a whiskey barrel in the corner of the
room. The top was open but covered with chicken
wire. Light was coming up from the inside. A
little sign said: "Warning, Baby Rattler."
I carefully peered into the barrel and saw a
bare bulb, a tuft of grass on the bottom, and,
resting on the grass, a blue rattle toy for
babies.

By the way, did I tell you about our quick
weekend getaway last month? Zag and I just had
to get out of town to decompress from all of
the stress with prepping our portfolios. We had
heard that there was a huge rattlesnake roundup,
an annual event in Sweetwater that brought in
snake handlers from various parts of the state.
There were pits full of rattlers. They'd been
drained of venom by hooking their fangs on the
side of a vial for medicinal purposes, then
their heads got chopped off, slit, and skinned,

and the meat -- still writhing, headless, gutless, and skinless -- was fried for hungry customers to snack on. A group of experts put on a show including tricks like how to get out of a sleeping bag packed with snakes, and how to use a snakebite kit. They said that 30% of rattler bites don't contain venom, 40% contain only a little, and 30% are downright poisonous. Snakes eat once or twice a year and can survive two years without food. Each time they eat, they shed their skin and add a rattle. I'm glad we went to the roundup after we arrived and camped out the night before, otherwise I would have been awake and paranoid all night imagining rattlesnakes slithering under my tent.

Anyhow, Carl had a Crock-Pot on the bar from which he spooned out his barbecued beef to make my sandwich. Then he took out an iced mug from an old Coca-Cola cooler, drew my beer from a tap, and brought me a scrumptious lunch that made me feel that life is good.

Had an unusual experience yesterday afternoon. Our lab received a call to photograph an armadillo race that the Pathology Department was hosting. Since I was the only available photographer in the lab at the time, I went. Outside was a big banner hung between two trees: "7th Annual April Fool's Armadillo Dash." It was weird and fascinating to watch doctors, researchers, and med students race armadillos. Right outside the Pathology Building, a good-sized festival was underway. Boy, armadillos are slow, but fun creatures to watch. I wouldn't mind having one for a pet. If I get any good pics out of this assignment, I'll send you copies. I learned later why they used armadillos. One of the pathologists uses them to study leprosy. Apparently, armadillos are one of the few animals that can carry this disease, and they're rampant in this state. Racing lepers -- what fools, only in Texas!

Whole lotta love,
Max

Characters in El Paso

Medical Legal Photography   Clinical photographs are basically medical-legal records. However, when you receive instructions to take photographs for litigation, be aware that this requires a more specialized approach than taking clinical shots. Special considerations are: carefully documenting your client's instructions; making necessary preparations before doing the actual photography; the photography itself; and then the administration of the photographs. Since photographs are taken in support of court claims for compensation for personal injury or crimes, many of them can have a much greater impact—financially and psychologically—on the client than clinical photographs. Improper handling of these medical-legal procedures could be construed as professional negligence. DO NOT RETOUCH THE PHOTOS!

M ax's friend Lukas straddled a rusted swivel stool at the counter of the Happy Jalapeño, a local café almost within spitting distance of the Rio Grande. It was 7:30 in the morning, and the Mexican waitress kept coming back to give them a written report on their stock:

"We out of green salsa."

"Chorizo sausage comming this afternoon."

"Sorry, no more blue torteeyas today—only yello."

Lukas didn't utter a word, not even writing a response on the waitress's check pad. Instead he replied calmly, in his most eloquent use of American Sign Language, "You illiterate fry-face, I've come all this way from Tokyo for some Tex-Mex food, and now you've picked today to run out of it. Is an American running this place or what?" The smoke overhead from his cigarette created a sense of fuming anger.

The waitress wrote, "Sorry, I not know hand language."

Max reached over to take her pad and scribble, "Two break-fast burritos—lots of cumin and cilantro. Bring out a bottle of Tabasco." He turned to Lukas: "It'll be as close to Tex-Mex as they can get."

Lukas gestured to the waitress as she was about to turn toward the kitchen.

"Two coffees." He mimed holding a saucer and sipping from a cup.

"*Sí*, I know that one!" she said with a smile.

Professor Lukas Volmont was a tall, thin man with a voracious appetite that defied all natural laws of weight gain in a man of sixty-five. Language and literature had been his calling for fif-teen years at one of RIT's nine colleges: the National Techni-cal Institute for the Deaf, the country's only technical college for deaf and hard of hearing students, where he pushed them to rise above American Sign Language, their native language—but not leave it behind. He packed Chaucer, Shakespeare, and Chekhov into their isolated deaf-world brains. He couldn't care less if they never learned to speak a word of English, Spanish, or whatever. To survive in America, they had to be able to read and write in a language other than their own (which couldn't be written on paper anyway).

His favorite phrase was: "Read, read, till your eyes bleed." Read everything you see, anything you can get your hands on, even if you have no reading material with you—there is always something to read in English in your present environment. Read the writing on bathroom stalls, the contents label on the can of your drink, your candy wrapper, your cigarette packet, the subway advertise-ments, bus stop posters, even the tags on your underwear. If it contains letters in the English alphabet—read it!

Lukas had given up on his students a few years ago, realiz-ing that his efforts were fruitless except for the occasional at-tentive student like Max, who—so he liked to think—tried to absorb everything around him. Lukas also gave up on capitalistic, egocentric, audio-centric America, and told people that he'd "Deafected" to Japan—typical Lukas, fooling with language like that. Japan's beauty, economy of space and materials, and its Zen aesthetics had caused him to stay there. Oh, how the Japanese Deaf adored Lukas! How many non-Asian deaf people actually study Japanese? They implored him to stay on with their theater. Lukas spent his time nowadays as a professional actor and lecturer on tour, not in it merely for the acting and adulation, but for the education of the masses. Hearing people worldwide needed to see that deaf people lead normal lives, he believed, and that they could even be artists on the stage. He was quite proud of being the oldest working Deaf actor on earth.

Actually, he'd been invited by the Japanese Theater of the Deaf to go on an international tour with them as a guest artist performing the role of a white professor in their nonverbal visual adaptation of *Kaspar Hauser*. One of the tour stops happened to be at the University of Texas, El Paso, where Max was on a special three-week medical-legal photography rotation. Zag was doing his three-week rotation in ophthalmic photography at the University of Texas, Dallas.

Max had kept in touch with Lukas since taking his Great World Drama course his sophomore year. Lukas was one of the most intelligent deaf role models he had ever met. With no access to any deaf people in his line of work, Max put a premium on any time he could get with Luke. It didn't hurt that he hadn't had a visitor who was Deaf for about a month.

"Theater is the best teacher of life," was one of Lukas's oft-repeated proverbs. Max had his doubts, though. Lukas always wore thrift-store clothing, and ordered the cheapest fare on the menu. How come he'd never learned to prosper beyond used clothing and second-rate food?

"What are you reading these days?" Lukas signed.

"Not much, a Patricia Cornwell paperback here and there—but mostly technical manuals on biomedical photography."

"Ah, studying diseased-dead flesh."

"I'm killing myself in the photo lab working and preparing for my RBP fifteen hours a day. Not much time for pleasure reading."

With half-framed reading glasses worn near the edge of his hawk nose, Lukas glanced over some Japanese writings from a hardcover book propped up by a napkin dispenser. Several napkins were filled with doodlings of Japanese characters as he tried to memorize the precise strokes and structures of various ideograms. Japanese was his sixth language.

The waitress set down their coffees and scooped out a handful of cupped creamers from her apron pocket. She gestured to the coffee, as though Max didn't know what the creamers were for.

"Shame." Lukas put his pen down and looked at Max. "You're going to spend the rest of your life working inside darkrooms and morgues? Very macabre."

"Of course not," Max said. "I'll get to work in a medical school environment . . . that's pretty prestigious in itself. And, usually with the country's leading researchers and doctors. Like right now I'm working with the one of the nation's foremost forensic pathologists! He's like that TV doctor, 'Quincy, ME.' He removes bullets and foreign objects from bodies, and I take the close-up photos that help him with medical-legal cases in court. I get my photos published alongside his articles in pathology journals and textbooks. He really likes my work. Says I know how to make photographs really sharp, with just the right exposure and contrast—better than the other guys." Max decided not to mention that the pathologist worked in the morgue with Tubesock, a stinky pet ferret that mostly hung out on one of his shoulders.

Lukas nodded and pulled out a fresh napkin from the dispenser. The waitress brought their meal to the counter.

"Food," she gestured, hand to mouth, feeling a little more confident with them.

Lukas looked at Max and then at her. Max intercepted Lukas's raised hand, knowing he was about to sign something inappropriate.

Max gave her a "thumbs-up" approval, and she walked off with jubilant purpose in her step.

At a table behind Lukas sat an obese man smoking filterless cigarettes. His bulk covered most of his belt. The man repeatedly spat bits of tobacco from his yellowish-brown tongue. Several pieces got caught on his stomach, missing the floor. His greasy gray hair had a copper tint near where it parted on the left. Between sips of coffee and puffs of smoke, his face was pinched from hacking so hard.

"You know, Lukas, just down the street there, they even let me go into the OR to photograph operations," Max signed, hoping he might think this was more impressive. "Imagine them letting a deaf person in the sacred world of the OR?"

"Why wouldn't they? You're a very capable intern learning the tools of the trade."

"Yeah, but the communication issue. The doctors in the OR all wear masks and hats covering most of their faces. It's completely sterile in there—they can't remove their masks."

"So?" Lukas sketched some new Japanese strokes on the napkin. When he looked up, Max continued.

"How do you expect me to lipread them?"

"I don't. I expect you to write back and forth with them," signed Lukas.

"That's exactly what I do. I always bring a pad and paper with me into the OR. Sometimes even the OR nurses help with the written communication."

"Elementary," signed Lukas.

"What was that about elementary school?"

"I didn't say anything about school. I said 'e-l-e-m-e-n-t-a-r-y,'" Lukas fingerspelled, as if emphasizing the letters with the bold clarity of alphabet blocks.

At a nearby table, a young mother was trying to feed her son. The little boy twisted around in his high chair and babbled to the heavyset man. The mother coaxed the boy to eat a forkful of scrambled eggs. He opened his mouth, took what he could, but didn't turn toward her. Lumps of egg fell to the floor like pieces of an old yellow sponge. The boy reached out toward the man, stretching the limits of his high chair belt. He squealed. The man lit another cigarette and coughed. The boy laughed. When the man talked to him, only his gums and tongue showed. Not having any teeth seemed to make it easier for him to converse in the little boy's language. They could talk back and forth all day long—a conversation across the ages.

After eating his breakfast burrito, Lukas lit up another ciga-rette. He turned a page in his book and peeled a fresh napkin from the dispenser.

The man started to babble and hack constantly, not giving the kid a chance to interject. The conversation overlapped now, with neither listening to the other. The mother loaded up another fork-ful of eggs, this time lacing it with ketchup. Her son back-handed the fork. The man quickly turned his head in the direction of the blood-like splats he heard land on the floor.

Max finished his burrito and swiveled on the stool to directly face Lukas. Lukas looked sideways at him, putting down his felt pen. The pen bled black onto the napkin.

"Hey, who's your buddy over there?" Max said.

"Who?"

"That guy behind you."

Lukas swiveled around and saw the man.

"Oh, him."

Max was playing Lukas's game. Whenever they got together in restaurants, he'd ask Max things like, "Who's your new girl-friend?" thumbing at a homely woman eating alone at a table. Max would give a wan smile and say, "Yeah, yeah, go on back to your dressing room where you belong." Just to break the boredom of being on international theater tours, Lukas would go up to the woman and, in sign language, say, "He loooooooves you." No one would need an interpreter to translate what Lukas signed. Any idiot would understand the way Lukas simply pointed at Max, crossed both hands over his heart, showing the well-known sign for "love," and pointed at the woman. Most of the time, people were speechless at Lukas's behavior.

"Hey, Luke, why don't you go on over and talk literature with him?" Max said, pointing at the man.

"I'll need an interpreter." Lukas took a long drag on his cigarette, squinting to shield the smoke.

"Hell, you never need one when you write back and forth with pretty women in bars."

"He can't read." Lukas took off his glasses and slid them neatly into a leather-bound case with the poise of an actor being filmed up close, very aware of his screen presence and effect on an audience.

"Uh-huh! You're pretty sure of yourself, huh?"

"Yes, I know he can't," Lukas signed.

"C'mon, you've never met him! How do you know?"

Lukas stood up and combed his wiry gray hair back with his fingers. He counted out a handful of coins and left a small stack on the counter, collected his napkins, and slipped them into his book as a bookmark.

Lukas looked at Max and signed, "Elementary. Look at his eyes." He gave Max a hug and an unexpected peck on his forehead.

As he passed the man's table, Lukas pulled out one of his doodled napkins, left it on the table, and walked out of the restaurant.

Outside, looking in through the plate glass window, Lukas signed to Max, still at the counter, "I'll write you . . . maybe in Japanese." He winked. "Sayonara!"

Max went to the window to get Lukas's attention before he crossed Paisano Drive to walk along the river back to his hotel. Lukas raised his brows, as in, "What's up?" His rugged face matched the cragginess of the Franklin Mountains in the distance.

"Hey, Luke! You know where you are?"

He looked at Max with professorial condescension. He sighed. "The Pass of the North."

Max gave him a puzzled expression.

"In 1581. The first Europeans passed through here. Before that, Indians traveled by for millennia. Long before the Mexicans claimed it as theirs."

"You lost me," Max said.

"It's all right there in that pile of brochures by the door," he signed. "If you ever take the time to read."

"No, I meant, do you know the sign for this city?"

"El Paso," Lukas signed, his right L hand shape moving past his other hand, shaped in an O.

"Do you know why that's the sign for it?"

Lukas shook his head.

"L pass O—get it?" Max winked back. Lukas gave him an "OK" gesture of sarcastic approval. Watching him walk away with that long gait of his, smoke trailing behind, Max wondered how long it would be till their next meeting. How much longer would Lukas still be alive? Would Max still be in Texas? Would he get a medical photo job somewhere in the University of Texas system after his rotation was up? He hoped it would be in Galveston.

The heavyset man in the café sensed that something had been put in front of him. He felt around the table until his fingers discovered the shape and embossed texture of the napkin. His eyes looked up at the ceiling. They moved in rapid little circles trying to decode this familiar yet foreign object that Lukas had laid before him.

The mother and her son had left. Max picked up his tab and paid the waitress. She motioned for him to wait while she wrote something on her check pad. He checked his watch and looked out the window across the street at the towering exterior walls of the university, designed in Dzong style, a distinctive type of architecture popular with Buddhist temples in the Himalayas.

The waitress showed Max what she had written: "How you do good-by?"

Max waved his hand, as in the universal "Bye-bye."

She giggled and copied him. "Bye-bye."

As Max left, he noticed with a start that the man with gray eyes had no pupils. The man held the napkin up to his nose and sniffed both sides. He rubbed the napkin between his fingers, searching, unaware that the mystery was Professor Lukas Volmont's Japanese characters.

May 5, 1982

Hospital cafeteria
  Hola y'all -- Feliz Cinco de Mayo!
  Picking up a little Spanish here and there
on the island. Not bad for a deaf guy, huh?
I'm eating an enchilada with refried beans and
Mexican rice. Mmm, mmm pretty good for hospital
food. Feeling festive 'cuz Zag and I are
getting down to the homestretch. Preparations
are under way to get ready for our oral exam,
which will be during the national Biological
Photographers Association convention to be held
at University of California, San Diego. Two-
thirds done. Didn't think we would make it this
far. Professor Robb has been (finally!) helpful
with my oral paper. He's determined that it come
out scientific and professional. Robb said that
Zag and I started our papers as if they were to
be presented to a camera club. When he read our
rough drafts, he actually tore our papers apart
-- in front of some doctors in the lab. He was
showing off. He yelled at us to start thinking
scientifically, and not for some 10th grade
camera club BS. I'm getting a real education
here.
  My department accepted a new resident to work
in the black-and-white print darkroom. He's
Hispanic and his name's Orlando. Actually,
he's here a bit early to begin his residency
(for next year's RBP certification), but since
we're having a hard time keeping up with the
demand of cranking out black-and-white prints,
Dr. Robb hired him to help out. Zag & I have
been too consumed with orals preparation --

perhaps overly consumed. Can you blame us? Our
presentations have been scheduled in two weeks
on a Friday morning. GULP!

I've been showing Orlando the ropes some
since I'm very familiar with the inner workings
of the darkrooms. Turns out Orlando's from
Colorado Springs. Because of the deaf school
there, he's a little familiar with deaf people,
and sensitive about how to communicate with me.
That's a load off me. He's kinda quiet, but one
thing we found we had in common is that we both
like to go running. So now I have a running
partner . . . and another party-going partner.
He's single and on the prowl to meet women (like
yours truly). We've gone to a couple of frat
parties already and met a few people -- not much
luck with the girls yet. I'm surprised medical
schools have fraternities and sororities --
they party just as hard as the students I knew
at RIT.

Orlando & I run out on the beach about 4-5
times a week after work (Zag doesn't go with
us 'cuz he hates running; prefers laps in the
pool). After work, I go to the Field House to
get changed into my running shoes and shorts. I
walk across the street to one of the frat houses
(can't remember the name -- Phi Krappa Zappa?)
where Orlando rents a room. From there, we run
five blocks to the beach, hang a left at the
seawall on the Gulf, and then run to the very
end of East Beach -- which is about 2 ½ miles
-- and then back to the frat house. 5.2 miles in
all. Orlando could run farther if he wanted to,
but that's about my upper limit. Must be that
Colorado air that makes him seem as if he could

run forever. He's not arrogant about it though -- just stops when I've had enough.

Back at his frat house, there's a vending machine with all sorts of beers -- no sodas. He loves Coors Lite, so for a quarter we each get a cold one and plop down on the front lawn. That's our cool-down procedure.

I wrote a little poem for you about running on the beach.

> *Trans-portation*
> I run naked on the smooth
> hard-packed sand of the gulf
> yet far out over the water
> I also hover by a cloud
> above a catamaran
>
> Behind me the surf laps
> quietly over my run
> down below the beach stretches forever
> under my feet the grit of blackened sand
> blends into the brown
> while the little red windsock
> on the mast top tickles
> my stomach

Let me know what you think (I don't actually run naked, you know!).

How're things on the homefront? Please write!

Mucho amor!

Yours,
Max

The Seawall

24-Hour Call   When you are on call, you are responsible for keeping the hospital photographically covered twenty-four hours a day during the extent of your call. Make yourself accessible by phone and pager. If you are at a place where noise would drown out the beeper sounds, call the hospital to leave the phone number of your location. Stay within a thirty-mile radius of the hospital. You should not be intoxicated while on call. If you become ill, ask another photographer to cover for you. If you are unsure how to shoot a particular situation, check the manual. When at the hospital, always maintain a professional attitude and wear a white lab coat with your identification.

Reynaldo slowly sat up in the backseat of his Gran Torino, yawned, and then bunched his sleeping bag up over his brand-new portable tape deck. He crawled over to the front seat. His foot knocked out the plastic dome light cover as he felt around for loose change underneath the litter on the floor. He found a dollar's worth of coins and got out of the car.

Inside the 7-Eleven, he went to the refrigerator where single cans were stored and got out a tall can of Budweiser. He spilled his change onto the counter, where the clerk carefully counted each grimy coin. Reynaldo hurried back to the car and took out a disposable pack of salt and his plastic container of reconstituted lemon juice from the glove compartment. After he filled his beer can to the brim with lemon juice and salt, he started up the car and headed for the hospital.

At the east end of the island on the bayside, the main towers of the University of Texas Medical Branch were lit with yellow spotlights. Preparation for emergency surgery was under way on the fourth floor in OR no. 2 for a burn victim brought in from an offshore oil explosion. Max, who was on 24-hour call, had been paged to photograph the burns on the patient's body for insurance purposes. He leaned against the wall waiting for the nurses to cut away the work clothes. The patient, in shock and under heavy sedation, sat on the stretcher and stared at the change in his body. The doctors stood with folded arms around a draped table ready with surgical tools. One whispered something into the ear of the other. They laughed under the cover of their face masks. Max yawned and checked his watch. He looked around for a stool to sit on.

A nurse came into the room and said something to the circulating nurse. Both looked over at Max while they talked. The nurse left and the circulating nurse came over. She wrote something in pen on her scrub pants for Max. He read the message on her thigh and nodded, gesturing "OK" with his fingers. He looked at the burn patient, then went out the door, leaving his camera equipment on a small table.

Reynaldo was waiting by the receptionist's window outside the sterile core of operating rooms. Max stopped halfway down the hall when he saw who was by the window. He shook his head and then proceeded. Reynaldo gave him a big smile and waved hello.

"You're not supposed to see me in this area," Max signed.

"You told me OK visit you hospital here."

"No, only in the photo lab—in the basement, I said. Remember? How did you find me here?"

"Jew Man told me. Me finish visit basement, you not there. He told me you here. Me need talk with you."

"I'm not supposed to be talking here. I could get fired. Now go. We'll talk later."

Max grabbed Reynaldo by the arm and pulled him over by the wall to make way for an orderly pushing a draped body on a gurney.

"He dead?" asked Reynaldo. "What happened?"

"Yes. Now, go on."

"Every day, you see-see that?"

"Yes, but we shouldn't be talking here. Now go. I gotta go back and take pictures."

"Meet lab later?"

"No, I prefer outside of the hospital. We talk too much at the lab. It's not good," Max said.

The receptionist stared over her computer terminal at the two men arguing with their hands. She motioned to another to wheel her chair over for a look.

"Why?" asked Reynaldo.

"Makes me look like I'm socializing all the time at work. Please, I'll meet you later. Just tell me where, I'll show up, OK?"

"Meet restaurant, near wall. Know where?"

"The seawall's ninety blocks long. How am I supposed to know?" said Max.

"You know, red, blue lights, pretty. H—something."

"Yeah, yeah, I know where. Go on. See you later. My beeper is vibrating, I gotta get back," Max said.

The streetlight glare along Seawall Boulevard gave the break-ing surf the color of bile. Offshore, oil rigs outlined with beacons continued to pump through the night. Cars and people drifted by slowly in the humidity. The only bright spot was the blinking neon sign, HOLLYWOOD CAFE, which hung behind the salt-misted window. Near the window, Max stared across the red Formica table at Reynaldo.

"Why did you steal it?" Max asked. He was chewing on his moustache.

"My son," said Reynaldo.

"But your son is too young to want one. Besides, he probably won't have any use for it until he gets older."

"I want sell, get money."

"What do you need the money for? Reynaldo, look at me."

Reynaldo rolled the salt shaker between his palms, a Gerber baby food jar with fork holes poked through the lids. The baby's smiling face on the label was almost gone.

"I want buy son hot dog," said Reynaldo.

"A hot dog?"

"On seawall, Saturday."

"I could've given you money for that, Rey. You know I would. I gave you my good shirt and pants, didn't I?"

A waitress with crossed eyes came over to take their order. Max couldn't tell if she was looking at him or Reynaldo. He went ahead and wrote on his napkin, asking for their list of Mexican beers. She shook her head and pointed to a Budweiser sign.

"They only got Bud here?" Max asked Reynaldo.

"Here cheap," said Reynaldo.

Max gave the waitress an "OK" gesture.

"I can't believe it, no Tecate?" Max asked. "This is a Mexican joint, am I right?"

"Yeah."

"You come here a lot?"

"Fridays. Free coffee."

The waitress returned with two tall cans of beer with pieces of ice floating on the rims. Max looked around at the customers. A couple of men at the counter near the window stared listlessly into the holes of their beer cans. A middle-aged couple at the other end were making out. In the corner booth, a dark, emaciated old man coughed hard. Bits of food shot out of his mouth.

"Your pants. Broken," said Reynaldo. His tongue toyed with a piece of ice.

"You broke my pants?"

"Zipper."

"Aw, I don't care. Reynaldo . . . Reynaldo, look at me."

"You disappointed . . . me?" he asked.

"Well, no . . . yeah, yes. Look at me. That doesn't mean I'm going to stop being your friend. What's your sign down in Mexico for 'friend'? I forget."

"Amigo," he signed.

"Yeah, that's it. Amigo. You and me, amigos. But if you get caught I won't have the bucks to bail you out."

Max slapped at a mosquito and flicked it off his arm.

"You photographer," said Reynaldo.

"That doesn't make me rich. And it doesn't mean you can feel free to steal tape decks or whatever from K-Mart 'cause your amigo can save you every time."

"You take beautiful skilled pictures."

"So?"

"Many dollars in your pocket."

"Uh-uh, I'm barely getting by. Hospital pays me like a janitor. Nobody's buying my freelance work, and you know what? Rey . . . I hate it when you look away. What're you looking at?"

"Poor man there."

The dark man in the corner picked up a plastic wrapper off the floor and used it to cover his hand to eat his roll. He slid on three pats of butter, took a bite, and washed it down with a swig from his brown quart bottle. Beer dribbled down his chin. He coughed again, spraying bits of bread. When he finished his roll, he crumpled up the wrapper and threw it back where it had come from. He hawked a wad of phlegm and spat it under the table.

"I'm still paying off my camera equipment, my bicycle, TV, and, on top of that, I've got rent and food."

"You rich."

"Come off it, I'm not rich. Now, where's the tape deck—in your car?"

"Yeah. In sleep bag."

"Are you still sleeping in your car?"

Reynaldo picked dirt out from under his fingernails with a fork.

"Look . . . your wife's family can't do this to you," said Max.

"See son two hours, Saturdays now."

"They cut down your visiting hours?"

"Told me court order."

"They're liars!"

"I good father . . . bring flowers for wife, tell her I love her. She not understand—mental retard, you know. Her mother, brother, sister protect her. They ask me, 'Where money? Where money?'"

"Do you give them all your money?"

"Mother take . . . for the boy."

"Do you give them all your money every Saturday?"

"Yeah."

"You work your ass off at the tackle factory; you clean the movie theater every night; and then you give your paychecks to that woman?"

"I want see my boy."

"Hide some of it. They won't know."

"They know. Son want see me bad. I deaf, he deaf—we same. I make son laugh."

Reynaldo rolled the pepper shaker, which still had its label intact. He stared at the baby's picture. Max looked at the black velvet pictures of valiant toreadors hanging crooked on the wall.

"Reynaldo . . . I'm leaving here next week."

"What wrong? Don't like here?"

"Nothing. I like Galveston. I like drinking beers with you in the movies . . ."

"Where you go?"

"California."

"California have Tecate, lime, salt?"

"Yes."

"Can I go with?"

"You can't."

"Why? You, me amigo. Live together, eat together, lie in sun together—"

"I'm sorry. I must go . . . alone. I'm taking a big test for my work."

"Test? You back, will?"

"Oh yeah, I'll be back here. In a couple weeks."

Max paid for the beers and handed Reynaldo a fifty-dollar bill. He gave Reynaldo a strong hug and then headed out the door. He stopped to look both ways before he crossed the boulevard to get to the seawall. Max watched the murky water fifteen feet below swish garbage around the boulders. He started to walk back to his car but stopped and looked back. Reynaldo was still sitting at the table playing with the Gerber baby food jars.

May 21, 1982

La Jolla Coffee Klatch

Greetings from sunny San Diego, "America's Finest City"!

Dear folks -- my oral examination was tough. I was supposed to have a sign interpreter, but she never showed up. The board of registry gave me the option of allowing me to postpone my orals until next year's convention. Yeah, right! I flipped an imaginary bird at them. Think I was gonna let that happen over a no-show? Told myself it was now or never. I wanted them to think that I could function just like hearing medical photographers. If they saw that I totally had to depend on interpreters, they'd see that I need them like crutches all of the time -- a real drag on department/hospital budgets, would slow things down, blah, blah, blah. Deaf stigma crap.

I said politely that I wished to proceed, and asked them if they could select someone from the group of five examiners as a spokesperson who could articulate words clearly. If the others would kindly channel their questions through the spokesperson during the inquisition, it would allow me to read lips easier. Fortunately, they obliged.

The title of my presentation was "Histotechnology and the Photomicroscopist." It was basically about how important it is for biomedical photographers to establish a good relationship with the Histology Department in their hospitals. Remember I did a two-week

rotation in our hospital's Histology Department
to learn how they prepare human tissue for study
under the microscope? They go through this
process where they take a half-inch piece of a
diseased part of the body, cardiac tissue for
example, and soak it in a variety of chemical
and dye baths that give the cell components a
specific color. This helps the doctor easily
examine the cells under a microscope and spot
abnormalities, which informs their diagnoses.
It's a whole 'nother inner world. My main
point was that if you're friendly with the
histotechnologist, they will make clean-cut
tissue slices and good color separation among
the tissue cells for you to create fantastic
photographs through the microscope. The key to
making great photographs for doctors who want
them for publication or presentations is to have
the technicians go the extra mile to prepare
microscope slides for photo documentation.
Sorry, am I talking over your head? Hope it
makes sense.

Anyhow, that portion of my presentation
went pretty well, except for a color slide
that the projector ate. GRRRRRRR!!!! It was
one of my most important slides, showing a
comparison between a routinely prepared tissue
section and one that was specially prepared
for photomicroscopy. I worked a long time on
laying that out and putting in the graphics.
And, then the #%&@-ing machine swallowed it
and kept it down. I was able to finally fish it
out, but the 35mm transparency was too mangled
to put back into the slide carousel. The board
understood and smiled. One of them said it

happened to all photographers. They were kind
and smart enough to look at the crumpled slide
through a loupe on a light box they had in the
room. After the presentation, they threw some
hardball questions about my topic as well as
my portfolio. I fielded them as best I could.
I left the room with a lot of doubt, totally
pissed about the dysfunctional slide projector
and the interpreter who went AWOL -- that really
threw off my game. They told me to wait in the
hotel lobby for the results of my orals. After
a half hour, they called me back into the room,
looking solemn.

Sssshhhh, everyone! Are you sitting down?

I PASSSSSSSSSSSSSSSSSSSSSSSSSSSSSSSSSSSSSSSSED!

First Deaf Registered Biological Photographer
in the world!!!!!!!!!!!!!!!!!!!!! Zag passed
too, of course! You should've seen us whooping
and hollering in the lobby. Hotel security came
running to see what was the matter.

We learned that there was going to be a
celebratory dinner for the newly crowned RBPs,
so we made plans to stay an extra night in La
Jolla to be around for the banquet. What did
the two newly minted RBPs do in the meantime?
Headed for the nearest beach! And what beach was
nearby? Black's Beach -- reputed to be a nude
beach.

We had to walk down a cliff to get there,
and once we arrived, it didn't take long to
let go of our inbitionsx inhibitions, drop our
clothes, and hit the surf. I had never felt so
good and relieved in all my life. After swimming
for a while without a care in the world, we took

a stroll to dry off au naturel. We saw a couple
of girls throwing a Frisbee back and forth.
Seeing them naked felt very natural -- it wasn't
erotic or anything. As we passed them, I made
a gesture for them to flick one to me. To my
surprise, one of them threw me the Frisbee. I
flung it back, thus starting a four-way Frisbee
toss. I let Zag do the talking and charming, as
I had left my hearing aids back in the hotel.
Didn't want to come across looking stupid and
not understanding anything they said. He later
told me that they were UC San Diego students.
He filled them in on our new titles and invited
them to join us later to party. We waved good-
bye to them and headed back toward our clothes
pile.

What I saw next drained the blood out of me.
Walking on the beach toward us were Dr. Robb and
his wife -- fully clothed! There was nowhere to
escape or hide to avoid detection. It was all
out there and hanging. He said, "Well, I guess
congratulations are in order." His wife was
trying to keep her gaze out toward the ocean. At
first, I thought he was being sarcastic about
us being out in the nude, then I realized he
was referring to us getting our RBPs. We stood
around for a minute or so mumbling thanks. Then,
oddly enough, we shook hands with him and his
wife, and they went on their merry way.

When we get back to Galveston, we need to move
out of our beach house. Memorial Day weekend
is coming soon and the rent will triple. It may
turn out that Zag and I will have to go into
town and find separate places to live. It'll

probably be hard to find something cheap with
two bedrooms at the last minute.

Love,

Dempsey Maxwell McCall,
Registered Biological Photographer #319

P.S. I take back what I said in my other letter.
I do run naked now.

Discovering Light at the Dmax Bar

Shooting on the Floors Photo requests usually come in over the phone. Ask for the following: patient's name, doctor's name (NO INTERNS! Get the staff doctor in charge), department doctor works for, type of shots. Ask if the patient can come down to the clinical studio. If not, request the name of the building, floor, and room number, and bring portable strobe equipment with you. If the patient has dressings, a nurse must be on hand to remove them so that you are able to shoot the wound and/or the healing process.

After searching through the university's list of available housing in the Galveston area, Max settled for a small, sand-cheap, peeling-paint garage apartment in a duplex on Eighth Street, a block from the seawall. He and Zag were not able to find a two-bedroom place together that was within their budget. Now that the island's tourist season had begun, over Memorial Day weekend, rent prices were jacked up everywhere. The real estate agency agreed to allow Max a month-to-month contract provided he put down the first and last month's rent as security deposit. He wanted a quick escape in case things didn't work out.

In the back alley, when Max rolled the apartment's old-fashioned garage door aside to park his car and unload his bike and belongings, the entire duplex swayed. He locked the door with a padlock and walked around to the front yard to get to the stairs of his apartment. He had an obstructed view of Broadway, the island's central artery, which ran east and west. The grass was about a foot high, chock-full of sandburs. Every now and then Max had to pick the stickers off his shoes and pants. He started a mental list of items he wanted to address with the Realtor: sand-burs and a wobbly apartment.

He smelled cigarette smoke and looked around to see where it was coming from. A fence divided his front yard from a larger yard fronted by an old two-story house with a bar on the first floor. The bar's back door was open. An elderly man with a cigarette dangling from his mouth came out carrying a bucket. He chucked a pail full of dirty water out on the grass in Max's direction. Their eyes met. Max held up his hand to wave hello. The man flicked his cigarette away, coughed, and walked back inside.

Later in the day, he saw the same man smoking while sitting out on the second-floor balcony of the house above the back of the bar. A woman about the same age came out and sat down next to him, lighting up a cigarette of her own. Both looked like bulldogs—rough, heavy, and grumpy.

"I'm here to report some problems with the apartment I just rented," said Max.

The realty office receptionist took out a pad and pen. "Your name, please."

"Max—I mean, Dempsey Maxwell McCall. I'm over on Eighth Street, in the garage apartment duplex."

"Apartment number one or two?"

"The one on the left, if facing Broadway," said Max. He didn't recall seeing any numbers.

"And what's the problem?"

"Well, the grass is over a foot high, with these sticker burrs all over. Somebody needs to cut the lawn real soon. The other problem is that the whole duplex sways whenever I open or shut the garage doors. That wobbling worries me a bit."

"OK, I'll pass this on to the owners," said the receptionist.

"The owners? I thought you guys would take care of this."

"No, we just handle rental contracts and administrative stuff for owners of rental properties."

"Do you mind divulging the owners' names and contact info, or is it some big state secret? Because I don't have it."

"You should have it—it's at the bottom of your contract."

"Oh—I guess I should've read the fine print. How about you helping save my eyes and my time by telling me how I can reach the owners?"

"Sure, just a moment," said the receptionist with a professional smile.

Max looked out the salt-misted window facing the seawall. The surf was riled up today, bringing multiple whitecaps to shore. At the lifeguard stand, he could see a red flag flapping madly. It was going to be a riptide day.

"Here you are, Mr. McCall. The owners are Mr. and Mrs. Rodriguez, of 501 Eighth Street. They're in the house right across from you. You've probably seen it. They live above a bar, which they own as well," she said.

Max had always wanted to live near a bar. He had this *Cheers*-like fantasy of frequenting a neighborhood bar where he knew everyone and the bartender considered him a regular, calling him by his name, knowing his drink, and so on. God damn Hollywood for conjuring up that fantasy! Now he had to face the Bulldogs. It wasn't so much about being assertive and addressing problems that were no fault of his own, but about the fact that he was going in with one strike against him—communication. Try lipreading bulldogs.

For the time being, Max let it go. What was important was that the hospital was a straight shot down Eighth Street—he could see the main towers. He could get there in five minutes by bike. Perfect for being on 24-hour call. The more calls he took, the more overtime pay he would rake in.

One Saturday, Zag came over to check out Max's new digs. Soon Zag was measuring the distance between the walls with his feet, alternately putting the heel of one shoe in front of the toe of the other.

"Good grief, it's a prison cell," he said.

It didn't help that Max had put up burglar-proof bars on the window by the stairs.

"The walls are so close you can smell your own breath," Zag said.

"Only you would want to smell your gefilte fish breath. C'mon, it's not that bad. It's ridiculously cheap."

"I see why," said Zag. "But, the positive is you're close to the seawall and the Gulf of Mexico—the 'Mediterranean of the Americas.' Babes galore!"

"Amen!" said Max. "And five minutes to work by bike—can't beat that."

"Radical. That twenty-minute drive to work from the beach house got old."

"Yeah, and the Field House—six minutes. You and I get to play more tennis."

"Whoo! More Max-and-Zag matches. Hey—what's that cigarette smell? You been smoking?"

"No, it's coming all the way from that bar over there," said Max. "I smell that all day and all night. I'll be lying in bed, nice warm breeze coming in from the Gulf lulling me to sleep, then the wind stops; I smell that shit, and wake up."

"Close your windows."

"Right, and turn this place into a steam room? I'm getting hot and humid just talking about this," said Max. "Let's get out and try a brew at the old neighborhood bar over there. I haven't had the balls to go in by myself. You should see the rough characters that hang out there—they look bigger and meaner than the Hell's Angels. I need a buddy to go in there with me."

"Sure, why not. Can't hurt to go in once and see what it's like."

"My landlord owns that bar. I'm hoping to catch him to tell him about a couple of problems I've been having with this place. Need you there to be my rock."

"Tell him to cut the fuckin' grass!" said Zag.

"That's first on my list!"

"I hate these Texas sandburs," said Zag.

Zag and Max could barely see anything when they walked into the Eighth Street bar. They stood by the door waiting for their eyes to adjust to the dark. After a couple of minutes, they still had trouble seeing each other or anything in the bar. The walls and ceiling were dark. Illumination was at a bare minimum, mostly coming from the neon beer signs. The brightest light came from a TV in the corner of the bar. Max noticed that the wood and bar stools were dark as well, probably from decades of absorbing cigarette tar.

Darkness is the enemy of deaf people. Can't read lips or signs. It reminded Max of summer nights outside with the neighborhood kids, talking and laughing though he couldn't follow a word anyone was saying. He might as well have been alone inside a mineshaft. At least, like the mine, the bar was cool and dry thanks to the air conditioning.

Just three men were at the bar, sitting side by side, smoking and nursing their beers while watching *The Dukes of Hazzard*. From behind the bar, Max saw an orange glow moving around. It was the bartender, who turned out to be the owner, Rodriguez. His cigarette bobbed up and down in his mouth as he asked Max and Zag what they wanted. He took his cigarette out, coughed, and then put it back in for another inhale. His coughing looked and sounded more like barking.

"Two Lone Stars, please," said Zag. Without using his voice, he mouthed to Max: "He looks like a bulldog."

Max put his finger on his nose and said, "B-i-n-g-o!" in the rhythm of the old farm song. He asked Zag to come up to the bar with him, to help interpret if needed. He beckoned to Bulldog to come to where he stood.

"Are you Mr. Rodriguez?"

Bulldog nodded.

"Hi, my name is Max. I'm the one renting your place across the yard." Max held out his hand to shake.

Bulldog said "So?" not offering his hand.

"I'm sorry, what did you say? I'm deaf and it's hard to lipread you with a cigarette in your mouth."

"He said, 'So?'" said Zag.

"Well," said Max. "I have a problem. My yard is this high with grass and sandburs. Is there a way that somebody could get my lawn cut? It's really bothering me."

Bulldog gave him a long stare.

"I don't believe you're deaf. You can talk," said Bulldog. He kept wiping the bar in the same spot over and over.

"I'm sorry, what did you say?"

"He said he doesn't believe you're deaf—you can talk," said Zag.

Max pointed to his ears. "See these things, Mr. Rodriguez? They're not earrings, not weight-loss gimmicks, but hearing aids. If I weren't deaf, why would I be wearing them?"

"How come he talks so good?" said Bulldog to Zag. Zag interpreted orally.

"'Cause I have a normal voice box like you," said Max. "I grew up at an early age with hearing aids and learned to speak well. But!

I do not hear as well as I speak. A lot of people don't understand that."

Bulldog uncapped two Lone Stars and pushed them toward Max and Zag.

"Umm, so, about the lawn," said Max, changing his tone. "Anything you can do about that?"

"Lawn mower's broken."

Zag gestured, "Lawn mower, broke" as if he were snapping a branch over his knee.

"Well, why can't you—?" Zag nudged Max away from the bar.

"Forget it," mouthed Zag. "Let it go."

Bulldog, wiping the bar, stared after them in disbelief as they returned to their seats.

After five minutes with their beers, Max and Zag found it wasn't possible to breathe without gagging from cigarette smoke. The place was a breeding ground for emphysema and lung cancer.

"That has got to be the worst fuckin' bar I've ever been to in my life," said Zag when they got outside. Both were taking in deep breaths. "How can they stay in business?"

"Cigarettes and alcohol—a lethal combination," said Max. "As long as smoking and drinking are permitted together, people don't care where they are. The world could be crumbling down all around them and people would still be sitting on bar stools drinking and puffing away to their heart's content."

"I got a name for it," said Zag. "The Dmax Bar."

"Dmax? You naming it after me or something?"

"Maximum Density. Dmax, remember that from photo science class?"

"Yeah, the blackest black on a photo print."

"That bar is it!" said Zag.

A month later, Max was given a phone message at work to go to a patient's room to photograph a tracheostomy. When he got to the room, he found Bulldog Rodriguez lying in the bed, his wife sitting next to him, holding his hand. Both looked up, but did not seem to recognize him as their tenant. Max picked up his chart and read that he had cancer of the throat. His larynx had been removed and a tracheotomy performed.

Bulldog grabbed an artificial larynx device from his bed table and put it up to his neck. Max heard mechanical voice sounds but couldn't understand what was being said. He asked Mrs. Rodriguez for help.

"My husband wants to know what you're doing here with that camera."

"I'm sorry," said Max. "Didn't anyone tell you?"

Bulldog put the device up to his neck and said something monosyllabic. Max assumed it was probably "no."

"No," said Mrs. Rodriguez.

"Thank you. I want to let you know that I am deaf, which was why I had trouble understanding your husband. My apologies for that. Please bear with me. I am a medical photographer and your doctor wants a photo record of your healing process with the tracheotomy. It will only take a minute. I am going to ask you to open your shirt some so I can photograph a close-up of the tracheostomy tube, the faceplate, the sutures, and the surrounding skin.

"I will be using a flash; I'll let you know when to close your eyes. And then I'll be out of here in a jiffy."

Nothing more was said in the room between the three. The Rodriguezes watched Max's every move. He sensed something slowly registering in their minds as he assembled his equipment. Recognition? Embarrassment? Shame? Eventually they stopped watching him and averted their gazes. Max sensed their defeat, and then their surrender to being photographed.

As he finished all of the necessary shots and then packed up his equipment, Max formulated what he wanted to say before leaving. It took all of his might to resist the urge to blurt out sarcastically, "Now, will you please cut my lawn?"

Sometimes, during a balmy June evening at twilight, Max liked to lie in bed by the window to watch the Galveston sky change colors in contrast with the bar's neon sign. It was about the only beautiful thing around that place.

And sometimes he got out his camera, turning over onto his stomach, steadying the lens on the windowsill, and taking long-exposure shots of the sign composed with the sky. He'd read somewhere—perhaps in a Kodak manual—that just as oils were the medium of a painter, light is the medium of a photographer. A painter must learn the properties of paint to bring ideas to life on canvas. Likewise, a photographer must understand the characteristics of light to create life on photographic film. If Max were to rewrite that Kodak statement, he would add that, for a deaf person, light is also life.

Then, when it got dark, the mercury-vapor light on the Rodriguezes' balcony would click on, and its sickly white glow would light the way for smoking roughnecks to come and go at the bar all night long, while Max tried to sleep.

June 9, 1982

Kitchen, 8th St. Apt.
Dear Ma & Pa McCall:
  Life has been looking up since I got my RBP.
I'm still settling into my garage apartment,
trying to organize things during my free time.
I love the apartment despite its rickety flaws
and high grass full of sandburs. It's just the
right size for me -- for now, that is. I want
to be as economical as possible. For shower
curtains, I took some large green plastic bags
from work, cut them open along the seams, and
duct-taped them together and onto the curtain
rod. The windows have white plastic kitchen bags
over them -- same idea as the shower curtains --
I cut them along the seams to make them one-ply
(so more light can penetrate). During the day, I
fold the bottom half up and tape it so I can see
outside, and then at night, I remove the tape
and let the bottom half drop down for privacy.
  Professor Robb invited me over to his place
the other day to check out a three-seater couch.
He said he had a good deal for me, and was
going to throw in a coffee table as well. After
measuring the couch dimensions, I asked how much
he was asking for it. He said, "Free! I told you
I had a good deal for you." It ended up that I
had to saw six inches off the back legs of the
couch in order to get it through my front door.
Later, I nailed the two pieces back on. All in
all -- not pretty, but not bad. Heck! I ain't
expecting Home & Gardens to come knocking on my
door anytime soon.

My new Sears Telecaption TV arrived two days ago. The first TV with built-in closed captioning. At long last!! Took out a small loan from my credit union for this TV. They'll deduct $50 a month from my paycheck until the loan is paid off. I could've paid it off with a lump sum from an upcoming paycheck, but figured a loan would help me build my credit references.

It was heaven to be able to watch ABC Nightly News with Peter Jennings in captions. Finally, I can get full access to my daily news . . . and to baseball games, especially Baltimore Orioles games when we get them down here. Remember when I was home and always asked what the announcers were talking about during the games? You would say it wasn't anything important. Now that I can read what they're saying, it IS important stuff about the players, the teams, and the strategies -- all inside info I had no idea about.

Just made arrangements to have a one-man photo show in the university's medical library. I figured why not? Backup duplicate prints had already been made from when I created my RBP portfolio -- can use them for the show. The historian who runs the gallery happened to see one of my prints at the photo lab and asked if I had more work similar to what she saw. After finding that I had plenty, she asked if I'd be interested in having a show. Of course I accepted.

Exhibits held in the library are seen by everyone at UTMB; most people tend to pass through the library. Also, the exhibits get publicity through the Galveston newspaper as well. I'm psyched!

Zag decided not to rent a place of his own. He had been looking for a job, flying back and forth to L.A., and landed one as a senior medical photographer. He negotiated a way to terminate his contract early with UTMB and will start his new job on July 15th. I was really happy for him, but will be awfully sorry to see him go. We are definitely going to keep in touch.

Will let you know of my plans for end of summer once I know them. Hope this finds y'all healthy and in good spirits.

All my luv,
Max

Tropical Storm Esperanza

Arthroscopy   If the image on the operating room video monitor is fuzzy, foggy, or bloody, do the following: 1) add more irrigation to keep the wound clean; 2) wipe condensation off the arthroscope; 3) suggest to the surgeon that he is holding the scope too close to the subject; 4) wipe moisture off the video camera—the camera only gets wet when the surgeon is careless and breaks the seal between the camera and the scope.

It wasn't until the second day after the surgery that Max started to feel pain from the repair of a partial detached retina. His left eye looked like it had been given a good pummeling in a boxing match. His vision was often watery. When he looked from side to side or up and down, there was an electric jolt; to avoid it he moved his entire head slowly, like a robot, whenever he wanted to look at something.

As the day progressed, apprehension crept up in him—the field of view out of his left eye seemed to be getting narrower, not wider, like it was supposed to. Hopefully it wasn't an infection. Max recalled the eye doctor telling him yesterday that he wasn't out of the woods yet. Bad metaphor—there are no woods in Galveston. Max was supposed to go back to the doctor in a couple of days to see how much had healed. If it didn't look good, more work would need to be done. He couldn't imagine reliving that Nazi experiment of an operation. Imagine a tooth being drilled for two straight hours right on a nerve, except in this case it was right in his eye. He'd had trouble breathing from being under a surgical drape the whole time, thinking he was suffocating in his own stale air, despite the oxygen flowing through a tube into his nostrils.

Now that his RBP certification was in the bag, he worried that his career was already ruined—six years of education and training in biomedical photographic communication down the drain. It exhausted him to think about it. Who would hire a one-eyed, Deaf medical photographer? His rebuttal would be: all you need is one eye to look through the viewfinder. But, people care mostly about appearances. Being Deaf was enough of a stigma to overcome; add a black eye patch, and what do you get? A Deaf pirate.

Trying to keep his mind off the horror show running a loop in his mind, Max made himself a tall glass of iced tea and sat down in the living room by the open window. The sky was overcast, with a layer of dark billowy clouds racing underneath. A steady wind blew in, making his white plastic-bag curtains flap. Even though a tropical storm was coming, the simple elements of light, color, wind, and the smell of the ocean put his mind at ease. It was just as well, since his teary eyesight made it difficult to read or watch TV.

Just as he was about to nod off in his chair, Max's door-light flashed intermittently. When he opened the door, he was shocked to see his friend Larry from RIT standing there nonchalantly with his arm around his hippie girlfriend, Flowersong. Larry wasn't a hippie or anything, but he'd gotten henpecked enough to allow his girlfriend to convince him to adopt her faux-bohemian lifestyle. Even though he'd received no advance notice, Max couldn't tell them sorry, no room, hitchhike back home. Besides, he was genuinely happy to see Larry, one of the few decent, hearing male friends he had from college who knew signs.

"What's up, Popeye?" said Larry.

"Can I use your bathroom?" asked Flowersong.

Max let them in and showed her the bathroom, which was off his bedroom. They brought in their backpacks and sleeping bags, smelling of body odor and cigarettes. Larry opened the refrigerator and pulled out a couple of Lone Star beers. It was as if they had just seen Max last week—when it had actually been two years.

"What happened to your eye, bro?" Larry voiced and signed. He knew Max liked hearing his voice while he signed words. Larry used to work as an interpreter for one of Max's photo classes. Both loved listening to the music of Bad Company and had become instant friends. Even though "bro" was spoken slang, Larry made up his own sign language slang and always used it around Max, who understood and appreciated it, even though not many other Deaf people did.

"A tennis ball disliked me, bro," said Max.

"How'zat?"

"I was playing a set and was having a good baseline volley when I decided to surprise my opponent by approaching the net. He hit a powerful return forehand that smacked me right in the eye. Started seeing brown spots and floaters afterward. Went to the hospital to have it checked out. They had to operate—reattached my retina."

"Whoa! Just like Sugar Ray Leonard," said Larry.

"Who's that?"

"Famous pro boxer—former Olympian?" Larry demonstrated with a little shadowboxing and pretended to hit himself in the eye. "Bam—detached retina."

"That's weird," said Max. "I was just thinking earlier that I felt like a boxer had punched me in the eye and knocked me out."

"A tennis ball, huh? Kinda faggy, don't you think? I'd rather tell people I got hit by a boxer in the ring."

"Thanks a lot! Put those beers back in the fridge, asshole, or I'll detach *your* retina," said Max, shaking a fist at him.

Max learned that to save money, Larry and Flowersong had hitchhiked from Rochester, New York, all the way down to Galveston. He was a musician and she was a songwriter, although both had originally studied to become certified ASL interpreters. Flowersong came out of the bathroom.

"I swear, I've never felt a house sway and creak so much," said Flowersong. "Are we getting a hurricane?"

"No, but a tropical storm is brewing. You guys made it to shelter just in time. Welcome to Max's Shelter for Homeless Musicians!"

"We're not homeless!" she said.

"Uh . . . Flowersong, he's joking," said Larry.

"Oh . . . in the bathroom while I was sitting on the toilet, I put my hand up on the window. I swear, I could feel the glass bend a little from the pressure of the wind."

"Are you sure it wasn't from you straining a little too hard to get your granola dooties out?" Max laughed and spurted out his beer, and then his hand shot up to rub around his injured eye.

"Ow. Damn, Larry. That hurts!" said Max.

"Larry—fuck you and the horse you rode in on!" said Flowersong.

"I didn't ride in on a horse. I rode a whore," said Larry, slapping her on the butt and winking at Max to let him in on the ribbing. Flowersong gave him the silent fuck-you gesture.

"Hey, what's this?" said Max, pointing to a bag on the counter.

"Got you some fresh chicken wings," said Larry. "Hope you got a frying pan and some oil."

"Oh yeah, I got all that stuff. I'll fry you some wings."

"My man! I was hoping you'd say that."

"So, Max—do you have a girlfriend down here?" Flowersong asked.

"No—been too busy prepping for my certification. And guess what?"

"You're now certified as an RBP?" said Larry.

"Get this guy another beer!" said Max. "Yes—as of three weeks!"

"Oh, Max, congratulations!" said Flowersong, giving him a hug.

"Thanks—first deaf person ever to get an RBP!"

"Lemme get *you* another beer, my man," said Larry. They all clicked their bottles together and then sat around quietly sipping. Max got up to close all the windows in his apartment. It had started to pour down rain, and the wind was blowing newspapers off the table and knocking over picture frames and boxes of Kodak film.

"To get back to your question . . . a lot of the girls on the island are BOIs," said Max.

"What's BOI—queer boys?" asked Flowersong.

"No, Born on the Island . . . locals who're born and raised here. Sometimes with their attitudes and outlook on life, it seems like they've never been off the island. They're kinda clique-ish and proud. That's why it's been a little hard to meet and really get to know a woman around here. They see me as a tourist or an outsider."

Max took the chicken wings out of the package and started to snap them in half to make it easier to cut between the drum and the wing. He chopped the wing tips off and threw them away. Larry found the frying pan and oil and got the burner going on the stove while Max whipped up the hot sauce; then he pan-fried a batch of wings Rochester-style. Certain Rochester people were fanatical about cooking wings their way—not Buffalo-style, which meant dumping a bag of frozen wings into a deep fryer. Flowersong wouldn't have any of it, proclaiming she didn't believe in the slaughter of animals. Max looked down at her leather Birkenstocks and wondered which animal had gotten killed for its skin. For the moment, he and Larry were secretly glad she had become a vegetarian; it meant more chicken wings for themselves. As for

Flowersong, they let her have as much celery, carrots, and blue cheese dip as she could stand.

While they ate, Larry heard a dripping sound coming from the bedroom. Of all the places in Max's apartment, it was the ceiling over his bed that had decided to drip water. The irony of it was that when he'd risked getting a waterbed, he'd worried whether the old garage apartment floor could withstand it, or whether the bed would spring a leak. Instead, the ceiling had sprung a leak, right above the bed. It was like bailing out water from a tarp over a swimming pool—until he decided to just leave a bucket on the bed.

"Too bad that leak isn't over your fish aquarium," said Larry. "Save you a lot of trouble having to refill it, eh?"

"Still a wiseass, ain't he?" said Max, looking over at Flowersong.

"Know what this reminds me of?" asked Flowersong. "The movie *Rocky*."

"How'zat?" said Larry, using another one of his signed slang words: he signed "What's up" with one hand, along with a back nod of his head like a homie.

"You know that scene where Rocky is lonely, all by himself in his cramped, dinky apartment? He talks to his little goldfish."

"Oh, yeah! Moby Dick! Max—do you talk to your goldfishie there in little tiny sign language?" asked Larry. Max managed a smile while massaging the skin around his eye patch. The electric jolts kept coming.

Two hours after Larry and Flowersong arrived, and with the storm in full force, the power went out. Max found some candles in a storage box and lit them. Throughout the night, Larry kept hearing glass breaking near the apartment. The man had such a phenomenal ear, he could have heard a mosquito fart outside. Whenever Larry heard a shatter, he and Max would go outside and check around the premises for broken glass. As it turned out, an apartment complex across the alley was getting it bad. The folks in the apartments whose windows broke could kiss their carpets good-bye, and maybe their floors, too.

In the midst of all this, Flowersong sat at the kitchen table with her journal, writing songs by candlelight and trying them out on her lips. Max was getting annoyed with her. She was useless around the apartment, except for remembering to flush the toilet every time she went to the bathroom. Although she looked halfway interesting on the outside and was fairly cute, with long brown hair and a tie-dyed shirt with a low neckline, inside she was dull, impersonal, and aloof. Max wanted to ask Larry what he really saw in the girl, but felt it was the wrong time to ask, especially in such close quarters and given the fact that the two of them did everything together—eat, sleep, bathe, watch TV, and go to the store. They even had the same part-time job, working for an interpreting agency in Rochester.

Max knew exactly when they made love. That first night in his apartment, when Max said good night and went to bed, they rolled out their sleeping bags on the living room floor in front of the TV. Because of the bucket on his waterbed catching the leak, Max slept on his bedroom floor. Just before he drifted off to sleep, he felt his floor shake with varying intensity. He sat up and put his hand on the wall behind him. Sure enough, the apartment was swaying in short, rhythmic, back-and-forth movements. He had never experienced an earthquake and was wondering if this was what it felt like. Then it stopped, only to start back up again, this time with a faster rhythm. He crawled over to the door between his bedroom and the living room and put his hand on it. The vibrations were stronger there. Larry and Flowersong were either fucking on the other side, or playing hopscotch. Max decided it was most likely the former, and left the door alone. They probably thought they could take advantage of Max's deafness and have sex with reckless abandon. Little did they know that Max, like most deaf people, was a vibration-detection expert.

He got up to go to the bathroom and downed a few Tylenols to deaden the pain in his eye. While holding a candle up close to his face by the mirror, he slowly peeled back the gauze bandage and took a peek to make sure his eyeball hadn't popped out. He was still terribly disturbed by a story that his boss, Dr. Robb, had told over a Mexican meal he'd treated Max to for having earned his RBP. Robb was once called to the ER to photograph a woman who'd crashed her car into a telephone pole. Her skull had cracked, exposing a part of her brain. She had a scalp flap, and one of her eyes was lolling out of its socket. The oddest thing was that she demanded to be let up off the stretcher so that she could get home in time for dinner. She would turn her head toward a nurse to insist on this, and her eye would sway over in that direction. Robb had to follow her on the stretcher to the operating room for more photo documentation of her case. Totally oblivious to her loose eye swinging to and fro, she'd kept asking the orderly to be released so that she could get home to cook dinner.

After emptying the bucket on his waterbed, Max blew out the candle, grateful that his eyeball seemed intact. He looked out his bedroom window to see if anyone in his neighborhood had power. With his palm on the windowpane, he could feel the pummeling of a hard downpour. It was still dark out all around, yet the sky had that faint gray cover—like a cataract—that gave enough illumination to reveal the dark outlines of apartment buildings and a little river flowing through the back alley. Every now and then, lightning, nature's strobe light, would freeze-frame rain droplets in midair. Water still dripped from the ceiling into the bucket. The storm wasn't letting up. He decided to lie back down for the count on the blanketed floor, close his good eye, and try not to fret over his post-certification future while thunder reverberated through his body and his vision started to heal.

Midnight, July 4/5, 1982
Living Room, 8th St. Apt.

Dear 'rents:
   This will be a rather short note as I've got
a bit of an eyestrain tonight, plus my left eye
tends to get tired easily from looking at any
one thing too long, like this letter -- ha!
Many, many, many thanks for sending the "CARE"
package. Ooooohhh . . . the box of brown-sugar/
cinnamon Pop-Tarts was so yummy it nearly
brought tears to my eyes. Speaking of eyes, my
eye patch came off last week. Practically wet
my pants in relief that my vision was 20/20 and
clear when tested. Wondering why I'm typing
late? Just got home recently from Galveston's
Independence Day parade of floats, military
vehicles, and street performers marching along
Seawall Blvd. After the parade, there was a
cool fireworks show (hence the eyestrain) over
the Gulf. Free entertainment -- wheeeee! Always
good during these budget-conscious days. Just
wanted to dash off a quick thank-you for that
package. Was thrilled you got me Stephen King's
new book Different Seasons -- can't wait to
start reading it.

Buenos ~~nachos~~ xx noches,
Max

Max and Maddy

Backgrounds and Environments   When photographing patients, it is important to show medical information in context, such as the patient sitting up in bed, or attached to equipment. If the photograph were to show a specific medical condition—for example, dermatitis caused by a bra strap—it would be helpful to include a shot of the strap next to the wound. Avoid messy backgrounds. Be aware that certain backgrounds with strong colors can reflect a color cast onto your subject matter. To play it safe, bring our neutral white and gray fabric panels with you to use as makeshift backgrounds. Ask the patient to remove any jewelry and makeup. All clothing should be removed from the field of view when possible. People are unaccustomed to being photographed naked. Obviously, you need to employ sensitivity and tact. Hair should be brushed away from the face. Use a hair band or bobby pins. Long hair can be put up in a bun, or swung over the shoulder away from the camera. Hair clips can help reveal lesions on the scalp.

Every year the Pathology Department hosted their big summer picnic at some outdoor location or other on Galveston Island. This year it was being held at Seawolf Park, a thumb of land sticking out into Galveston Bay. A World War II submarine was berthed there as a memorial, and there was also a fishing pier and a playground for kids. All of the picnic tables were decorated with Texas-themed tablecloths. Red-white-and-blue Lone Star flag napkins, cups, and plasticware were set up in neat rows. Only the women in the Pathology Department were involved in the decorating—after all, it was Texas, and the state was quite a few years behind the Northeast in the women's liberation movement.

When Dr. Robb had gone back to RIT for his annual recruitment lecture, he'd found another applicant that he liked. Her name was Bertha, and she was hearing-impaired. She'd lived in Photo House in the dorms when Max was a resident advisor. He remembered her as smart and ambitious, a bit overweight, but with a self-deprecating sense of humor. Probably what had worked in her favor in getting selected was that she could speak and hear quite well, having grown up with an oral deaf education. In Deaf culture, she was considered "hard of hearing." With hearing aids, she spoke just like a hearing person, could hear well over the phone, and did not have to face people to lipread. She was proud of this accomplishment, and during her time at RIT felt that she didn't need to learn signs at all. She hung out with a small group of like-minded oralists—the A.G. Bell Society, Max liked to call them. He made a mental note to sit down one day with Dr. Robb and convince him to consider future Deaf applicants—just as intelligent, perhaps more so—who might not be able to speak as well as Bertha or himself. Or who chose not to speak at all. Nevertheless, Max was pleased in a way, because he had blazed a trail for another educated person with hearing loss to become employed in biomedical photography.

Somehow, someone in the department got wind of the fact that Bertha knew how to play the trumpet. She was asked if she could perform "The Star-Spangled Banner" at the picnic. Bertha happily obliged. This led to Max being asked if he could sign the words to the song while Bertha played the melody. Max reluctantly obliged, as he needed a good reference for when his contract ended. He didn't want a refusal to turn into a reason for not being offered a possible job at the university, should one open up. Bertha and Max practiced a few times in her apartment; she'd ended up living next door to Max in the other garage apartment on Eighth Street.

Before Bertha moved in, however, a lovely, blonde, natural-looking, hearing medical student named Viveca had lived next to him with Argos, her golden retriever. She was always friendly to Max, with a "hi" and a wave. Sometimes they talked a little bit, but they'd quickly run out of things to say to each other, because, for some reason, each was a little uncomfortable with the other. Maybe a cultural abyss needed to be bridged before a longer conversation could get going. Or maybe it was because he couldn't pronounce her name properly. He had trouble with the letter *V*— and especially two *V*s close together. No matter how hard Max tried, he ended up saying "Hi, Fibeca," which elicited wan smiles from her. She tried to help alleviate this awkward matter by suggesting that he just call her Viv. When he tried that, it came out as "Fib," which was worse, so he went back to Fibeca.

Once, he got up the nerve to ask her and Argos over to his apartment for dinner. He made a spinach-mushroom quiche, as that dish was practically failsafe for any guest. For Argos, he had some big leftover hambones from a soup he'd made. Viveca came over and rang his door-light. In hindsight, Max was not sure if it had been worth the trouble to rig all three rooms in his apartment with flashing lights for the door and telephone. First of all, the rickety apartment shook a little whenever someone walked up the steps. This let him know someone was at the door. Second, there was a window beside the door. Anytime someone passed the window, he either saw the person's head, or a big head-shadow crossed the wall. And then there was the 150-watt bulb going off over the doorway. It brightly illuminated every room as if it were in the middle of a Major League Baseball park at night. Rigging the other two rooms with flashing lights had proved to be an unnecessary waste.

Viveca came in smelling like she had just showered. Her hair was slightly wet and gave off the fragrance of Herbal Essences. She wore a white V-neck T-shirt that showed humbly sized breasts with a bare hint of cleavage. Argos rushed in smelling like the ocean and immediately went off to sniff every corner of the apartment.

Max had wine chilled in the fridge and glasses all set. Viveca politely declined the wine and asked for juice. Strike one. They sat down at the card table, which he had set with paper plates and napkins.

"Where did you get that tapestry?" she asked.

"Oh, I got it real cheap at some street bazaar in Houston."

"It looks nice up on the wall there," she said.

"Thanks. It saved me the time and trouble of having to paint these filthy walls."

She smiled politely. Argos was sniffing around in his bedroom, where he had just put fresh sheets on the waterbed. He hoped Argos didn't smell anything he might have dribbled on the floor from watching a porno video the night before. He could've kicked himself for doing that. If things got hot with Viveca after dinner, he might not have as much ammo to shoot with, and she would see him as some sexually dysfunctional deaf dweeb.

Max took the quiche out of the toaster oven and sliced it into quarters.

"OK if I put out the hambone for Argos now?" he asked.

"Sure, sure, go ahead."

Good timing. Max didn't want Viveca to think something weird was in his bedroom, because Argos was spending an unusual amount of time in there, licking the floor, sniffing the drawers, etc.

"Careful, quiche is hot. Would you like more apple juice?" asked Max.

"Sure, please. Thank you."

"Do you mind if I help myself to some wine?" he asked.

"No, not at all. It's your home!"

"Well, yes and no. It belongs to the Rodriguezes, remember?"

"Oh, I hate that man!" she said. "Such a slumlord. When is he ever going to get our grass cut?"

"Next year?"

"No! It's already halfway through the summer!"

"He's a tightwad. Doesn't want to spend on gas, repairs, nor on anyone who can cut the grass for him."

"The sticker burrs are driving me crazy. Every night I have to pick them out of Argos's fur."

"We should file a complaint to somebody, but I don't know who," Max said. Finally, a topic to talk about that took the focus off each other.

"I don't know, either. I've been so busy with medical school that I don't have time for things like that," said Viveca.

"Maybe I can look into it and find a way to lodge a complaint. If I do, then I can just show you a letter and you can sign it if you agree."

"Oh, sure, that would be a huge help." She smiled. He noticed that her teeth were rather small and somewhat gray. He thought he could overlook that flaw.

"Bon appetit," he said, double-knocking on the card table, which wobbled a little when he pulled up closer to it. "Sorry about the table—one of these days I'll get a real table, after a couple more months of pay at the lab."

"Oh, that's OK! My dining table is my lap when I sit on the sofa. Hmm, this is good," she said.

Max wasn't so sure. She kept picking out the diced onions and corralling them to the side of her plate. OK, so she didn't like onions. Strike two. At least Argos was chewing on her bone with blissful abandon. Viveca was done with her slice, leaving a little pile of translucent squares on her plate. She finished the last of her juice.

"Well, that was good. Thank you so much for having us over." Argos looked up, predicting her mistress's departure, but kept her head down, gnawing with the side of her teeth.

"I'll have to have you over sometime," she said, getting up.

"I'd like that," said Max. "Are you sure you don't want to stay for dessert? I made a banana yogurt pie." He suddenly realized that he'd made two pies for tonight's meal. Why do these revelations always surface after the fact?

"No, thank you. I have to watch my weight," she said.

"Weight? You have a perfect figure—I mean, you have no fat at all. At least, I'm not seeing any. Not that I'm looking. Sorry, Fib, I mean Fibeca—that came out kinda strange."

"That's OK. I know what you mean. I just have to watch my weight. I can balloon up real fast." She stroked Argos hard behind the neck, as if urging her: Come on, let's get out of this man-joint.

"Well, take the hambones for Argos. I don't plan on chewing them."

She laughed courteously.

"Here, let me put them in a Baggie for you. And I'll let you know if I make any progress with Rodriguez."

He held the door open for her as she left and went down the steps and back up the same number of steps to her apartment next door. He could still smell her Herbal Essences.

It turned out that she never did invite him in to her apartment for a meal or a chat. And he never found a way to formally file a complaint against Rodriguez, who kept saying the lawn would be cut sometime within the month. The sandburs were as high as ever, and Viveca and Max were back to their obligatory "hi's" and waves.

Before long, one day he noticed a rental truck outside. Viveca and some guy were moving out her belongings. She'd never told Max she was planning to move. Well, he wasn't exactly her boyfriend or closest confidant, but as a neighbor he'd kind of gotten used to fantasizing that they were very familiar with each other, and that he knew what she was doing from day to day—going to her pediatric medicine classes, coming home to walk Argos along the beach, eating dinner, studying, and then going to bed.

"So you're moving out, huh?" he asked.

Viveca stopped on her way back up the steps. "Oh, yeah, I meant to tell you," she said. "I got a residency in San Antone."

The guy walked up behind her and put his arm around her waist. He whispered something in her ear. She nodded yes. He continued on, gave Max a nod, and went into her apartment.

"I see. Wish you luck," said Max. His fantasy that he would slowly but surely work on this simple, cute, homey girl had completely shattered to pieces. Here she'd been with this guy all along, who was probably sucking on her humble tits and banging her brains out next door while Max watched porn videos to tide him over until she was ready.

That was when Bertha—the hard of hearing, chubby, pimply-faced, thick-glassed Christian pathology photo resident—moved in next door. She was sweet and dorky and rather unfeminine. One couldn't help but like her because she was real and all there, up front. It was just that he couldn't get his little guy to even squirm when he tried to imagine her undressed. Nevertheless, Bertha and Max became friends through work and their alumni connection.

In Bertha's sparse apartment, he sat on a folding chair and watched her assemble and tune up her trumpet.

"Do you know the words to 'The Star-Spangled Banner'?" she asked.

"Of course!"

"Sorry, I didn't know. Some deaf people don't know any songs, so I was just checking. Didn't mean to offend you."

"No offense taken. How do you wanna do this?"

She was wearing a white crew neck T-shirt with no bra, and a necklace with a small wooden cross pendant. Had Viveca left her white T-shirts behind? Bertha's breasts were big and floppy, and swayed every time she blew on the trumpet. Nope, the little guy still wouldn't move, but Max found it fun to watch the physics of her breast movement while she played the trumpet.

"I'll nod my head when it's time for you to start signing the first word," she said.

Of all the musical instruments he had heard up close (with his hearing aids on), the trumpet was one of his favorites. It had pure tones that his residual hearing picked up quite clearly. The same went for drums. He found it easy to follow the rhythm of the national anthem and, after a few run-throughs, Bertha and Max had the song down pat.

At the picnic, Dr. Robb introduced them to everyone and announced that they were going to perform "The Star-Spangled Banner." Max felt like they were in a dog and pony show. He got the impression that most of the employees were seeing him and

Bertha in a different light outside of the lab, as if they'd thought they had no other aspects to their lives besides work.

A microphone was set up near Bertha, and another one was placed near Max. Max looked at the AV technician and shook his head. The technician looked at him with a puzzled expression. Max gestured that he was going to sign, not sing. Was he going to perform sign language to a microphone? Everyone laughed. The technician came forward and removed the mike and quietly apologized.

Bertha looked at Max to indicate she was ready. He gave her a wink. The first few undulating notes came out to him from the portable public address system near them. The trumpet sounded hauntingly beautiful, almost like "Taps," perfectly juxtaposed with the memorialized submarine, the USS *Cavalla*, in the background, and the U.S. and Texas flags fluttering together, up high in a blue, cloudless sky. Beyond the *Cavalla*, the Galveston–Port Bolivar ferry was making its hourly commute across the Houston Ship Channel.

Bertha gave Max a nod, and he began signing the first verse. Unexpectedly, everyone began to sing along with his signs, almost as if they knew what each sign meant. Bertha, in her own musical world, looked up from her trumpet keys and became red-faced, but she continued on. Seeing the others singing bolstered his energy and made him exaggerate some of his signs to impress them more. Max was so into the moment that he completely blanked on the last few lines. Shit! He looked at Bertha, who gave him a look back to continue on. The words wouldn't come to him. Hell, who would know the difference as long as he kept moving his hands in the air in a pretty way? No one would have a clue that he had forgotten the last lines of the anthem.

When the song ended, everyone clapped vigorously. The women wiped tears from their eyes. The men looked at their feet, clearing their throats. Dr. Robb came up to shake Max's hand, and then hugged Bertha. Over Robb's shoulder, Max gestured a "thumbs-up" to Bertha.

Some of the guys came up to Max and slapped him on the back without saying anything. A couple of the women hugged Max, saying how beautiful his signs were, and how they felt they knew every sign for the whole song. This was actually the first time that Max, as a Deaf employee, was shown genuine respect. How ironic that it had taken music to garner that.

Max slowly came to terms with the fact that he would have no luck with women throughout the residency year. He would ride out the remaining time working at the lab and teaching his sign language class until the end of August, and then seek his chances elsewhere. A week after the picnic, during a break from a class lesson on animal signs, one of the women from his sign language course slipped Max a note inviting him to her house for a small gathering. She wanted him to meet her deaf cousin from Austin who had recently been hired as a costume assistant for an outdoor summer stock theater on the west end at Galveston Island State Park. Hearing people often told him that they had a hard of hearing grandmother, an uncle who was hearing-impaired in one ear, a deaf dog, or a deaf whatever, whom they hoped he would meet one day. He guessed they thought people with hearing loss were one big family. Since she was one of his good students, he was willing to meet this woman's cousin.

Max remembered having hiked through the state park when he'd lived out at the beach house. It was on a Sunday morning, in the middle of a Galveston winter, which usually got down into the thirties for a few weeks. He'd needed a break from his portfolio work and had to get out of the house for a long walk in fresh air. As he hiked along the boardwalk trail that went over the swamps, he'd discovered beyond tufts of marsh grass an outdoor amphitheater overlooking a bayou. It was right smack in the middle of miles of wetlands and beach. Seats were arranged in high, tiered rows like the outfield section of a baseball stadium. A row of seagulls squatting on the seats watched Max walk across the dirt stage. There was no one around. No boats out in the water. Just palm trees; a steady, cold wind; and the gray sky.

Behind the theater was a Quonset hut with the large, faded word PEPSI painted in blue and white across the corrugated steel. Beside the hut was a row of identical one-level apartments, like a lone motel on a country highway. A sign over the boarded-up box office read: "Come back next summer! See Broadway-style musicals every night under the stars: *The Lone Star; Annie Get Your Gun; Hello, Dolly!*" He'd felt like he was in a deserted town wiped out by a plague.

When he met Madison, the costume assistant cousin of his student, it was like arriving at an oasis he had been seeking for months. For him, she was a tall, cool drink of water—an intelligent, attractive Deaf woman he could relate to, at long last. He learned that her parents and siblings were also Deaf, as were five generations of relatives. She rarely moved her lips when signing. It took Max some getting used to, for he had become so used to speaking and to reading the faces and lips of hearing people. He didn't need to wear his hearing aids with her; instead, he had to get accustomed to turning off his voice and reading her unique Southern sign style. She loved to fingerspell, which took a bit of extra concentration for him. To him, fingerspelling was like reading fancy cursive. After a while, he got the hang of reading it.

Maddy, as she preferred to be called, had a natural, old-fashioned beauty that reminded him of a 1940s movie actress—like Hedy Lamarr or Lauren Bacall. She had smoky blue eyes and long blonde hair parted on the side and held up by a barrette. When she formed her hand shapes into words, it was graceful and poetic, even when she was talking about mundane things. Her goal was to become a professional actress for stage and film, but to achieve that, she needed to work with costumes to learn all about how stage productions worked. She believed that the best way to learn the craft was to work in all areas backstage.

She was intrigued by the kind of work Max did at the hospital, and wanted to know more about it. They agreed to meet to give each other tours of their workplaces, and the following Saturday morning Maddy pulled up to the main entrance of UTMB in a

1966 aqua-colored Chevy step-side pickup truck with Texas plates that read: DEF PWRD.

"Good morning," signed Max. "Nice truck! Lifted body and fat Super Sport tires—gorgeous! Is that a three-speed column stick shift?"

"Are you talking about my body?" asked Maddy. "Yep. Love old trucks. They're good for a traveling girl like me."

"What's your license say?"

"Deaf powered!" She put one hand over her ear and the other hand out the window in a fist.

"Radical! Shouldn't it be Deaf power, though? What's the 'd' for?"

"The truck is powered by me!" she said.

"Ahhh, now why didn't I figure that out?"

"Maybe you haven't had your morning coffee yet."

"You're right! Was waiting to see if you wanted me to pick up some coffee before we go to my lab."

"I get my morning caffeine from Pepsi. Is there a machine around?"

"Oh yeah, vending machines are all over the place. We've got medical students everywhere."

After they got their coffee and soda, Max gave Maddy the grand tour. He introduced her to Orlando, who was alone doing some work for a neuropathologist on some black-and-white prints of dissected brains to be published in a journal. Max cautioned her that the photos might be upsetting to look at.

She waved her hand at him like he was a nuisance: "Get outta here, I've seen it all," she said.

"Oh really? How's that?" asked Max.

"My father used to work as a mortician's assistant."

"Wow! My grandfather was a mortician."

"Check that off on the list of things we have in common," said Madison. She held up her soda can to toast. Max held out his coffee cup.

"Wait, wait," she said. "Deaf toast!"

"What's that?"

"Hold your cup out and bend your wrist to touch my wrist. You know, Deaf people must feel; can't hear our drinks clink together."

"Ah, learn something new every day," said Max. "Cheers!"

Back at her truck, she told him she would drive, and would be happy to bring him back to the university. Max protested, but she insisted, saying she was born to drive.

"So, you'll be my c-h-a-u-f-f-e-u-r for the day?" he said, finger-spelling each letter as clearly as he could. He was testing her with this word choice, wondering if she would understand it. He'd been accused by some deaf people of trying to act "hearing" by throwing out "big" words.

"I'll be happy to be your chauffeur," she said, fingerspelling the word back so fluidly that the word was like a sign in itself. This confirmed to him that she was indeed a well-educated deaf woman with strong bilingual skills—a rare find now that he was out in the hearing world.

Maddy told him to hop into the cab. He put his camera bag on the floor of the truck and climbed in. She backed out of the Pathology Building parking lot and went down a narrow side street to get to the seawall. She eased her big truck into the stream of traffic on Seawall Boulevard with the confidence of an eighteen-wheel-truck driver.

"You're a helluva driver," he said. "I noticed you barreled right through tight spots without batting an eye or backing off on the accelerator."

She laughed and gave a dimpled smile. She took her eyes off the road and momentarily caught him admiring her. Max asked about her background. She'd gone to the Texas School for the Deaf for a while, but found it way too easy. Next she went to an oral school, where they drove her insane with speech therapy. And then she'd gone on to a mainstreamed school where she was placed in a gifted program. After high school graduation, she'd enrolled in the honors program, studying theater and dance at the University of Texas in Austin. She lived with her parents near the deaf school for a while, and was a part-time teacher's aide there until she was ready to strike out on her own.

"Funny you mentioned the word *chauffeur*," she said. "I had a dream last night that I was a chauffeur for famous people. They told me they liked my driving."

A car towing a speedboat suddenly cut in front of her. Maddy honked her horn and stayed on it for a good fifteen seconds. "*Idiot!*" she signed. "Hearing people can't drive." She tailgated the car, staying several feet behind the boat's propeller.

Signing away with one hand on the wheel, she said, "A chauffeur, imagine . . . me a deaf woman whom these stars trusted to drive them anywhere. In my limo, there's Ryan O'Neal and his girlfriend Farrah Fawcett . . . that's what, over sixty million dollars riding in the back seat? Jack Nicholson and his latest mistress in another row of seats in front of O'Neal and Fawcett—thirty-five million . . . what's that come to?"

The front of the truck was getting closer to the boat propeller. The speedometer pointed to 70 mph. The left lane was wide open for passing. Max didn't say anything because he didn't want to offend her by commenting on her driving skills; their relationship was budding nicely, and he didn't want to nip it off.

Maddy beeped the horn again a few more times. "Ninety-five million dollars—imagine!" she said. She went on and on about the celebrities and how she was driving a gold mine in her block-long stretch limo. The brake lights on the boat trailer lit up. Her sandaled foot with red painted toenails was nowhere near the brake pedal. This time she held down the horn and let it blare continuously. Max was about to put a damper on the relationship by letting her know that they were dangerously close to a gory pileup on the seawall.

Slowly, the boat trailer veered off onto the highway shoulder. They passed the vehicle, mere molecules from metal scraping metal.

Shifting gears, Maddy talked about how she hadn't done much reading lately. She wanted to get back into it, though she had been

reading off and on a book about the works of some writer named Piraro that he didn't know about. Then it hit him.

"Didn't he draw some cartoons called 'Bizarro's World'?" Max asked.

"Yes, yes, he did!" She was flushed in the face. "Not many deaf men would know that," she said.

"Well, ahem," said Max, adjusting an imaginary sports coat and tie. "What can I say?"

She turned the truck into the entrance to the state park and maneuvered a windy road leading to the amphitheater parking lot. He studied her profile and tanned complexion. When she looked over at him, he averted his gaze. She stopped the truck and put it in park.

"So, what were you looking at, Mr. Max?" she asked.

"Well, I was thinking you have a nice, unique face for a portrait."

"What're you waiting for? Get that camera out!"

"Stay right there. Your arm resting on the wheel, and you looking at me, is perfect. You parked in the right spot—nice background of the bayou and palm trees framed by your truck window."

Maddy started to remove her barrette to fix her hair, but Max told her to leave it. He liked her hair's down-to-earth look, with a few stray wisps of blonde hair hanging over the side of her face.

"Aren't you going to use a flash?" asked Maddy.

"Nope, ambient lighting," Max answered.

The costume shop near where Maddy parked was located in one of the stables he remembered seeing from his walk. Rows upon rows of period costumes and wigs were on stands. Dressmaker dummies with fabric swatches pinned to them were everywhere. Max got lost at times looking for Maddy on their little tour of the costume shop. Behind one of the dummies, he saw her arm stick out and beckon him to follow her. She showed him a row of industrial sewing machines and patted them on their behinds. "My babies," she said.

Next she showed him a little room in the Hitchcockian Bates Motel setup behind the theater. The room was adorned with Christmas lights and sheer fabric hanging over the strings of lights to cheer things up. Her dresser top and windowsill were full of empty Diet Pepsi cans. She admitted to an addiction.

"Right now we are doing a play called *The Lone Star*. Want to see the wings where the actors bring props on stage?" Maddy asked.

"Sure, would love to see it. I've never performed on a stage or gone backstage."

"This is a natural stage—no wood or raised platform. Kind of like the old Greek theater. Makes it easier to bring on set pieces, like cannons and horse carriages. We even use live horses. That's why we have those stables over there beyond the wings."

"Very interesting. You know, I hated theater when I was grow-ing up," said Max.

"Why is that?"

"My parents once took me to an outdoor show in Roanoke Island, North Carolina. We were in an amphitheater very similar to this one, sitting way up in the nosebleed section. I must've been about nine or ten years old. All of the actors were as small as ants to me. Ever tried lipreading an ant?"

Maddy smiled. "Well, I can get you front row seats here, but we won't have any interpreters around. This island is like fifty years behind on accessibility issues," she said.

"It's not that bad," said Max. "The hospital has been good to me about that, but that's another story. Anyhow, I'm in this outdoor theater sitting practically up in the clouds, bored out of my mind, when suddenly my parents get up and start exchanging remarks with someone behind us. Then, for no reason, we leave. In the car, my mother takes her shirt off. I smell something weird. Find out a lady sitting behind us threw up on my mother."

"No wonder you hate theater!" Maddy laughed. "Well, here we are. This whole property used to be a cattle farm."

"They sure made good use of these old barns for wings—brilliant," said Max.

"People I work with have told me there's a ghost that goes back and forth between the two barns. One of the farmer's sons hanged himself in the hayloft. They say you can hear the rope creaking and swaying. And sometimes you can see the shadow of the body swinging."

"Have you seen it?" asked Max.

"No, just what I've been told."

"I don't believe in ghosts. I think it's a hearing thing. Most ghost stories are all about sounds—creepy sounds."

"You've got a point there," said Maddy.

"I've never seen any ghostlike movements or anything. I work in a place where people die all the time. How come I don't see their ghosts around when I'm working in the lab?"

Maddy nodded in agreement.

"Let's get out of this hot weather and go back to my room where it's cool and dry," said Maddy.

"I bet it's nice to see a show here," said Max.

"It is. Even if you can't follow the words, you can sit back, drink a Pepsi, and enjoy the warm Gulf breeze, the sunsets, herons flying by."

"You and your Pepsis!" Max said.

"It's not just me. Pepsi is a big sponsor of our shows here."

"Oh, that explains it!"

"So, when the actors fight for Texas's independence," Maddy continued, "it gets pretty lively—really visual, with gunshots and cannon fire. No words are needed. I'll get you a comp ticket if you want."

"That would be real nice. Would you be able to sit with me?"

"Sorry—no. I have to work backstage during the show. Actors have to make quick costume changes, and I help them with that. Sometimes an actor's costume will rip or they'll lose a button. I have to be ready for emergency sewing. Then after the show I have to launder all of the costumes."

"I think I could manage going solo," said Max. "Would you be around after the show, I mean, after you do the laundry?"

"Hmmm, I'm usually the only one around after the show. I could throw a load in the wash and we could hang out till it's time for me to go back and do another load. Have to do three loads."

Maddy opened the door to her room and let him in first.

"I wouldn't mind waiting," said Max. "Would you have space for me to wait in your room among all of these Pepsi cans?"

Maddy closed the door. She swiped all of the cans from the windowsill and closed the blind. She stood there and looked him directly in the eyes. "Yes," she said. "I think I have space for you."

Max swallowed hard. His throat clicked. He took a few steps toward her and took her hand. He gently rubbed her long, slender fingers, and lifted them to his mouth. He could smell a light, honey-lemon scent. Maddy took a step closer to him. Softly, Max nibbled each knuckle on her hand, starting from the thumb to the little finger. Before he got to the little finger, Maddy moved her head in to intercept his lips. She pressed her pelvis against his, and when she did this, Max reciprocated and put his other hand inside the back pocket of her jeans and pressed harder. She opened her mouth to let his tongue have intercourse with it.

After a bout of animalistic lovemaking, Maddy slowly woke up on Max's hairy chest. Although she couldn't hear it, she could feel Max's heartbeat along the side of her face. Max was already awake, lightly rubbing the palm of his hand slowly up and down her back. He was trying hard not to plan too far ahead into his future with Maddy. Doing so in the past had brought bad luck.

She fingerspelled to him: "D-o n-o-t s-t-o-p."

Max fingerspelled back: "S-t-o-p w-h-a-t?" He rubbed her breasts.

"T-h-a-t," she said.

He massaged her ass cheeks.

"A-n-d t-h-a-t." She gave him a warm kiss, and looked over at her clock. "Stop! Oh no, I've got to hurry and get you back home. Have to start setting up costumes for the actors before tonight's show."

Both quickly put on their clothes, kicking Pepsi cans in the process. Max asked if he could drive her truck—he had always wanted to drive a pickup with three-speed stick shift. He also wanted to avoid another near-miss on the seawall. She agreed.

Max kept the truck within the speed limit while Maddy sat close to him, holding his hand, her head on his shoulder. Off to their right along the beach, the surf curled and pounded forward. Palm trees swayed their heads in unison from the trade winds, making Max feel serene. Since the sun was lower in the sky, he asked Maddy if he could turn off the air conditioner and roll down the window. He felt her nod on his shoulder. Warm, humid air rushed in, bathing the two of them with the feeling that—at least for this moment—all was natural and right with the world.

July 24, 1982
Bedroom, 8th St. Apt.
Dear folks,

   Since I last talked with you over the phone
about Maddy, my relationship with her has been
developing nicely. I wasn't sure where it was
going to go, but things have been looking good.
I have never met a Deaf woman, or any woman for
that matter, who understands me as much as she
does. I've included my favorite photo of her --
taken in her '66 Chevy pickup. Dad -- what're
you looking at? Keep your eyes on the truck!
   I wrote a poem about her, but not sure if it's
right yet. Want to send it to you for feedback
before I give it to her.

Cracking the Cryptology of Love

by
Dempsey Maxwell McCall

for Maddy

her sleeping puckered lips
invite me in to connect
to take away her baby's breath
instead I lean over to kiss
the hollow of her cheek
a pulse in her neck taps out
she turns and stirs with her feet
a lover's secret code about—

. . . if only I could decipher.

Is it too sappy? Let me know what you think.

Zag has left for L.A. We had one last hurrah out on the beach with beers, barbecue sandwiches, and body-surfing.

Still not sure about end of summer plans. Want to see how things pan out with Maddy, especially with her work ending in August . . . and mine too!

Siempre el amor,
Max

Toll for the Ferryman

Small Cavities   For small-cavity and deep wounds, use the ring flash instead of the handheld flash. The handheld flash would create shadows that could obscure pertinent information. With the tube of the ring flash around the lens, you will get flat, even lighting without shadows. Be aware that ring flashes create circular reflections on wet surfaces. Warn the surgeon, or appropriate medical personnel, beforehand about difficult or unusual photo setups.

It was four o'clock in the morning when the vibrating pager went off. When he was on 24-hour call, Max usually either had trouble getting to sleep or slept sporadically, with vivid dreams. Before the pager startled him awake, he had been in the middle of a dream in which he was being interrogated by two doctors from the university. In the dream, he was off for the evening when Drs. Folse and Leatherberry came to his 8th Street garage apartment and pressed the button that activated his door-light. A hearing friend of Max's had been at his place, working periodically over a couple of weeks on pen and ink drawings. He couldn't remember if it was Orlando, Zag, or Larry, or maybe Bimbo. On the night that the two doctors came over, the kitchen sink was the messiest it had ever been. Whenever Max's friend came over, he always used the sink to wash his pens and trays—but on that particular night, the ink had coagulated in the drain, causing black goo to overflow onto the counter and the floor.

The doctors wanted to talk with Max about his medical-legal work on a recent case in which a patient's face had been mangled by mechanized surgical equipment—an automatic surgical suturing machine—completely programmed by a computer. It looked

217

like a large, stainless steel, industrial sewing machine fastened to a vertical track. Max had been recording the new automatic suturing procedure on videotape in the operating room when the machine went haywire and rapidly pulverized the patient's face. Max kept seeing the thick needle impale the man's skin, up and down, back and forth across his entire face, wrapping it with blue surgical thread. The patient was left for dead on the table, alone with Max and his video camera. The surgical team had vamoosed.

The dream continued: the media had somehow gotten wind of the malfunction and learned that Max was the photographer on the scene. They ambushed him on campus just before he went in to work, begging for a copy of the videotape. Max found himself suckered into an impromptu press conference, trying to answer interview questions from a bevy of international reporters as best he could in the glare of bright lights, and without an available ASL interpreter. He found that every time he tried to answer a question, he spoke with a mouthful of wet sand. And when he spat out the sand to speak more clearly, the words came out in a foreign language that nobody understood, not even himself.

The two plastic surgeons waiting in his apartment leaned forward, glowering at him, their postures stiff. After a long silence, Dr. Leatherberry finally said: "You're a pretty good biophotographer, but you've got a horrendous voice!" Then Dr. Folse clipped a metal cuff around Max's neck and tortured him with electric shocks. That was when Max suddenly woke up to the vibrations from his pager.

It was difficult to sleep with the pager clipped to his underwear, and then there was the ever-present worry about missing the call because he didn't feel the vibrations. Missing a call would be the death knell of his long struggle to achieve the elite responsibility of handling 24-hour call. He had worked hard to convince people at the hospital that he could take calls as well as his hearing counterparts, provided that the right accommodations were made: a vibrating pager and a Telecommunication Device for the Deaf, one for him and one for the main switchboard operator at the hospital, to allow the two to converse over the phone. Max had gotten Dr. Robb and Dotty, his old Affirmative Actions friend, to help him wrangle with the administrators to secure the necessary communications equipment.

Max envied the other photographers who took turns at 24-hour call. First of all, they earned overtime pay just for wearing a pager on their belts. Then there seemed to be a sense of prestige that came with wearing this small brown electronic device, listening to important words come out of it. Communication was quick. Phone calls were made to retrieve more information. Wearing the device raised one's status almost to the holy level of doctor. When Max had first received the accessible equipment for taking calls, Dr. Robb had arranged a test run by having the main switchboard operator at the hospital page Max. Max had felt the vibration and called the switchboard via his TDD. The typing of the reply message from the operator was slow, but at least the line of communication had been opened. He was ready for his first full weekend of 24-hour call.

Ironically, when the third call of that weekend arrived, he paid through the nose to gain equal access. It was around 3 a.m. on a Sunday; he'd finally been able to drift off to sleep when the pager went off. Max immediately put on his shirt, pants, and shoes, and then wondered why he was doing all of this before even calling the main switchboard. He didn't need to have his pants on to make a phone call. Shaking off the grogginess, he sat down, picked up the phone, and dialed the number for the hospital. He pushed the receiver into the rubber coupler of the TDD and watched the cursor on the LED readout blink off and on intermittently, which indicated the phone was ringing:

HELLO? UTMB OPR GA

HI MAX HERE GA

YOUR CALL IS FOR O.R. #12 STAT! SIAMESE TWIN SEPARATION GA

Max stared at the LED readout. Had the operator just typed a non sequitur? Siamese cat separation? What was there to separate on a cat? Besides, UTMB didn't deal with veterinary medicine. Max reread the readout: SIAMESE—TWIN—SEPARATION. Through the three o'clock fog he got it—there must have been a birth of two babies physically joined somewhere on their bodies. GOT IT BE THERE ABT 20 MINS THANK U GA COME PREPARED TO STAY ALL DAY GA TO SK SKSKSK

He hung up, switched off the TDD, and tore out the printout of the conversation. He quickly put on his shoes while running through a mental checklist of necessary photographic items— extra batteries and film, a wide-angle lens, a 200mm telephoto lens, an extra camera body with a motor drive. He downed a glass of orange juice and put a packet of granola bars in his pocket. Then he hopped on his bike and headed for UTMB.

After double-checking with the operating room dispatch desk on the location of the Siamese twin separation procedure, Max donned a set of surgical scrubs and went to OR no. 12. When he entered the room, there were twice as many people as usual, including a TV cameraman and a photographer, obviously from the local media outlets. Everyone seemed to be in high spirits, bustling about with energy. Dr. Casey, one of the pediatric sur-geons that Max had taken pictures for, approached him and mo-tioned for a pad of paper and pen. He wrote that in addition to the specific close-ups that he wanted of the separation procedure, he would like a variety of shots around the room for a pictorial essay. Max enjoyed taking photos for him. He was a good doctor to work with: open-minded about working with Max, yet very precise about what he wanted, always economical with words. His movements on the operating table were also essential and exact. When he was off the table during a change in dressing or proce-dure, Dr. Casey often kept his gloved hands together in prayer formation and made small rocking motions.

Two anesthesiologists were working to get the twins anesthe-tized. It took longer than usual—everything was taking more

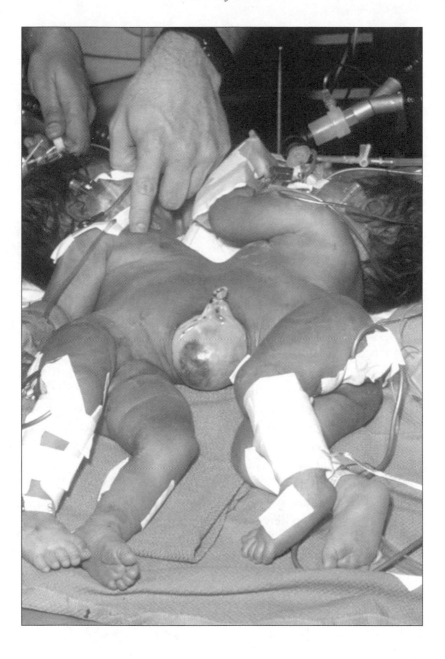

time—as they were dealing with two patients. Max could see that the twins were conjoined at the abdomen. He read on their chart that they shared a liver, breastbone, and diaphragm. After three hours, Dr. Casey began cutting, slowly and methodically. Every now and then he would stop, have the scrub nurse wipe up the blood in the field, and beckon for Max to shoot some close-ups. Max had to keep taking short breaks to go to the bathroom or drink water to stay alert. His stomach tightened into a knot for lack of food. He wondered if the others felt the same. He was sure they could hear his stomach gurgle and rumble, but he couldn't hear theirs. After a while, the novelty of photographing the separation wore off, and it became just another day in the OR. He stepped in every now and then to take the requisite shots the doctor asked for. Then the moment of the actual separation came. Suddenly, the novelty and flurry of activity returned, with everyone scurrying around to take care of two tiny individual patients in the room.

Finally, after nine agonizing hours and six rolls of film, the circulating nurse dismissed Max. She wrote to him to put in a rush order on processing the film, and to send the results to Dr. Casey's office. Hungry and exhausted, he dropped the film off at the lab for development, then climbed wearily onto his bike to head home. When he woke up the next day to go to work, he learned that, hours after the separation, one of the twins had died.

The next early-morning call—4 a.m.—was for a medical-legal case in the ER. When he got there, he notified the admitting clerk that he was the medical photographer on call. She was on the phone and held up a "4" hand shape. She buzzed the security door to let him in. As he was going in to examination room number four, a nurse stopped to warn him that the patient was no longer alive—had died about a half hour ago. The body was waiting to be transported to the morgue, after the medical-legal photos were taken. Max thanked her and parted the curtains.

The first thing he saw upon entering were blood-soaked gauze pads all over the floor. When Max looked up, the hair on his neck stood up. It was Reynaldo on the table, with the crash cart next to him. In a way, he wasn't surprised. Yet seeing Reynaldo this way jolted Max deeply. Max had not seen him for a while, mostly because he had been spending a lot of time with Maddy. A terrible sense of guilt washed over him. The last time they'd been together was when Max had treated Reynaldo to lunch at IHOP a couple of months ago. Rey was beside himself, and had needed to vent about the threats made to him by his ex-wife's protective brothers. He'd tried to insist on more time with his son. Max suspected that this might be why his friend was on the table—he'd gone too far with his demands for visitation and had gotten street justice for it. The family probably thought that they could easily get away with murder, since no one in the police department was going to waste much time investigating the death of a homeless deaf man.

Rey's hair was disheveled; his usual brown face was pale and gray. Tubes stuck out of his open, crooked mouth. White EKG lead pads dotted his chest, and an IV line was stuck in his arm. Max saw a small gunshot wound in the chest near Reynaldo's heart. He wished he were back in the urology exam room with him, interpreting the absurd situation with his penis—anything but this.

Max wanted to rush out of the room and ask the admitting desk to call another photographer to take over, but something told him to tough it out. Put up the wall and do the job. Doctors and nurses did it all the time. Why couldn't he? Determined to document as much clear evidence as possible for a medical-legal case, he first photographed a wide shot of Reynaldo's entire body, for orientation. Reynaldo's feet were outstretched—rigor mortis had quickly set in after resuscitation efforts failed. They had cut open his blue oxford shirt down the middle. While Max was focusing and setting the proper f-stop for exposure, he slowly realized that it was the shirt he had loaned to Reynaldo for the Mardi Gras party. Reynaldo's eyes were wide open, in a frozen, cloudy stare. Why hadn't the ER team closed Rey's eyes?

While studying for his written exam, Max had read about post-mortem procedures and related folklore. It was ritually important to close the corpse's eyes quickly, as the eyes were among the first organs to rigidify, and leaving them open was considered a threat to the dead person's kin. One way to keep the eyes closed was to put coins over them. Some felt that the coins were a toll for the soul, so that when it crossed the river Styx into the afterworld, Charon, the ferryman, got paid. Seafarers did something similar by putting a coin under the mast of a ship in case the ship sank and all hands drowned. In many cultures, coins on the eyes of the dead represented a feeling that money, so important in life, might also be important in death. Knowing Reynaldo, Max thought he would probably have liked that.

Max grabbed a stool and stood over the body to take a medium shot of Rey's torso. Replacing the normal lens with a macro lens, he went in close to the bullet wound. Tears ran down Max's face. Images of his abused high school photo buddy, Billy Hendricks, were superimposed over the scene. He blinked, swallowed hard, and recorded the wound at various magnifications, and then got down from the stool. He noticed a wallet under the ER table. Opening it, he found a couple of dollars and a photo of a little boy smiling. It was Reynaldo's deaf son, the source of so much agony for him. He put the wallet back in Reynaldo's pants. Max had the strange urge to get on the table and give him a bear hug. Instead, he took a couple of quarters out of his camera bag and closed Reynaldo's eyes with them. Before he left the room he noticed that the IV bag was still dripping fluid down into Reynaldo's arm.

August 7, 1982

Dear Mom & Dad:

I'm writing with a heavy heart. My Deaf friend
Reynaldo died last week. Had to photograph him
in the ER. Apparently, he was murdered. Gunshot
wound in the chest. I suspect it had something
to do with Reynaldo demanding partial custody
of his son from his ex-wife's family, though
I have no way of knowing for sure. The case is
still under investgax investigation. I've been
told that I will have to testify in court to the
validity of the photographs of his bullet wound.
I don't know when yet. It might be in a couple
of weeks or it might be in six months to a year.
I am not looking forward to that because of
complex communication issues involving the use
of ASL interpreters in the courtroom. It's too
complicated to explain in a letter, I'd rather
not get into that. Reynaldo had no money; lived
a hand-to-mouth existence. The hospital has
been trying to locate his family in Mexico but
has not had any luck. They're holding his body
for ten days. If no one claims it, the hospital
notifies the Anatomical Board of the State
of Texas, who will determine if the body is
suitable for donation to medical education. Zag
flew in from L.A. when he heard the news. He and
I are taking up a collection. We plan to claim
Reynaldo's body, have it cremated, and give him
a proper send-off, probably at the seawall near
the LeRoy Colombo memorial. Just wanted you to
know what's going on. I'm basically fine, but
still a bit shocked that Reynaldo's gone for
good.

I miss you all very much.

Love, Max

Of Serendipitous Things

Photo Log   Filling out your photo log is a very important part of your job. After you shoot a picture, make sure you write down: patient or subject's name, date you shot the picture, department the photo will be billed to, date delivered, name of doctor or scientist the photos will go to (NO INTERNS OR MEDICAL STUDENTS!), and a good description of what you shot. If the photos are slides, label the top slide in each series; thumb-spot all slides in the stack; put the slides in a glassine envelope or wrap them in a paper cover fastened with a rubber band. If the photos are prints, put them in a corresponding-sized manila envelope and label it with the doctor's name and department, and date; file away slide and print orders in their respective sections in the delivery cabinet.

During an early Sunday morning in mid-August, Max grabbed his camera bag on a whim and went out to do his favorite form of photography: "street shooting." It was a technique he'd learned from one of his biomedical photo classes at RIT, where he'd been given an assignment called "Serendipity." He'd had to look up the word after class: an accidental discovery of things in a happy or beneficial way. At first, this puzzled him, as everything he'd learned to photograph during his four years at college had been planned and factual. But Max learned to relish the freedom to go out in the countryside, to the water, the mountains, the city, even the suburbs, and shoot anything that seemed unique to him.

With the RBP certification in the bag, and his contract expiring at the end of the month, Max knew his days on Galveston Island were coming to an end. Since so much time over the past year had been spent photographing images inside the hospital, he wanted to shoot as many images as he could outside to take with him wherever he would ultimately end up. One afternoon he walked west along Seawall Boulevard till he got to Fort Crockett, where the old military casemates overlooking the sea used to protect the island. Bimbo had pointed out this historical landmark during Max's first week here. The concrete bunkers jutting out from the grassy hill were eye-catching. He took out his Nikon F and screwed on his 35-105mm zoom lens. He began snapping pictures until he realized that he was at the end of the roll.

As he rewound the Kodachrome and loaded up a fresh roll, he relived yesterday's trip out to the west end of the island with Bimbo, who had gotten a little friendlier and more respectful since Max had received his RBP. Bimbo had been eager to show him a surprise at his trailer. Max couldn't imagine what it would be—except perhaps a total fumigation and decontamination of the place. When they arrived at the trailer home, Max was shocked to find out how close the answer was to what he had imagined, although in a twisted way. In fact, the trailer home had burned down. The framework and stilts were still there, but everything inside was charred and mostly gutted. Max looked at the sofa in what used to be the living room, where he'd slept for two weeks, almost a year ago, when he'd started the residency program. He remembered his first morning waking up to an army of fire ants crawling over his stomach. Now the sofa was just metal and ashes. Across from the sofa was the melted TV. Max couldn't figure out why he'd chosen this specific moment, but Bimbo went over to the TV and wrenched a Mickey Mouse figurine out of the warped plastic.

Bimbo suspected that the fire had started as a result of a faulty water heater. He'd woken up on the night of the fire at around 3 a.m. and seen that a good blaze was eating away his home. He'd run out the door to a neighbor, who called the fire department.

For some odd reason, Max felt terrible and emotional about it all, yet Bimbo was smiling and taking it all in very well. He simply said that there was nothing he could've done about it. He planned

to rebuild the place while staying in a cheap hotel until he got back on his feet again.

Leaving the fort to proceed west down the boulevard, Max spotted an old cemetery surrounded by a wrought iron fence. The grass was overgrown. Many of the gravestones were chipped or cracked; a headstone here and there was turned over. He noticed faded silk flowers that had blown away from the gravesites, through the fence, and onto the sidewalk. They seemed to be stuck, twirling around and around in their own little purgatories, caught between the wind of passing cars and the breeze from the Gulf. Max wondered if people bought these fake flowers to put on graves so that they wouldn't have to keep coming back to lay down yet another fresh bouquet of flowers. Grieve once and be done with it.

He unscrewed the 35-105 and replaced it with a macro lens. Down on his knees, he homed in on a couple of yellow and purple flowers stuck around a stand of iron. He thought of Reynaldo, of how hard life had been for him. Then he focused on the little pieces of silk unraveling around the edges of the petals and shot a bunch at different angles.

Max walked across to the other side of the boulevard, to the seawall, and sat down, his legs dangling over the wall near a section that intersected with a man-made jetty. The long, even row of seaweed-covered granite blocks was used as a breakwater to help hold down the beach. Waves crashed against the granite in a constant battle for occupation. He looked east and west along the boulevard at all that was man-made—restaurants, hotels, condominiums, cars, telephone poles, traffic lights, and even the seawall.

Max realized that what it all came down to was that Galveston was primarily a sandbar resting between the Gulf of Mexico and the bay—a shifting barrier island. So many lives, relationships, buildings, discoveries, and creations—medical or otherwise— had been delicately constructed on it, shaped like a massive sand castle—only to, perhaps, be washed away in a day by a hurricane. Yet the human animal, with its innate will to survive, kept coming back to rebuild and renew—like the child who returns to his devastated castle and begins a new one. For what else is there to do?

The ocean was all stirred up. Surfers were out taking advantage of the higher than usual waves. The Gulf winds blew a fine salt mist over Max's face. Toward the east, the seawall curved inward around a bend, revealing more sand and beach. Over the water were the oil rigs pumping on the horizon, and passing in front of them were shrimp boats with their outriggers towing their trawl nets. The sea spray created a soft-focus quality in the air with a monochromatic blue-gray hue. He liked this natural mise-en-scène and lifted his camera to compose it.

A tourist in an obtrusive yellow hat walking along the beach entered the frame. He waited for what seemed like ten minutes before she found a shell and moved on. As he held his breath before pressing the shutter release, he felt a blossom of rejuvenation unfolding from within, a sense of renewed confidence. When he pressed the shutter open, he captured all of it. Then he put the camera in his bag, got up, and walked farther west.

August 31, 1982

Well, Mom & Dad . . .

This is it. Time to move on to bigger and
brighter things. I'm heading for California. I
told you that Zag got the job as a medical photo
supervisor at Cedars-Sinai Medical Center --
the "hospital of the stars." He wrote to tell me
that there was a position vacancy for a senior
medical photographer.

I immediately faxed Cedars an application and
resume, which resulted in an invitation to come
out West for an interview. It all happened very
quickly. Zag pulled some strings. His department
needed a photographer bad. I flew out last week
for the interview and was hired on the spot. I
was the only applicant who had an RBP next to
his name, so naturally they went with the most
qualified person.

It's going to be awesome out there. It's
sunny -- and dry! -- all the time. Warm, even
temperatures in the 70s-80s most of the year.
Everyone looks healthy and upbeat. Mom -- you
would enjoy walking around Beverly Hills, a
stone's throw from the hospital. Actually, the
hospital looks more like a fancy hotel. There's
an OR suite on every floor -- highly unusual.
Most hospitals have one floor with a central
core surrounded by operating rooms. The morgue
looks like a regular clinical lab. Very clean
and sparkly -- not drab at all!

Zag forewarned everyone in the photo lab about
me so that when I first met them, they were
already friendly and "deaf-awared." I felt very
comfortable there -- it's going to be a good

fit. Can you imagine Zag as my boss?? Margarita
lunches, here we come!

Folks who knew me at UTMB threw a little
farewell party at a local Chinese restaurant.
At the end of the luncheon they gave me a little
roast. Then we opened our fortune cookies. Mine
said: "One day you will meet a beautiful deaf
Chinese girl." I looked around the table to
figure out who'd done that. Everyone was poker-
faced.

Dr. Robb gave a short, cheesy speech taking
all the credit for pulling this poor deaf guy
up through the ranks to the exalted status of
an RBP. Even Bimbo had a tear in his eye. I told
Orlando, one of our residents (and my running
buddy), that I was passing the "RBP baton" on
to him since he's next in line to go up for his
certification. He said, true, but it wasn't
going to be a "Deaf baton." I asked what he
meant by that.

Then, this simple, quiet man, who normally
doesn't say too much, got up and gave this
impromptu speech in voice AND signs. The
signs weren't great but at least they were
understandable. This was his reply as I remember
it:

"Max -- the doctors and scientists that I
work with will not be making any special, extra
effort to communicate with me, this normal
everyday hearing person. The people working in
the OR, or wherever in the hospital, are not
going to be on their toes, aware of the special
ways of dealing with you, though I think they
work better when you're around. I don't have
your unique perspective on life and work. You

have that innate ability to visually absorb the
world around you, for that has been the only way
you have learned to do what you need to do to
survive. You have your beautiful Deaf culture
and ASL within. No one can take those away from
you. You have what I call 'the Deaf heart.'
So, that's what I meant when I said I wasn't
going to be receiving a Deaf baton. It's going
to become a hearing baton when I touch it. The
days from here on out at work will be ordinary
without you."

I'll tell you -- there wasn't a dry eye in
the room. I gave Orlando a hug and said, "Aw
shucks! Been holding back on me. I'm surprised
you knew all those signs." He said he'd picked
them up from me, and from Reynaldo, whenever he
visited the lab. Then I looked at Dr. Robb and
said, "You've gotta hire another Deaf resident.
Orlando hates 'ordinary.'"

Dr. Robb whispered, "Well, what about Bertha?
She's deaf."

I glanced over at Bertha, who was munching
on an egg roll, chatting with one of the lab
workers without the need to lipread. If you look
at her, she passes for a hearing person. I was
about to explain to Robb about what a capital
D meant in the word Deaf and all of the deep
cultural references that went with it, but I
stopped myself. Not now -- this was my moment to
bask in and enjoy; maybe another time when I'm
alone with him. At least Orlando got it, and in
much less time with me than Dr. Robb.

And Maddy? Her contract with the theater ends
after Labor Day weekend. She already has a
job lined up . . . you're not going to believe

where. In HOLLYWOOD! She got hired as a wardrobe mistress for American Theatre Arts, a small 99-seat house near Hollywood and Vine. Somebody from the amphitheater got her connected. What luck! We're going to follow each other to L.A., camping along U.S. Route 10. It'll be a blast!

Well, Mom & Dad -- I'm signing off here. Look out for a letter and some motel-made postcards from me (probably from Las Cruces or Tucson) as we wend our way to the West Coast.

Thanks for being there and keeping me company this whole year. Ready to begin the California scrapbook? I've enclosed one last photo to close out your Texas scrapbook -- a shot of the seawall, Galveston, and the Gulf.

Always, with love,

Max